SHY GROVE
A GHOST STORY

Scott A. Johnson

ISBN - 978-0692982594

Interior artwork by Lily K. Coy-Johnson

Printed in the USA

First Edition

For Katie. Thank you for giving me back my life, my work, and for being my muse. This book exists because of you.

ACKNOWLEDGMENTS

There are so many people without whom this book could not have been possible. First, my teachers and classmates at Emerson. Also, the faculty, staff, and students at Seton Hill University.

But most importantly, there are the people in my life that encouraged my behavior, and without them, I'd never have gotten a single word written. To Nikki, Ward, Jake, Wes, Kristin, Jarred, Clint, Heather, Hadley, Callum, Corbin, Matt, Meg, Tim, Lucy, and Gary, I thank you from the bottom of my black little heart. You are the family I've chosen.

To my mom and dad, to my brother and his family, thank you. You keep me grounded and push me to be better.

Finally, and most importantly, to Katie, Zoe, and Anna, you are my reasons for writing. You lift me up when I am low, encourage me when I need it, and make me feel alive. I love you all.

The asphalt gave way to gravel and shale, potholes and ruts. Manicured trees gave way to wild pecans and oaks that reached across the sky and choked out the sunlight.

"Not far now," said Mr. Andrews as he juggled the steering wheel and a crinkled map. "I think."

"You've never been here?"

"Nope," he beamed. "Seen pictures, though. Your aunt liked her privacy."

Gary sat back in the seat and tried to ignore the ancient Cadillac's creaks and moans. It smelled musty, old, with stale cigarette smoke and Armorall, but it was better than letting the hot Texas air in. At least the air conditioner worked, otherwise the heat would've baked them in the car like a couple of pizzas in an oven.

They'd left the highway half an hour ago, came to the tiny town of Shy Grove, and worked their way through the neglected streets until they found the unmarked road, if it could even be called a road, obscured by a thicket.

"You're sure about all this?" Gary surveyed the landscape. "I didn't even know the woman."

"Read it yourself," said the lawyer as he plopped a thick folder into Gary's lap. "No children of her own, no surviving relatives, and only one sister, your mom, who had only one child. You. No mistake."

The car lurched to a halt.

"We're here. Come take a look."

The lawyer shifted and grunted his way out of the car and closed the door with a loud hollow bang. Gary sat for a moment. Aunt Ester. *Crazy* Aunt Ester. Well, at least the town fit.

Gary got out and followed Mr. Andrews up the front path.

The house was huge by Gary's standards. Two stories, a sleeper porch upstairs, large columns covered in the rotting skeletal remains of ivy, it was more than his teacher's salary would've afforded him. But it was his now, all the same.

"Everything you can see," said the lawyer. "You've got about twelve and a half acres. That dirt road we turned on? Consider that your driveway. Come on in and have a look around."

He fumbled with the key and, after a minute or two, managed to get the door open.

The stale air inside smelled of must and roses, lavender and mold.

"Do the lights work?" asked Gary.

"They should," said the lawyer. "Sent a crew around to check out the electrics." He flipped a switch on the wall. The lamps responded with a soft glow.

"What about phone? Gas?"

"Gas works," said the lawyer. "No air conditioning, no phone. Hell, way out here, you're lucky to have running water and indoor toilets."

The place felt like a museum, a shrine to a dead woman's tastes and passions. In front of him, the great room sprawled with antique couches, a grandfather clock, and an upright piano that looked like it was more used as a coffee table than a musical instrument. The tattered rugs and ragged curtains spoke volumes about their previous owner.

"No one's been here since she died," said Gary.

"Nope," said the lawyer. "Everything's just as she left it."

It was uncanny, the feeling that, at any moment, he would walk around the corner and find Crazy Aunt Ester doing whatever it was she did. Dishes in the sink, laundry in the hamper, a yellow pad on the table. He imagined the pen might still be warm from her touch. There was something else, though, just beyond the feeling of a life interrupted, that pulled at him, made him feel at once like the place belonged to him. More, that *he* belonged *there* in a comforting embrace.

"So what am I supposed to do with all this?"

"Don't know," said the lawyer with a wide *aw-shucks* smile. "That's not my area. All I'm supposed to do is make sure you know it's yours now."

"I could sell it, couldn't I?"

"Maybe all the stuff," snorted the lawyer. "But the house? Not likely. Not in this economy. Besides, Shy Grove's mostly dead anyway. I don't think anyone would want to live out here."

"So, what? I'm stuck with it?"

"Like I said, not my area."

Angela might like it. Zach wouldn't, but he didn't like much these days unless it went through the Internet. Still, the place was huge. With some work, a lot of work, it could be very nice.

"There's more," said the lawyer. "You've got a great big barn out back. No animals, though, and the barn needs work too, but it could be nice. I don't know what's in it, but whatever's in there belongs to you too. All the land out here, I guess you could sell for farming, unless you're planning on becoming a farmer yourself."

"I'm a teacher," said Gary with a laugh. "I teach middle school English. I don't know anything about farming."

"Just as well," said the lawyer. "Ain't much that grows out here anyway."

Gary looked out the kitchen window toward the weather-worn barn. It might've been red once, but the harsh weather and heat baked what was left of the paint to a sickly pink. The bare boards that showed through were dead gray. From where he stood, the old building looked sturdy, but he knew even less about construction than he did farming. For all he knew, a swift kick would bring the whole thing to the ground.

Still, there might be money to be made. The antiques, the land, whatever else they found in the house might be worth something. And it was closer to his work in Luling. If nothing else, it might be a good way to spend the summer. Zach could do with a little offline time. At fourteen, he spent most of his time jacked into his computer. As far as he was concerned, stupid things like parents shouldn't even exist. The kid was a stranger to them. Maybe a little time together might bring back the old Zach, the one who used to laugh and seemed to actually like his parents. Not likely, but it was worth a try. And who knew? If Angela liked it, maybe they'd just sell the house in San Antonio, move out here to the boonies. Yeah, fat chance of that, too.

"So what do you think?" Mr. Andrews' smile seemed forced. Sweat rolled down his cheeks, and he looked like he couldn't wait to get back to his air-conditioned office.

"Is this everything?"

"There is a considerable amount of money," said the lawyer. "When we settled up her accounts, took our fifteen percent, it left you with just over a hundred and fifty thousand."

"*Dollars*?"

"I ain't talking pesos," laughed the lawyer. "All I need is a signature and we can head back to my office."

"Where do I sign?"

Gary glanced in the rearview mirror. Zach's face was turned toward the window, his dark hair over his eyes. Little white wires lead to his ear-buds. No matter what, the kid wouldn't hear him. Even if he did, Gary doubted he would respond. Angela sat reading in the passenger seat. How she never got car-sick mystified him, but it didn't matter. So long as she was happy.

When they left I-35, Zach pulled his cell phone from his pocket and jabbed the keyboard. Gary wondered who he was texting. Probably one of his so-called friends. Bunch of pot-heads, the lot of them. It didn't matter either, though. Another half-hour and there wouldn't be anyone to text, no computer to hide inside.

"You're doing it again," said Angela without looking up.

"What?"

"Staring at him in the mirror. Can't you two just get along?"

It was an old fight, one he didn't feel like having again. Whether it was just his age or not, Zach still needed to take responsibility, needed to be considerate of other people. Anymore, it seemed like he felt the world revolved around him, only existed for his amusement. Or scorn.

"Just making sure the trailer's still with us," he said. She nodded and continued reading. Maybe his relationship with his son wasn't all that needed fixing. Maybe some work in an isolated house might do wonders for his and Angela's as well. Married couples fought, after all. Sometimes all they needed to get over the problem was a little bonding time. He hoped it was the case.

"Where are we?" mumbled Zach.

"Almost there," said Gary. "Wait'll you see this place. You won't believe how big it is!"

"Whatever," said Zach, his customary reply to just about everything. He sunk back down into the seat and resumed watching the world outside pass him by.

They pulled up in front of the house just before noon. Gary got out, walked up to the front porch and spread his arms wide.

"So? What do you think?"

Angela got out of the car and smiled. Her smile was one of the things Gary loved the most about her, the way her whole face lit up. It was good to see her smile again.

"Wow," she said. "Zach, honey, get out. You should see this."

The rear door opened and Zach's lanky frame unfolded, his eyes locked on his cell phone.

"I get no signal," he said without looking up.

"Nope," said Gary. "Cellphones don't reach out here. Too far out. There's no internet either."

"Lame," muttered Zach as he stuffed his phone back into his pocket. He looked up at the house. His face said he was unimpressed.

"So?"

"Why couldn't I stay with Grandma?"

Why indeed. Maybe it was because Angela's mother liked drinking until she passed out most nights. Maybe it was because Grandma didn't feel like putting up with his shit either. All true, but the *real* truth was Gary wanted Zach with him, wanted to try to salvage whatever was left of his son before high-school turned him into even more of a stranger.

"C'mon," said Gary. "It'll be like going to camp, but indoors. Think of all the treasures we might find."

"Whatever," said Zach as he slammed the door and stalked around to the trailer.

"Give him time," said Angela. "He'll come around."

"I hope so."

He seemed so excited. Nevermind the fact that all her friends were in San Antonio, or that the house was in a serious state of disrepair. Gary wanted them to give it a shot as a *family*. It was important to her husband, so it was important to her. San Antonio wasn't that far away, only about three hour's drive, and she'd always dreamed of having a place in the country. A house as big as this must have a place where she could set up her studio. And, she had to admit, she didn't like seeing Zach slip away from them any more than Gary did. But she felt protective of him, even from his own father.

Angela walked around the yard as Gary tried to get the door unlocked. He looked so goofy, with his white legs and khaki shorts and flip-flops, his long brown hair and his Texas State t-shirt. At least he hadn't started wearing black socks and sandals. He was trying, and it made her love him all the more. If only she didn't have to play referee all the time.

In the back of the trailer, Zach already had the doors open.

"Need a hand, tiger?" she said.

"Why do we have to be here?" he hissed. "It's *his* aunt that died. Why'd he have to drag us out here too?"

"Because we're a family," she said. "Please, just *try* to make the best of it, okay?"

"But it's summer! I'm supposed to be hanging with my friends and having fun!"

"It's three months," she said. "It won't kill you. Besides, I kind of like the idea of having us all together."

"You would," he mumbled as he went back to the task of pulling boxes down.

"A bad attitude isn't going to help anyone," she said. "If you're determined to be miserable, you will be."

"Got it!" called Gary.

"Terrific," muttered Zach.

It was going to be a long three months.

Superdad had to go screw things up again. Three months without his cellphone? Without going online? Without seeing any of his friends? And where were they anyway, the buttcrack of Texas? It wasn't fair. They could've left him at home. He was fourteen. Fourteen, for chrissake! It wasn't like he was a kid anymore. All because some obscure relative kicked off, Dad got a bug up his butt to do the whole family-bonding thing. Perfect. And there went Mom, defending Dad again. Like it was *his* fault, like he should be happy out here in redneck land with bugs and snakes and no one his own age to hang with.

Besides, the house looked creepy. Sure, it was big, but something about it just made his skin crawl. Maybe because the old lady died here. Maybe that was it.

He hefted a box marked "Kitchen" onto his shoulder and made for the front door. As he stepped onto the porch, into the shadow of the house's roof, he shivered. It was almost like he felt eyes on him, watching, judging, taking his measure. He shook the feeling off and walked through the door.

"Smells like old lady in here."

"It was an old lady's house," said Dad. "We'll air it out. Kitchen's through there."

"Why is it so hot in here?"

"No air conditioner."

The thought struck him as ridiculous. Who didn't have air conditioning in Texas? No phone he could *almost* see, no cable television too, but no air conditioning? How could anyone survive in this heat without it?

"Relax," said Dad. "Soon as we get the perishables out and unhook the trailer, we'll go pick up a couple of window units, okay? You won't have to sweat to death while you sleep."

Dad smiled when he said it, which made the comment irritate him even more.

"Whatever," he said as he made his way to the kitchen. "Which room is mine?"

"I don't know," said Dad from the doorway. "I haven't looked through the rest of the house. There are four bedrooms upstairs, so you can pretty much have your pick."

Zach grunted as he put the box on the counter. Dad hated it when he didn't talk. Good.

"Tell you what," said Dad. "Let's unhook the trailer and get those window units. We can get some lunch while we're out. Sound good?"

"Whatever," Zach shrugged.

Dad let out a deep breath and went back outside. Lunch sounded good, but there was no way he was going to show them even a glimmer of happiness. They ruined his summer, and if he had to be miserable, so did they.

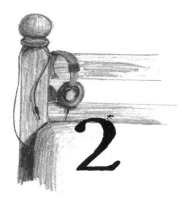

2

They bought four window-mounted air conditioners. One for each bedroom, one for the breakfast nook, and one for the room Angela claimed as her studio. Once he got them installed, Gary and Zach pulled the beds out of the trailer and moved them to their respective rooms. There were already beds, of course, but the thought of sleeping on them, without knowing who'd last used them or how long ago, seemed creepy.

After he got his boxes and bed in his room, Zach closed the door and didn't come out for the rest of the evening.

Gary lay on the comforter in his boxers and let the cold air wash over his body.

"We can start going through stuff tomorrow," he said. "Where do you want to start?"

"Downstairs," she said. "Start with the furniture. Maybe we can get an appraiser out."

"No phone, remember?"

"Well, then," she said. "I guess I'll just have to drive into Austin. You and Zach will be okay by yourselves, right?"

"Uh..."

"After all, you're the one who wanted bonding time with him. A little father-son time, right?"

She had him there, even if being alone in the house with his son wasn't quite what he had in mind. Still, how bad could it be? If nothing else, he'd let the kid explore, see how far out the property went. It wasn't like there was anyone around to bother him. Besides, the sunlight and fresh air might do him good.

"Yeah," he said. "Okay. But don't be gone too long."

She stood in the bathroom doorway and smiled. She wore an oversized t-shirt and her long dark hair was down.

"What?"

"You're the only man I know who can make boxers look sexy."

"I hope so," he said. "Wouldn't want you making eyes at other guys."

She climbed onto the bed and lay down beside him. The cold air blew over her face, carried her scent with it.

"I'm glad we did this," she said.

"Me too." He gave her a hug. The wind from the air conditioner made the hairs on her arms prickle and her nipples stiffen under her shirt.

Zach lay in bed without sleeping, headphones blaring dark and turgid music. The room he chose, the least offensive of the four, was still hideous, with old-lady wallpaper and a vanity. At least there were no clothes in the closet, only boxes full of who-knew-what. He wasn't sure he could've slept in a room with some dead woman's clothes. It was hard enough with pink flowers staring back at him from the walls.

Mom and Dad took the room downstairs, the one with the only working toilet in the house. He took his time in the bathroom before he went to bed, just to let them know how inconvenienced he was.

He glanced at the clock. Ten forty-five. He should be out right now, hanging out with Mickey and John and Monique, cruising in Mickey's mom's car, hanging by the river, smoking weed. Instead, he was stuck in pink hell.

He turned his music off and rolled over and waited for sleep to claim him.

From below, a sound caught his attention, a voice like a guttural moan, but quiet, like a whisper. He clicked off the air conditioner to see if he could make out what it was. There it was again, and again, rhythmic grunting. It wasn't until he recognized the squeaking of bedsprings that he realized who and what he heard. He turned the air conditioner back on, full blast, and turned his music back up. It wasn't as bad as walking in on them, he figured, but damned close.

Angela woke bathed in sweat. Her heart pounded behind her eyes and her throat burned with heavy breaths. Her dream faded, blown like smoke by the air conditioner.

There was a man, she remembered that much. A tall, gaunt man in black. A priest, maybe. But he couldn't have been. There were others there too, all of them on their knees, all of them feverish. She was naked, she remembered that too, and that in her dream, she wasn't afraid. Not when the others stood and dropped their robes, not when the priest laid her on the altar, not when the others converged on her.

She wasn't afraid, not in the slightest. It had been a long time since she had such an intensely erotic dream. She rolled over and reached for Gary in the darkness. His sweat-slicked skin glistened against the moonlight. He took her hard before they both fell asleep, maybe that was it. She loved him, and he her, but the intimacy just wasn't there lately. The strange place awoke something in them both, and as far as she was concerned, it was a good awakening.

She put her head on his shoulder and smiled, and wondered if his dream was as good as hers.

Zach awoke to find his player's charge had run out. The room was frigid, moreso than he thought possible with a window unit. He reached up and turned the switch to "low," then he stopped and listened. No sounds, no squeaking bedsprings. Good. He lay back on his pillow, arms behind his head, and closed his eyes.

Thump.

It was so quiet, he wasn't sure he'd really heard it. But there it was again, louder this time. He listened to the sound until he was sure it wasn't from inside the house, then he crept out of bed, over to the window. The cold air from the window unit on his bare chest made him shiver, but he paid it no mind as he moved the curtain aside.

Outside, the night was clear. The moon shone down on the

yard, brighter than he thought possible. San Antonio streetlights never let moonlight touch the ground, always made the stars seem pale and few. But the night sky twinkled like a million pinpricks in a deep blue blanket. The moon hung low, pale and yellow without halogen streetlights to filter through.

He scanned the back yard until he saw the source of the noise. The door of the barn yawned for a moment, then slapped shut against its frame. It looked almost like the old structure was breathing. Zach turned to go back to bed when a shadow darted out of the barn. He froze and stared. Two more dark figures zipped out and disappeared around the front of the house.

Another sound, this one behind him, made him jump and turn. In the doorway stood his father, head down, wearing only his boxer shorts.

"Dad. What're you..?"

"You should be asleep," said his father. His voice sounded strange, almost like a whisper, but harder, more forced.

"I was," he said. "But I heard a noise and..."

"There's nothing to be afraid of," said Gary. "Go back to bed." He made a stumbling turn and slouched down the hall, his head never rising.

Zach went to his door and watched for a moment as his father moved down the stairs. He walked like a movie zombie, slack arms and stiff legs, not quite balanced enough to walk properly. When he disappeared off the landing, Zach realized his father was asleep. He crept down the hall and watched as his father reached the bottom step, amazed he didn't fall, and returned to his room. When he heard the door close, he hurried back to his own room, shut the door, and climbed into bed.

Dad didn't sleepwalk. At least, he never had before. He pulled the blanket up close under his chin. Like the house wasn't creepy enough, now there were shadows in a breathing barn and Dad was acting weird. He closed his eyes and wished he were back with his friends.

3

Angela left early, which gave Gary a chance to start things off on a positive note with Zach. Breakfast was always a good start, he figured, and maybe a ham and cheese omelet would serve as a good peace offering. The eggs were half cooked when Zach came down the stairs. His shaggy hair stood up at unnatural angles and, for a moment, Gary saw him as a ten-year-old again.

"Morning!" he boomed. "Hungry?"

"Not really," yawned Zach.

"Well, I'm making breakfast."

"Is there any coffee?"

Since when did Zach drink coffee? Fourteen-year-old kids didn't drink coffee, did they?

"Um...Yeah. Fresh pot. How do you take it?"

"Black," he said as he slumped into a chair.

Gary poured him a cup. No sense making a big deal of it. He couldn't remember when he first started drinking coffee, but he bet he was right around Zach's age. The eggs smelled wonderful as he scraped diced ham and cheese into it, folded it over, and slid it onto a plate.

"Breakfast is served," he said. Zach looked at the plate with disinterest.

"Don't we have Pop-Tarts or something?"

"We do," he said. The kid sure knew how to push his buttons. "But I thought I'd make something special for you this morning. You used to like my cooking."

Zach shrugged as he took a sip of his coffee.

"Where's Mom?"

"Austin. She went to get an antique appraiser."

"She went to Austin without me?"

"You were asleep," he said with forced patience. "Besides, it's not like she's going shopping. She'll be back soon."

"Whatever," said Zach. He pushed his chair away from the table, snatched up his coffee cup, and stormed out of the room.

Gary stared at the steaming plate for a moment, a mixture of anger and sadness brimming in him. He tried, dammit, and the kid threw it back at him. There was no winning with him. He'd give it a few days, give him a chance to dry out from his electronic addiction. Once Zach got over being mad, accepted where he was, he'd try again. He left the plate on the table, just in case, and set to washing the pan. He thought about cooking an egg for himself, but wasn't hungry anymore.

Zach came back downstairs dressed in a black t-shirt and torn jeans. He paused just long enough to get himself another mug of coffee.

"I'm going outside," he said, then gave the door a violent shove and let it slam behind him.

Gary let out a deep breath and picked up Zach's fork and plate. No sense letting food go to waste. Even if he wasn't hungry, it did smell good. He took a bite.

"You're welcome," he said to no one in particular.

The eggs did smell good, but he was too pissed off to eat. Trapped while his mother went back to civilization. Even for a few hours, even if they did nothing but drive until he got cell phone reception, she could've taken him. He expected such a move from Dad, but Mom? How could she?

He stomped toward the barn, images of breathing doors and darting shadows still fresh in his mind. Whatever was in there, he bet it was cool, or at least cooler than going through some dead old-lady dresser. Besides, inside the house, he felt funny. Not bad, but like he wasn't alone, like eyes followed him down the hallways. Creepy things he liked, but the house was different. It wasn't like watching a horror movie with the lights off, or visiting a spook house. This was real, intrusive. Inside, he couldn't get away from the feeling.

He expected the barn door to move easily, but when he tugged the rusted hinges held tight. He had to put his shoulder to the wood to get the door to move, and when it did, the hinges let out an awful squeal. So why didn't he hear it last night, and if it wasn't the wind that moved the door, what was it? The shadows?

He stepped through the doorway and paused while his eyes adjusted to the relative darkness. Although light filtered through the loose boards, most of the cavernous structure's insides hid in deep shadows. He took a couple of tentative steps into the gloom, mindful of the floor. It didn't feel like dirt. It was hard like stone, but uneven. How anyone could get anything done without lights was beyond him.

Another couple of steps. Something brushed his face. He panicked and swung his arms in front of his face. His hands found a noose. No, not a noose, just an old rope with a knot in the end. He grabbed it and gave a good solid yank. More creaks filled the air and the hay loft door above him swung open. Sunlight poured through the opening. He shut his eyes against the sudden brightness. When he opened them again, the darkness retreated to shadowy corners. Dust motes drifted through the air, golden specks suspended in time. One side of the barn held stalls, for horses he guessed. All he knew about barns came from movies, but they looked like horse stalls to him. Instead of horses, however, the stalls brimmed with other treasures. The first held more antiques like the ones inside, but these were damaged with water and neglect. The second was stacked high with books, piles of newspaper, and what looked like old ledgers. From the look of them, rats used them to make nests. The third held tools, the likes of which he'd never seen in person, though he knew what they were. Long wicked curved blades, pitchforks, a plow and several evil-looking things that resembled bear traps, but smaller, hung on the walls. The floor was a littered mess of horseshoes, chains, and other farm equipment, all of it rusted, weathered, and useless.

The last stall caught him by surprise. Instead of more junk, the floor of the fourth was covered in a blue blanket, littered with empty and crushed beer cans. He leaned through the open gate to get a better look. The beer was a cheap brand, the blanket worn. Around the edges saw a familiar and welcome sight: the burned tips of hand rolled joints. So there was weed to be had, and all he had to do was find it.

He turned to face the other wall and stopped short. How he missed the great blob of white tarp, he couldn't begin to guess, but the shape it concealed was unmistakable. He grabbed the heavy cloth and gave it a yank. As it fell to the ground, his heart fluttered.

Gary started at the door and worked his way back into the main room, a clipboard in one hand, a pen tucked behind his ear. By the door, a hall tree made of what appeared to be cherry wood stood with a two-foot tall mirror attached. He wrote it down. By it, a standing floor lamp with a cut glass shade. Further into the room, a couch, loveseat and chair, matching, surrounded a torn rug in front of the soot-stained fireplace. If anything in the house was worth anything, the total value might make his inheritance look like chump change. He bent to examine a side table with a pink marble top.

Lift up your voice and sing unto the Lord...

The voice drifted through the room, barely a whisper, almost a weak echo. Gary straightened and slowly turned.

"Hello?"

No answer. It might've been Zach trying to creep him out. Fat chance, tough guy. But the voice didn't sound like his son's, and he wasn't prone to quoting church services.

Sinners beget sinners, blood begets blood...

Gary whirled in search of the voice. It came from everywhere at once, inside his head and under the couch, up the chimney and down the hallway.

Come unto me...

The couch. That time he heard it clear. The voice came from under the couch. He knelt on the floor and looked, but found nothing. He reached up as far as his arm would go, felt around the moldy rug until he was sure there was nothing but warped boards and dust. Maybe Zach hid something up *inside* the couch, up off the floor and out of sight.

He felt around for a tear in the fabric, but found none.

"Dad!" Zach burst into the room before the back door had

time to slam shut. Gary jumped and scraped his shoulder on the jagged teeth of the couch frame.

"Jesus Christ! What?"

"You gotta come see this! Out in the barn! It's so cool! Come on! Come on!"

It was more than he'd said to him since they arrived yesterday, and the boy only talked a mile a minute for two reasons: scared or excited. The grin on his face told Gary he wasn't the former, so whatever got him excited enough to actually speak must've been something spectacular. He dropped the clipboard on the couch and scrambled after his son, who'd already disappeared again through the back door.

Outside, Zach stood in front of the barn, practically jumping up and down.

"Hurry up!" he squealed. "You'll never believe what I found!"

"Let me guess," said Gary as he slowly crossed the distance. "A severed head? A mummy? A baby elephant?"

As he got to the barn door, Zach stepped aside, grinning from ear to ear.

"Just look!"

Gary peered into the barn and blinked. Rusted and pitted chrome stared back at him with round headlamps.

"Isn't it the coolest thing?"

The old truck had seen better days, but was still in good condition from what he could tell. The split windshield and curved back glass told its model and make.

"It's a 1951 Chevy Stepside," he said. "Wow. I haven't seen one of these since that car show we went to in Beaumont. Remember that? You sat in the Batmobile!"

"I was nine."

"Oh. Yeah. Well, this one looks like it belongs in a museum."

"Can we maybe fix it up?" The kid begged with his eyes. "Please? I promise I won't give you any more shit...uh...lip for the rest of the summer! C'mon, Dad! Please!"

"Let's look at it first," said Gary. He let the swear slide. Had it been he who found a classic truck in the barn, *shit* would've been the tamest thing he said.

Apart from a few spots of rust and pitting, the outside looked okay. Even the back wrap-around glass was still intact. The wood planks in the bed were rotted away, but they were easy enough to replace. He opened the driver's side door.

Inside, the seats and dash were covered in dust, but looked in otherwise new condition. A set of keys dangled from the ignition.

"I wonder..."

He turned the key, half expecting the ancient vehicle to roar to life. That it sat inert did not surprise him.

"It'll take a lot of work to fix," he said.

"I can do it!" blurted Zach.

"What would you know about fixing a car that was built half a century before you were born?"

"I can learn," said Zach. He sounded exasperated, but still hopeful. "There's gotta be books or something about these things. If I had an Internet connection..."

"Tell you what," said Gary. "You want to fix her up? Be my guest. I'll help if I can, but she's your baby. And I'll do you one better than that. You fix her, she's yours."

"Really?"

"Yeah, I guess so. I inherited everything on this property, so I guess she's mine to give. And I'm giving her to you." He knew Angela would never go for it, not at first anyway. But it was every boy's dream to have a classic car. It was his, anyway, when he was Zach's age. It felt like a bribe, to buy the kid's love with the old truck, but Zach broke out into a wide smile and made it worthwhile.

"Yes!" Zach hugged him, actually hugged his mean old bastard of a father. For a moment, Gary had his son back.

"Climb in," he said. "See how you like it."

Zach wriggled into the front seat. His feet reached the pedals and he could see over the steering wheel. If he could get the thing running before he got his learner's permit, he'd have one hell of a sweet ride as his first car.

"Where's the gear shift?"

Gary laughed and tried to explain the concept of shifting gears with "three on a tree."

It was after two before Angela returned. The appraiser was a stodgy old fart with roaming eyes and a ratty cardigan. But he knew his business, so she endured his leering long enough to set an appointment to get him out to the house. By the end of the week, he said, which meant they had only three days to catalogue all the antiques and furniture. It would be tough, she figured, but with the three of them working together – and what were the odds of that? – it was possible.

She parked the car in front and made her way through the front door.

"Hello!" she called out. "I'm back! We have until Friday!"

Silence.

"Gary?"

"Back here, babe!" Gary's cheerful voice echoed from down the hall.

"I found the appraiser," she said as she made her way toward their bedroom. "The guy was a real pig, wouldn't quit looking at my boobs, but he knows his business."

She opened the door to the room they shared to find it empty. Though the air conditioner was off, a chill lingered in the air.

"Gary? Are you in the bathroom?"

"Come here," said the voice. "I want to show you something."

"What?" His voice sounded strange, fragmented as if it were broken against the walls.

"Something wonderful."

She hesitated, but stepped into the room. As she crossed the threshold, the fine hairs at the base of her skull prickled, her flesh crept. Something wasn't right.

"Where are you?"

"I'm in here," said Gary's voice from the bathroom. "You need to see."

"Angel?" Gary's voice, solid and whole, came from the back door in the kitchen.

Angela turned and ran down the hall, away from the strange voice in the bedroom. When she saw Gary in the kitchen, she burst into tears and threw her arms around his sweaty neck.

"There's someone in the house," she hissed. "In our room."

Gary moved her behind him and hurried to the bedroom. The door was closed. She was sure she'd left it open when she ran out. He put his finger to his lips and quietly turned the knob, then threw the door open. It banged against the wall behind it. The sound made her jerk.

"Where?"

"Bathroom." She pointed to the closed bathroom door.

Gary reached beside the bed and pulled his Louisville Slugger from underneath. He held it up in one hand, ready to strike, while he opened the door with the other. Inside, sunlight shone in through the open window. There was no one there.

"I heard him," she said. "I heard a voice. He sounded like you, but different."

"There's no one here now."

"I know what I heard, damn it!" Fear gave way to anger too quickly in her. She hated feeling helpless, hated feeling weak.

"Okay," he said. "I believe you heard something, but there's no one here."

"Maybe he climbed out the window."

Gary turned toward the fifteen-inch wide pane and cocked an eyebrow. "Not unless he was thinner than Zach."

"But how..?"

"Dad!" Zach's voice came through the window. "Where'd you go? I need you!"

His voice sounded strange, bounced from tree to stone from the barn and across the yard.

"Maybe you did hear me," he said. "I was in the barn with Zach. You've gotta see what we found!"

He kissed her cheek, tossed the bat onto the bed, and started out of the room. "Come see," he said.

She didn't move or release his hand, only stood with a frown on her face. He turned and his excited features softened into genuine sympathy with just a touch of humor.

"Oh, hey," he said as he put his free arm around her and hugged her close. "That really scared you, didn't it?"

She nodded.

"Old quirky house, remember?" he said with a little chuckle. "You heard me outside through the window. Mystery solved, okay? Now come outside. Zach needs to show you something."

It could've been the weird acoustics, she decided. But the cold, and it sounded so close. She followed Gary out, unwilling to stay in the room alone for the time being.

The sunshine outside warmed her prickled flesh smooth,

chased the chill from her bones. As she crossed the back yard toward the barn, Gary's explanation made more sense. It was an old house and they didn't know all of its quirks yet. But something about it felt wrong. There *was* someone in that room, she felt it. But for the moment, she wrote it off as a strange combination of acoustics and her imagination.

She rounded the corner into the barn and stopped short at the sight of her son naked to the waist and leaning into the engine compartment of an ancient truck.

"It's a truck," she said.

"Not just any truck!" beamed Zach as he climbed out. "It's a 1951 Chevy Stepside! Dad said if I can get it running, I can keep it!"

She shot a look of disbelief toward her husband, who offered her a sheepish grin.

"He's almost old enough for a learner's permit," he said. "I might even be able to wrangle a hardship license for him."

But Zach was so young! *Too* young! He was only...fourteen. When she looked at her son in front of the truck, it was hard to deny he was growing up, but until that moment, she'd always considered him a child, still wanted to protect him and kiss his skinned knees and make them better, the way only a mother could. But he got older and, somehow, she missed it.

"It sure is..." she searched for the right word. "Green."

"I know, right?" He looked happy, more than he'd been in months. As much as she wanted to pull him away from the rusted hulk, she couldn't. She forced herself to see him as he was, a young man.

"Don't worry," said Gary. "He's got a lot of work to do on it before it'll even turn over. It's a good project car."

"I don't think so," she said.

"C'mon, Mom!" said Zach. "Please? There's nothing else to do here! And I love classic cars! Remember that time we went to the car show in Beaumont?"

Gary cocked an eyebrow and smirked.

"What's the problem?" Gary grinned. "We're not talking about a demolition derby car here, it's a '51 Stepside! C'mon, let him be a *guy*!"

"Okay," she shrugged as a little piece of herself died on the inside. She'd not been on the receiving end of the two of them ganging up in a long time. It just didn't happen anymore. She wondered if Gary felt like this all the time. "Get to it. Have you boys eaten lunch yet?"

Gary looked up, startled.

"What time is it?"

"It's after two." Of course they'd lost track of the time. That's what men did when faced with something shiny that had the potential to be dangerous and go fast. "I'll go make some sandwiches. But then we need to get to work on the house. The appraiser will be here Friday."

"Uh-huh, yeah," said Gary, already joining Zach under the hood and up to his elbows in ancient engine and grime. She smiled, shook her head, and walked back to the house. If nothing else, it was good to see them working together, bonding.

She stepped through the back door into the kitchen and stopped. The room looked normal, the way it was supposed to. No ghosts, no intruders. No phantom voices. But she still felt on edge, like someone was watching her, just out of her sight. She shook it off and went about making sandwiches. At least the refrigerator was clean when they got there. There was food left, but it all had to go. She couldn't stomach the thought of eating a dead person's food for some reason.

She pulled a knife from the butcher block to slice a tomato. The blade rang as it came out, loud and wicked. She stopped and stared at the knife. It was sharp, so very sharp. It would make short work of the tomato, or meat, or anything that got in front of it. For a moment, the blade dripped crimson, painted along its edge up to the hilt. It seemed natural that it should wear a sheath of blood. That was its job, after all, to cut and tear.

She blinked and the knife shone clean again, the blood gone. It was a tool, not a weapon. How could she think of it used for anything else? She dropped it on the cutting board as if the handle burned, and backed away, her eyes never leaving it. Fear trickled down her spine as she backed out of the kitchen into the main room.

Thump.

The sound hit her at the base of her spine and churned her gut. She spun, looking for the source, but found nothing.

Thump.

The floor shook that time, enough to shift the furniture just a bit, enough that she felt it through her shoes and into the soles of her feet.

Thump.

Below the house. It came from beneath the floorboards. Something was under there.

Thump.

Angela backed from the sound slow, into the kitchen, as if a sudden move might make the floor rise up and take her. Then she turned and ran to the back door, threw it wide and ran out onto the porch, down the steps, into the sunlight. Only when she was safe in the day's brightness did she turn. The kitchen door stood open like a yawning mouth, the overhang sagged a bit, almost like an angry man's brow. For a moment, the windows seemed to cut through her, as if they stared through her flesh and into her fear. The house was wrong, diseased. Every instinct she had screamed to get out, get away.

But she was being silly. It was just a house, after all. There had to be some rational explanation. Ancient pipes under the house, too little sleep, something. The house was just a house, wood and brick, and nothing more. First the voices, now strange pounding from the floorboard. If she told Gary, he'd make fun of her in his good-natured way, then walk through, big strong he-man, to make sure it was safe for his cowering wife. But Angela Carter-neé-Wysocki cowered from nothing, not if she could help it.

"We're coming already!" shouted Gary with a good natured laugh. She spun to see her husband and son walking out of the barn together with Gary's arm around Zach's shoulders. Both of them wore enormous smiles. They were like old pals instead of constant bickering partners.

She turned back toward the house. The windows no longer stared, but were just glass and wood. The overhang stood straight. It seemed like any other house, like nothing happened.

"How..?"

"How what?" Gary put his arm around her and grinned. As he read her expression, his face melted to worry. Her eyes registered a flicker of...something. She looked afraid, as if she were about to burst into tears or hysterical screaming. But then it was gone, shooed away with a quick breath that let him know that whatever it was, she didn't want to say anything. It was the same look she had before, when she thought there were voices in the house, but what could have frightened her again?

It was nerves, that was it. It had to be. Weird-house jitters and too little sleep. She told him about the weird dreams last night, hadn't she? Maybe whatever scared her was an extension of that. Whatever it was, Gary didn't need to know, didn't need to think is wife was terrified of every little creak and bump in the night, or in the middle of the day for that matter. He'd tease her about it for one thing, and while he meant nothing by it, she let him know on more than one occasion that she didn't like being the butt of his jokes. But for another, he knew how much she didn't like to feel helpless.

"How... do you want your sandwiches?" she said with a forced smile.

"Roast beef?" said Zach. "With pickles, mayo and provolone!"

"Better make it two," beamed Gary. "And make mine toasted, if you please."

"Coming right up," she marched up the steps and back inside.

4

Zach lay in his bed asleep after an exhausting day. Mom and Dad stayed inside after lunch and worked on the house inventory. He, on the other hand, stayed outside in the barn until the light made it hard to see. While they wrote down every item of interest, he wrote down rust spots and the parts he could name that needed replacing. Oil, spark plugs, belts he knew, but he didn't know how to test the engine seals or even where they were. By the time they sat down to dinner, spaghetti and meat sauce, his muscles ached and he was exhausted, but happy. Imagine, that a thing like an old truck could make him happy. He took a shower to wash off the grime and engine grease, then went straight to bed without another word.

As he drifted off, he heard Mom and Dad talking about something, noises or weird things they noticed, but he didn't pay attention to the details. They weren't yelling and they weren't fighting about him again, so he didn't care. He closed his eyes and fell into a fast slumber.

In the darkness, his eyes snapped open, his heart raced. He lay in bed, still as stone, and listened for whatever woke him up. Over the air conditioner, he heard nothing. No squeaking bedsprings, no thumping barn doors, not even a whisper from the house. He glanced around the room until he saw a large shape in his open doorway. He couldn't make out any features, it was too dark, but it was of a rough size that he knew.

"Dad?" he whispered.

His skin prickled. Though he couldn't see the figure's face, he was sure it stared at him.

"What're you doing?" he whispered again.

The figure didn't acknowledge that he spoke, only pulled the door closed as it backed out of the room. Even over the air conditioner, the figure's shambling footsteps sounded as it walked down the hall and descended the stairs.

Dad was sleepwalking again. Two nights in a row. That was strange. But he spoke the night before. Zach wondered why he didn't this time. For a moment, a horrible thought, that it wasn't his father but someone else, flashed through his head. But he dismissed the notion as just being goosey and snuggled up in his blanket. He still didn't sleep for the rest of the night.

The lawyer was right. Shy Grove looked like it teetered on the edge of death. What passed for downtown had few real earmarks of progress and instead showed many tell-tale signs of decay. The only fast-food restaurant, or any restaurant for that matter, was an old Dairy-Queen with a faded sign across the street from the only gas station for miles. As their car crept along Center Street, Gary counted only a pathetic few shops. One was an old-fashioned drug store. Down the way a bit stood the general grocery, a Kroger, the sign to which still looked wooden. The shops between were empty, some boarded, as those who lived here either died or moved away. The only things left, he bet, were farmers and a few who made their living selling to them.

They parked where a sign read "Town Square," which was more of just a four-way stop. Angela kissed Zach and Gary and headed down to the general store for bread and coffee and a few other things she discovered she needed. Gary and Zach walked the other direction for a couple of blocks until they found the shop they wanted. On one side of the street was a huge building that looked like an airplane hanger with "Schulky's Feed and Supply" painted on the outside. On the other side of the street sat the only modern storefront in the town: The Hi/Lo auto parts store. Zach got to the door a full ten steps ahead of his father and raced inside. Gary chuckled. It was good to see the kid excited about something that didn't have a monitor attached to it.

As they walked down the aisles, Zach pulled out his list and started grabbing items off the shelves. Gary resisted the urge to give even the most well-intentioned suggestions for fear of stepping on the boy's toes or making him think SuperDad was trying to take over his project.

"I don't know what else I need," said Zach after a while. "Isn't there like a Haynes manual or something?"

"Beats me," said Gary. "Go ask behind the counter. Someone there's bound to know something about it."

Zach nodded and went to the counter. He stood for a few moments and waited, but when no one appeared from the back area he rang the little brass bell beside the register.

"Just a second!" a brassy voice exploded through the dark curtain. When its owner stepped through, Zach lost his voice and his cool.

The girl behind the counter was a tiny thing, in a Ramones t-shirt with hair the color of a new dried wheat and eyes that sparkled blue. She couldn't have been too much older, if at all, than Zach, who stood shuffling from foot to foot like he had to use the bathroom.

"I...uh...I need...uh..."

The boy's ears went scarlet as he let his hair fall down in front of his eyes. The girl, to her credit, said nothing, but a tiny trace of a smile crossed her lips. Gary took a step forward, intent on saving whatever was left of the boy's dignity, but Zach pulled out his list and set it on the counter.

"My dad and I found an old '51 Stepside," he said. "We're trying to get it running."

The girl's smile got bigger as she took the list and leaned on the counter to talk to him. Gary didn't want to eavesdrop, or worse, embarrass the kid, so he went back to the front of the store and pretended to look at bumper stickers.

Zach met him by the rack a few minutes later with an armload of parts and a huge embarrassed grin.

"So," said Gary. "Get the parts you needed?"

"She has to order some of them," he said. "But she'll deliver the rest."

"Did you give her directions to the house?"

He shrugged. "She said she already knew where it was."

"Did you get her name?"

"Cindy. Said she'd be by when she got off work."

Things were looking up. Not only did the kid have a project, but the girl certainly seemed to have his undivided attention. He wondered if Zach still pined for his friends in San Antonio, or if maybe, just maybe, the trip might be worth it after all.

They left the shop and walked back toward the car. Angela stood beside it, upset and without any bags in her hands. Her arms were crossed and Gary could tell she wanted to be somewhere else.

"They didn't have what you needed?" he asked as he unlocked the doors with his remote.

"Let's just go," she said. Angela was never terse. Something must've really rattled her.

He threw a glance to Zach, who was still off in his own little world where classic cars and pretty girls ruled the day, then got in and started the engine.

"I don't want to go back there again," she said. "The people are... weird."

He waited for an explanation. Best to let her tell what happened in her own way.

"There were only maybe three or four people in there, all older women. When I walked through the door, they all just stared at me. Like they'd been in the middle of a conversation, but they just stopped when I walked in."

"Well, we're new here," he said. "They probably know everyone around, and we kind of stick out."

"Yeah, that's what I thought," she said. "But I tried to be friendly. You know, introduce myself? But when I told them which house we were in, they got really cold. One of them drew back, like *physically* drew back away from me. Like I'd done something wrong!"

"Ester was weird," said Gary. "Maybe she got a reputation around the town or something."

"Yeah, but when I mentioned we might try to sell the house, they all started talking at once. They were yelling, Gary. Saying I couldn't sell the house."

"Did they say why?"

She shook her head. "They just turned really nasty, so I left."

"You have a list of what you needed?"

"Sure," she said as she pulled it out of her pocket. "But why...?"

Gary snatched the list from her hand and got out of the car.

"Back in two shakes," he said, and stormed toward the store. He despised rudeness, especially toward his wife and son. It didn't matter whether his aunt was the town loony or not, theirs was the only grocery store for miles. He certainly wasn't going to trek all the way back to San Antonio for ice cream. He hoped the whole thing was just some kind of misunderstanding.

True to his wife's word, when he stepped into the store four heads snapped up, as if they'd been caught doing something. He stopped and turned to each set of eyes.

"I'm Gary Carter," he said in as loud a voice as he could manage. "My wife and I just inherited my Aunt Ester's place. We're just here for a couple of months while we straighten up her affairs."

"Take longer than that," said the old woman behind the meat counter. "Lots of affairs to straighten."

He put Angela's list on the counter and smiled.

"I'd like this order filled, please. Unless, of course, you'd rather we spend our money elsewhere."

The old woman scowled and took the paper.

"It'll be a couple-a-five minutes," she said, then bustled off to gather items. As she disappeared through the swinging doors, Gary turned to look at the other three. One stood beside the dry goods. The other two either didn't work there or were on a break, as they sat with needlepoint frames in their hands.

"How's everyone doing today?" he asked with a broad smile.

"That lady," said the woman behind the dry counter. "She said you was going to sell the house."

"We might," said Gary. "Haven't decided yet. We might just decide to live there." It was a challenge. He wanted to see if any of them would give a reaction.

"Better off burning it to the ground," said one of the needle-point women.

"Why's that?"

The woman stopped sewing and looked up at him over her glasses. Though her wispy hair was grey and the wrinkles on her face told her age, her eyes were dark and sharp and bored into him like augers.

"Because land has memory," she said.

He was about to ask what she meant when the butcher came back around with a cardboard box full of the items on Angela's list.

"Here's your things," she said. "Pay at the front."

As he took the box, one of the needlepoint women got up and waddled to the cash register. That they accepted credit cards surprised him, but the little plastic box, though out of place, took his payment. He picked up his box and went to the door.

"Be seeing you ladies," he said with a broad wave. "Don't be strangers now, y'hear?"

Maybe he laid it on a little thick, but he got his point across. Whether they stayed or not, became locals or stayed outsiders, he wouldn't be intimidated. None of them would. Ignorant redneck farmers didn't scare him, and none of their voo-doo hocus-pocus garbage scared him either.

He knocked on the window for Angela to pop the trunk. She and Zach looked deep in a conversation, most likely about the girl. What was her name? Chrissy... Christie... Something with a "c" sound to it. Once he put the box in the trunk and closed the lid, he got back in, thankful for the cold air inside the car.

"Supplies secured, ma'am," he said with a salute.

"Did they...?"

"Weird. Just like you said. They'll warm up to us or they won't. I don't care either way. Oh, by the way... Did Zach tell you about his new *girl*friend?"

"Dad!" The boy's ears went crimson again.

Zach sat in the barn and kicked at the rough stones that made up the floor. He already looked over every square inch of his truck four times, and couldn't find anything else to do but wait for the parts. Cindy said she'd be by right after work, and he wanted to be outside with his truck when she saw him. Maybe the truck might make him look cool. At least, he hoped so.

While he waited, he poked through the stalls. Nothing in there could possibly be nearly the find the truck was, but maybe there were other treasures to be liberated. Besides, Mom and Dad told him the barn was his job. Rather than protest, he was grateful. Sure, the barn was hot and the light wasn't great, but at least Dad wasn't breathing down his neck every five minutes, and he didn't have to watch his parents pretend to not fight. And in the barn, he didn't get the same feeling that something watched him, that the house could fall around him at any moment and swallow him up.

He pulled a heavy trash barrel to the last stall and sifted through the debris. More than a twelve-pack's worth of crushed and empty beer cans littered the floor. Those he threw into a separate bin for recycling. Dad was all about the money, and if they even got a few cents for recycled aluminum, who was he to argue? Money was money.

When he lifted the blanket, the smell of old hay and feed mixed with beer and pot smoke wafted up in a cloud. It rolled his stomach and made his eyes burn. No telling what else was on the blanket, but it looked like the thing saw quite a bit of action. It went into the trash barrel. Then he scanned the rest of the stall for bits of treasure, little white twisted pieces of paper that he could pull together into a proper joint. Every bit he found looked burned to nothingness.

He pulled a rake out of the next stall and pulled all the old bedding out, careful to watch for any other prizes. He found a couple of quarters and a cigarette lighter, which was empty, and a pair of women's underwear. Those he picked up with the rake and held them the length of the handle.

"Very nice," said a voice from the front of the barn.

His head snapped toward the voice to see Cindy, one hand on her cocked hip, an amused smile on her face. It took him another moment to realize the pair of underwear still dangled from the rake in his hands. He threw it back into the stall.

"Sorry," he said.

"The truck," she said. "Very nice. You could do a lot with a truck like this one. What did you have in mind?"

"Get it running," he said. "For starters. Where did you...?"

"Your dad told me where you were. He's nice."

"Yeah...so, um...here's the truck."

"The parts are out front," she said. "I'll pull around."

He watched the swing of her hips as she walked back up the driveway. When she pulled back around, it was in a dually, the

Stepside's modern progeny. She looked almost comical as her tiny frame swung down out of the giant beast.

"Gimme a hand?"

He realized he'd been standing stationary as a piece of stone. With an awkward jerk, he hurried around back of the truck to help unload.

"I brought you these," she said as she hefted a tripod with dual lights onto her shoulder. "Might make it easier to see what you're doing."

She smiled as he lifted the light's twin and carried it into the barn. When they finished bringing the other two boxes in, they sat in uncomfortable silence while they examined the parts under artificial daylight. He had to say something, anything, to let her know he was interested without *saying* he was interested.

"How old are you?" He wished he could suck the ham-fisted question back into his mouth. She turned and cocked an eyebrow at him.

"Old enough," she said, then grinned. "I'm sixteen."

"What're you doing working in a Hi/Lo?"

"It's my dad's," she said. "He lets me work there during the summer to make some money."

"Sounds kinda lame." Again with the foot in the mouth. Something about her made him even more stupid and awkward than usual.

"You're not very good at this, are you?" The way she giggled when she said it let him know she didn't take offense, but he still felt stupid.

"Come away from the window."

Angela wrote down figures in her notebook while Gary peered out the window like a lecherous neighbor. Since the girl knocked on the door, the goofy grin stayed plastered to his face. It was cute for the first few minutes. Now it was damned irritating.

"They're going into the barn," came Gary's play-by-play.

"Good for them," said Angela. She wasn't completely comfortable with the idea of a girl in Zach's life, especially one who looked so...mature. Still, she trusted her son, and the girl seemed nice enough.

"Got the lights up!"

She slapped her pencil down on the table and stood up. Only then did Gary tear his gaze away from the show in the barn.

"What?"

"Leave them alone," she hissed. "How would you feel if your dad had watched you and your first girlfriend."

"He did," said Gary. "I hated it."

"Well?"

"Fine." He stomped away from the window and started going through yet another box of knick-knacks. She knew he wasn't really angry, more stung that she'd called him down.

"Hey," she said as she sat on the couch next to him. "Have you noticed anything weird about this place?"

"Like what?"

"I don't know," she said. *Has the house tried to eat you?* "Weird noises... Maybe you've seen something..."

"Is this about the voice in the bathroom again?"

"No," she said. Just like him to be dismissive. "Just forget it."

She went back to the table and sat down, her pencil poised, but with nothing to write.

"I'm sorry," he said. His hands felt good on her neck. Strange that she didn't notice him get up. "It's just an old house. There are bound to be noises and stuff. I promise, it's nothing to worry about. I'm sure of it."

"But I heard banging. Under the floor. It was really loud."

His fingers kneaded her shoulders, squeezed the tension out of them in a delicious little ache.

"These old houses are built up off the ground," he said. "Dollars to doughnuts, there's a raccoon or a opossum under there. If you like the place, we can call an exterminator."

"Maybe," she said. The more he massaged her neck and shoulders, the more she felt inclined to believe him. After all, what else could it be? A ghost? Ridiculous. "It still scared the hell out of me."

"I bet," he said. "I'd have probably pissed myself."

She laughed and reached to touch his magic fingers. But she felt only her own shoulder, her own shirt. She turned to find Gary still seated on the couch in the living room, and the phantom fingers no longer worked her tense muscles. She twisted in her seat, but could find no one else in the room. The hair on her arms prickled as her heart sped to a stronger rhythm.

"Hon? What's wrong?"

Her dry mouth wouldn't make any words, her throat clenched against a scream that stuck somewhere in her chest. Gary made a quizzical look, then stood up.

"I'm sure it's nothing," he said. "It's been a long day. I'm going to take a shower and hit the sack." Then he walked out of the room like nothing happened, as if he didn't notice the look of sheer panic that must've been on her face. The bastard.

She threw herself upright and walked out the back door. Girlfriend or not, she headed outside to see Zach. She didn't want to be in the house.

Cindy leaned over into the engine well of the truck. It was all Zach could do to not stare. Her tight t-shirt hugged her firm young body, and rode up just a bit to reveal her lower back. He wished he could be cool, think of the right thing to say to make her like him. But his brain stopped at *you're pretty* and *wanna see my videogames.*

"Your eyes are going to pop out if you keep staring at me like that," she said.

His ears went nova as he jerked his head to look at anything but the curve of her leg and the way her jeans hugged her butt.

"It's okay," she said as she slid down off the truck. "You *can* talk to me, you know. I'm not going to bite you."

"Sorry," he said.

She sat down on the bumper.

"So where're you from?"

"San Antonio," he said.

"That's not too far away."

"Far enough. Might as well be on the other side of the planet. What about you?"

"Shy Grove, born and raised," she said. "And I can't wait to get out of here."

"I hear that. This place is like...dead."

She nodded. "Didn't used to be. Just started withering away about fourty years ago. So, your aunt lived here, huh?"

"My dad's. I never met her."

"Lots of crazy stories about this house." She said casually, as if there were nothing to the comment. But something in the way her voice dropped, the way her eyes stayed riveted to his, let him know there was something there, stories that needed telling.

"Like what?"

"How're you kids doing?" Mom stood in the doorway, arms wrapped around herself like she was cold, even in the stifling heat of the summer evening.

"Fine," he said with as much emphasis as he could. "We were just talking about the truck."

"I'm Angela," said Mom as she shook Cindy's hand. Just what he needed. Finally about to get somewhere, and out comes mom to meddle and pry.

"Cindy. Nice to meet you Mrs. Carter."

"Yeah, Mom. Glad you could come out to meet her. We're kind of busy."

"Don't mind me," she said. "I'm just taking a break."

She twitched, ever so slightly, at the corners of her mouth. The smile was fake. Something was bothering her. He hoped she and Dad weren't fighting again.

"It's getting late," said Cindy. "I'd better get home."

"Will you come back by?" God, he sounded desperate.

"Of course I will." She flashed him a smile. "Like you can fix that truck all on your own."

For a moment, he thought she really meant it, but the smile put him at ease. She liked him. Enough even to tease with. Maybe Shy Grove wasn't so bad after all.

He watched her climb back into her truck. The engine roared as she cranked it up, then with one more wave, she pulled around and drove down the driveway.

"She seems nice," said Mom.

"Yeah. Thanks a lot."

"Honey, I'm sorry. I didn't mean..."

"Forget it. I'm going to bed."

Panic flashed across her face, like she didn't want him in the house. Dad liked to yell, but he'd never gotten physical before.

"What?"

"Nothing," she said after a pause. "I love you."

"You too." He stalked across the yard and into the house. The screen door slapped against the jamb as he disappeared inside and left his mother standing in the barn.

Gary was snoring by the time she mustered the courage to go back inside and climb in bed. She locked the outside doors and turned off the lights as she went through the house. With each extinguished bulb, her heart beat a little faster, her nerves felt a little more raw. It was irrational. She hadn't been afraid of the dark since she was a child in pigtails. But as the light retreated and the darkness grew more black, she imagined shapes in the living room, phantom feet on the stairs, fingers reaching out from under pieces of furniture to grab her ankles. By the time she reached the bedroom, her heart pounded and sweat that had nothing to do with the heat beaded on her upper lip. It wasn't like her.

The bathroom door stood open, just a crack, with darkness on the other side. Across the room, the closet door was also ajar. She closed first one, then the other then slid into bed and pulled her feet up tight. No matter how old she got, the creature under the bed and the closet monster could still scare her, especially if she'd already creeped herself out. She snuggled up behind her husband in the darkness and buried her face against his back, alert for any noise or any sign of an intruder. But the house was quiet, except for the drone of the air conditioners. Before long, she drifted into an uneasy sleep.

In the dream–it had to be a dream–Gary stood over her, his face slack, his naked body glistening in the moonlight. She tried to sit up, but it felt as if hands pressed her down, held her fast to the mattress. In his hand, the carving knife, the one she used to cut tomatoes, dripped with something dark and thick.

It had to be a dream. If she were awake, she'd scream, wouldn't she? She'd sit up and ask Gary what he was doing. She'd move or cry or anything but just lay pinned to the bed like a useless piece of stone while her husband stared at her with a knife in his hand.

He wasn't bleeding. She wasn't cut, and he wasn't bleeding. So why was there blood on the knife? The answer clicked in her head in an instant and she threw herself forward. She sat up in bed with her throat raw from her screams. Gary shook her, his face etched in panic. There was no knife, no blood. Zach stood in the doorway, wide-eyed, worried and alive.

"Wake up!" screamed Gary. "You're dreaming!"

For a moment dream and reality mixed, and she flailed at her husband, sure that he meant to hurt her, or worse, her child. But as it faded, she stared into their faces.

"You're safe!" said Gary as he wrapped his arms around her. "It's just me. You're safe."

She pulled away for the space of a heartbeat, then collapsed in a fit of sobs into his arms.

"Get your mother some water!" he barked. Zach jumped like he was stung, then ran from the room. When he came back he had a plastic tumbler full. She took it from him and gulped it down.

"What happened?" Zach lingered just inside the doorway.

"Just a dream," she said between swallows. "Nightmare. I'm okay. Go on. Go back to bed."

He paused and stared, then turned and eased his way out of the room. When their door was closed, she pulled away so she could see Gary's face. There was emotion there, not the stone blank from her dream. He'd never hurt them.

"Must've been one hell of a dream," he said.

"You killed him," she said. "Stabbed him."

"'Him' who? Zach? I'd never..."

"I know," she said. "But it was so real. I thought..."

"What? That I would really do something like that?"

"You were holding a bloody knife." She let the words hang while he fought for a reply. "You were just... standing over me with that bloody knife. And something was pinning me down. I couldn't breathe or move."

"Sounds like sleep paralysis," he said. "Have you ever had anything like it before?"

She shook her head.

"Do you think you can go back to sleep?"

"No," she said. "I don't want to. Not for a while."

He sighed and pushed himself out of bed.

"What're you doing?"

"Making coffee," he said. "It's going to be a long night."

"You don't have to..."

"What kind of guy do you think I am?" He smiled and gave her hand a squeeze. "Coffee'll be ready in a minute."

Well *that* was weird.

Zach lay in bed and tried to force the echoes of his mother's screams from his ears. When he heard them, he ran downstairs, certain Dad flipped out. But it was a dream, only a dream. She never had nightmares in San Antonio. At least, not ones that could've woken up a whole city block.

They were both acting weird. Dad and his sudden sleepwalking. Mom and her nightmares and acting paranoid. Thank God for the truck, or he'd be stuck inside with both their crazy asses. Instead, he got to hang with Cindy.

The thought of her made him smile. Just like him, she couldn't wait to get out of this pest-hole. She was pretty, and despite his own clumsy ineptitude, easy to talk to. Maybe she liked him. Maybe that's why she brought the parts herself. It couldn't be normal, for her to deliver car parts. It had to mean she liked him too, didn't it?

And she was so pretty. Pretty enough to already have a boyfriend. And she was older. He rolled over onto his back and stared at the ceiling. Girls like her could get any guy she wanted, and that never meant guys like him. But still, she might like him.

He wondered if she was laying in her bed thinking about him as well.

Angela breathed deep in sleep, her head in Gary's lap. He stroked her hair with one hand and sipped his coffee with the other. She was so beautiful asleep, so at peace. His angel.

He looked down and brushed stray wisps of hair away from her ear. So beautiful. So trusting. So vulnerable.

The thought shocked him, but even as it registered, other thoughts flooded in, things he *could* do, were he a cruel man. Hot coffee down the ear canal, that would wake her up, teach her to disturb his slumber. But why would he think such a thing?

Because she deserves it.

Surely not.

Is not a woman's place, to stand behind the man, to serve and honor him?

Biblically, maybe, but these were modern times. She was her own person, and he supported, not lorded over, her. But the thoughts wouldn't leave him alone. Hot coffee and spittle, a carpet tack or a worm, a long pointed icepick...

He jerked and sent coffee down the side of the couch.

"Huh?" Angela stirred. "I'm sorry...I dozed off."

"It's okay," he said, though somewhere in the back of his mind, he didn't mean it. "C'mon. Let's go get back into bed. A couple hours of sleep is better than none."

He stood and the malicious thoughts toward his wife vanished, as if they'd never happened. He put his arm around her and together they walked back to the bedroom and shut the door. Dreams or not, he was just flat-out tired. She had bad dreams, but he didn't. In fact, he slept more soundly in the old house than he did in San Antonio. Keeping the house looked better and better.

The rest of the week went by fast, and without incident. Zach kept to himself in the barn with his truck, until Cindy came to help, then his sullen face broke into a wide smile that only a girl could've put there. Gary stayed diligent with marking every piece of cloth and wood in the living room, emptying drawers and cataloguing their contents. His treasure hunt, he called it. By the time the appraiser arrived, the downstairs was finished. They slid all the furniture and boxes to one side of the room. The other side looked more than empty without furniture. It looked lonely, almost eerie.

When Gary went to roll the tattered carpet out of the way, he discovered it was nailed down, most likely by his aunt, to keep it from sliding around. It took him the better part of an hour with a claw hammer to dislodge the nails, but the thing smelled and had to go. Beneath, the wooden floors were scuffed and warped. They'd have to be replaced, whether they decided to sell the house or keep it.

The appraiser arrived at noon, clipboard in hand. Gary made a point of introducing himself, and told Angela to make herself scarce. It was one thing for a man to appreciate his wife's beauty, but to drool over her and stare with open lust was more than he was prepared to endure. Far from being insulted, Angela went up the stairs to the little room she claimed as her studio.

Of the upstairs rooms, Zach claimed the largest at the far end of the hall. Angela's was smaller, right at the top of the stairs. Its faded yellow wallpaper and rotted lace curtains didn't bother her, so long as she had a place to set out her tools and clay.

Angela never knew what figure would come out of her workings. Unlike many who sculpted from photos or used a form, her models lived in her head, existed only as vague ideas that took form as she added bits and smoothed away creases.

She turned her CD player on and let the music wash over her. Today, she felt jazzy. As the smooth wail of Dizzy Gillespie's trumpet poured from the speakers, she closed her eyes and put her hands on the clay. The beat moved her fingers across the pliable surface and told her where to push in, where to drag, where to cut and smooth. It was comfortable, to fall back into her rhythm.

The first song ended and she opened her eyes to look at her handiwork. It was a blank head, without features so far. But it had a unique shape, a strong chin and, despite the absence of a nose, a strong profile.

The second song started, *Lover Man*, and she closed her eyes again. But something wasn't right. His horn didn't soothe her mind the way it usually did, but filled the darkness behind her eyelids with flashes of color, bursts of red and purple, lightning streaks of white and orange. It frightened her, but exhilarated at the same time, for the music to affect her so much. Her fingers twisted and pinched in time with the music, guided more by the great player's horn than her will. She wanted to look, but the spell might be broken, so she kept her eyes shut tight against the music. As the song reached its crescendo, her knuckles ached and complained. Whatever the shape on her board was, she felt it not just with her hands, but as if it sucked at her life, pulled the breath from her lungs. Sweat beaded across her forehead and the muscles in her jaw ached against the effort. Her breaths came in ragged gasps, as if it were she who blew the trumpet. She wanted to stop, had to stop, but she couldn't. Her fingers continued to ache and poke and carve until the last note held and rang away. As it faded, she let go of her breath, as if she'd been released from an iron grip. Her hands throbbed and hung useless at her sides. Whatever came over her left with the music.

But what did it leave?

She forced her eyes open and stared at the tiny head in front of her. It was crude, nowhere near finished, but she knew the face, knew the curve of its nose and even the sneer on its lip. Even without knowing the image's name, it terrified her.

It was the face of the man from her dream, the priest, who stripped her bare and offered her up to the carnal lusts of his parishioners in the name of the god they served.

Her first instinct was to crush the thing, to ball it up and throw the glob away for fear that somehow, whatever she sculpted next, his eyes might still look out at her. But that was just silly, wasn't it? It was only clay, made by the clever spell of jazz and her own hands. She should tell Gary, but she knew what he would say. She dreamed him, and on a subconscious level, translated that dream into her artwork. And, of course, he would be right. It was the only explanation that made any sense.

But still, though only half-formed, there was something unsettling about it. The way it smiled, so full of lust and malice, the way its brows turned down in the middle, it almost had life to it. And the eyes...given the right amount of darkness and some ominous music, it wouldn't have surprised her at all to see the thing wink.

She threw a dishtowel over it and stood to leave, but then she stopped. Why did it scare her? After all, she *did* enjoy the dream. So much lust and open abandon, a far cry better than the one where Gary wanted to kill her, that was for certain. Gary didn't need to know. If she told him, he'd want to know about the dream, and it was hers, not his.

She lifted the cloth off the little head and took another look. Still only clay. She sat back down. Dizzy was almost at the end of another song, *On the Sunny Side of the Street*. It was a shame to leave it unfinished, her little man. It shouldn't take too long, not with heavenly jazz to guide her fingers. Heavenly jazz, odd that she'd never thought of the phrase before. But it fit. She took another long look at the statue and lifted her hands to the table. They burned, but more with the need to coax the figure from the clay than from fatigue. She closed her eyes as Dizzy began another song.

When the appraiser showed up, Zach stayed long enough to get a good look at him, then retreated to the barn. The man looked like he expected from Mom's report, older, piggish. Mom went upstairs to her room, and he to his barn.

His barn.

The heat, the smell of old alfalfa and oil, even the dust and dirt was somehow a comfort to him. He wondered how it was that he'd come to like the old structure, but it was no real mystery. It was Cindy. She came to visit when he was out here.

He opened the gate on one of the stalls and waded into the pile of old junk. That old guy inside said people were willing to pay for old crappy furniture. Dad seemed to think the living room set alone could get them more than a thousand dollars. If the guy paid by how old something looked, the stuff in the stall would be worth a small fortune.

He picked through the items, but found nothing of real interest. Though it was full and piled high, he couldn't stay focused on any of it. None of it looked any good, just old and worn out. There was so much of it, too much for one old woman. He wondered about the pieces, the lives attached to them.

He continued to pick, pulled out items that seemed at least to be in one piece, and threw bits he knew to be broken into the trash barrel. Toward the back, he found old glass bottles shaped like cars and buildings. Though empty, they still had a faint scent of the perfume they used to hold. They were, at least, somewhat cool. Not that he wanted to keep them, but they were better than the third rocking chair with a rotted-out seat he found.

As he continued sifting through the debris, the air stilled. For a moment, he pretended not to notice, but then he noticed a strange sound, almost buzzing, as if a thousand moths beat their wings at once. It wasn't a harsh sound, more of a whisper, a chorus of whispers, dozens of voices all at once trying to tell him their secrets. Zach stepped out of the stall and into the main area of the barn. The whispers seemed to come from higher up, falling down through the dusty air.

"Stupid wind," he muttered, though some part of him swore that what he heard wasn't air rushing between boards, but real voices. He swallowed hard, then turned back toward the pile of old furniture. Voices or no, he wasn't going to let his nerves chase him from his sanctum, the one place in this whole God-forsaken town where he felt at ease.

As he leaned down into the stall to pull out more junk, he heard another sound, this one familiar. The low rumble and rev brought a smile to his face. Cindy was back. As the engine shut off, he raised up out of the stall. She climbed out of the truck and the sight of her made him, again, aware of how his hands hung and of the position and placement of his tongue in his mouth. Today she wore bluejeans with holes in the knees and sneakers, along with a t-shirt that read "Chevy Queen." With her hair done in twin braids, she looked like the typical redneck girl with a whole lot of country and just a little bit of naughty inside. He liked that little bit.

What he didn't like were the two large boys who climbed down out of the passenger doors. They both looked to be near his age in their faces, but from the neck down they were bigger than any teen-aged boy should've been. Thick tanned arms came out of a tight stained tank top on one, out of a *Skoal* t-shirt on the other. They both looked like they would be more apt to bench-press her truck than ride in it. Next to them, he looked like a scarecrow.

"Hey, Zach!" she called as they approached. "This is Toby. He wanted to see the Stepside. Is that okay?"

The boy in the tank top grinned and stuck his hand out. Zach shook it and felt the bones in his hand shift.

"Yeah," he said. "Sure."

"He's good at fixing trucks. Thought he might be able to lend a hand."

"Wow," said Toby. "What a pile of shit! Bet we could make it into something real sweet, though. Right?"

"Who's that?" Zach nodded toward the entrance.

The other boy stayed just outside the barn, hands in his pockets. Blonde shaggy hair peeked from under his torn and stained ball cap. He seemed nervous, the way his eyes shifted across the doorway, to the roof, and back down to the floor.

"That's just my little brother," she said. "C'mere Chris. Don't be rude."

The boy shuffled up and nodded without speaking. Zach nodded, but the boy's eyes darted about the barn from shadow to shadow, as if he were afraid of being attacked.

The sanctity of the barn was spoiled. It was, as far as Zach was concerned, his barn, his place where he could be alone with Cindy. But the presence of two more guys, especially Toby with his farm-boy physique, made him feel inadequate. He wondered if they'd dated.

"Well, the engine don't look too bad."

Zach turned to see Toby already in the engine compartment up to his shoulders.

"My dad said I could have it if I got it running."

"That's cool," said Toby. "Truck like this, you'll pick up chicks by the bucket-load."

He flashed a look to Cindy who smiled back.

"Chris!" yelled Toby without looking up. "Get me that socket set from under the seat."

The boy didn't make a sound, but turned and trotted out of the barn.

"Is he okay?" asked Zach.

"Yeah," said Cindy with a laugh. "He's just nervous. He's never been out here before."

"And you have?" The image of the women's underwear and crumpled beer cans flashed through his head.

"Sure," she said. "Lots of times. Folks tell all kinds of stories about this place."

"What kinds?"

"Creepy stuff," she said with a playful smile. "To tell the truth, I was surprised when you told me you were living here."

"Why?"

Chris jogged to the entrance with a black tool case in his hand, then slowed to a cautious walk as he entered.

"Small town," she said. "Lots of stories."

He thought about the blanket and beer cans. It made sense, if she'd been out here, that she'd been with someone. It seemed likely that person might've been Toby. He tried not to think of her with her arms around him, or worse. Then another thought occurred to him.

"So...you've been out here before."

"Yeah."

"Were those beer cans yours?"

"A few," she shrugged. "I guess."

"What about the...other stuff?"

"Like what?" She crossed her arms and her eyes narrowed.

"You know." He didn't want to say it out loud. Not that Mom or Dad would hear him, they were busy, but he didn't want to sound stupid. He pinched his fingers together, raised them to his mouth, and inhaled sharply.

Her nose wrinkled as she smiled again.

"What do you have in mind?"

He shrugged.

"Toby," she said. "Gimme the can."

Without looking up, he reached into his back pocket and flicked a mint tin at her. She caught it and opened it up. Two twisted joints were inside.

"Let's go up to the hay loft," she said. "I bet your momma isn't quite as cool as mine is."

She led the way to a rickety wooden ladder that went up to the second level. It hadn't occurred to him before that moment that there even was a second level. He'd been so busy with the truck and the other discoveries that he hadn't even thought about exploring the rest of the barn. The whispers came from up here somewhere, if they were whispers at all.

"Save some for me," yelled Toby from beneath the truck's hood.

The ladder creaked and moaned as Cindy made it take her weight. Zach waited until she made it to the landing before climbing up himself, partly because it was afraid it might collapse with their combined mass, but also because he was transfixed by her shapely form climbing above him. He hoped she wouldn't notice.

As he passed through the opening, Zach took his first look at the hay loft area. Just like below, it was a mess of storage and disuse. What few actual hay bales there were sagged and smelled of dampness and rot. He wondered where the strange whispering noises came from when a lighter clicked and Cindy took a sharp toke.

"So you were saying?"

"About what?" She passed him the joint.

"Stories. About this place." He sucked in. The smoke tasted sweet and burned in his throat and lungs. He held it in until he felt the tiny rush, then let it all go.

"People say this place is haunted," she said. "Not so much the barn, but the house. But kids around here like to sneak up here. You know, call each other chicken and dare each other to spend the night or something. Lots of stories. The old woman who lived here, your..?"

"Great aunt," he said as he took another hit and passed the joint back to her.

"Everyone was piss-scared of her. Said she was nuts. But the stories the old folks tell are about before the house was built."

"Like what," he snickered. "Built on an Indian burial mound?"

"Not exactly," she said as she walked over to the rail. "Chris!"

The boy's head popped out from under the truck.

"Grab that broom and sweep up the floor."

"Nuh-uh. Ain't my floor!" The boy's voice was higher than Zach expected.

"I want to show Zach something! Now do as I say or I'll whup your ass!"

He crawled out from under the truck and went to do as he was told.

"Little brothers," she said with a snort. "Twice my size and I can still kick his butt. C'mere."

Zach moved to the rail and looked down.

"The old story goes that, a long time ago, there was a church on this land. The church was where the house stands and the barn was where part of the churchyard was."

"Yeah, right," he laughed. "That kind of stuff is never true."

"Oh yeah?" She jerked her head down toward her brother as he swept the flagstone floor clean. "Take a look."

The floor was more haphazard than he realized, with large stones of every shape and size.

"Yeah? So?"

"Look closer." She pointed toward a clean area. Zach scooted closer to see exactly where she pointed. "Don't those rocks seem shaped funny to you?"

He scooted closer still.

"They look like rocks to me."

"Closer," she said. "Look at that one by the wall."

He sighted down her arm, close enough to feel the warmth of her cheek. She smelled nice too. He looked down the length of her slender arm to her fingers. No polish, no long girly nails, just pretty, long fingers. Then down, past her finger, to the spot she meant. The stone on the floor was odd shaped, sure, just like the rest of them. But there was something familiar about it, like something he saw in a comic book or a television show. Something that made the hairs on his arms prickle. Round on one side, flat on the other, just like a...

"Is that supposed to be a grave stone?" he asked, the spell of Cindy's beauty broken.

"It *is* a headstone," she said with a smile. There's a bunch of them down there. They just flipped 'em over and used 'em to lay the floor."

"Why would they do that?"

"Old folks say it's because that church was bad. They say that living in that house drove your aunt nuts."

"According to my dad, she was nuts to begin with."

There were more, just like Cindy said. Now that he'd seen one, he couldn't stop seeing them. The truck, with Toby's legs sticking out from one side and Chris's out the other, was surrounded with five of them. There were more along the outside. He counted at least an even dozen before he stopped looking. The sight made his skin crawl. Were the bodies still under the floor? Did he walk on them every day? Did they still whisper to the living?

"What happened to the church?"

"People say it burned down. The wrath of God or something on account of them being wicked. I don't know for sure, but that's what they say."

"I don't buy it," he said. "You're just trying to scare me." Ghosts weren't real, those *weren't* headstones, and the whispers he heard were just the sounds of wind through loose planks.

"You don't seem like the scared type to me," she said. "Just thought you might like to know."

"Hey!" Toby stood below looking up at them. "Don't y'all be getting too close up there!" He had a devil's grin. Zach's ears heated up as he realized how close to Cindy he stood.

"Shut up, Toby!" She balled up a fist. "I ain't your girl no more. I can do what I want."

"You and him?" Zach's shoulders sagged.

Cindy rolled her eyes and smiled.

"It was a long time ago," she laughed. "He's just yanking your chain."

"Yeah, well, you and loverboy might want to come down and look at this!" He waved a rusted part over his head. Chris's legs still stuck out from the other side of the truck.

Cindy shrugged and made her way back to the ladder. Zach took another look around at the odd shapes and caches of treasure. There were lots of shadow-filled corners, where broken boards could hide and the wind could hiss through. He made a mental note to explore more thoroughly, then followed her down the ladder.

The appraiser wasn't nearly as friendly when Angela wasn't around to ogle. The second she disappeared up the stairs, he became all business, which suited Gary just fine. Not that he blamed the man for looking, but a look and a leer were two different things. Had he not needed him, Gary might've thrown him out. In fact, he might've done worse. *Thou shalt not covet thy neighbor's wife.* But after almost two hours, the appraiser retreated to the kitchen with his notebook and a calculator to go over his figures. Gary got a cold soda from the refrigerator and looked out the window. That girl was back, what was her name? And this time she brought a couple of guys with her. Poor Zach didn't stand a chance with the likes of those two Greek gods around. Served him right though. Gary tried to push him into football, baseball, anything that didn't involve sitting in a dark room with a computer screen his only source if illumination. But the kid wouldn't budge, and now look at him. Skinny, pale, he looked like a vampire, only not as appealing as the movies would have people believe.

Gary was right, had been all along. Not that anyone would recognize it. He glanced at the table where the appraiser looked lost in thought, then took his soda back to the living room. Music filtered down from upstairs. Angela was hard at work, which left him nothing to do but wait.

Of course they're playing while you're working. You've got to do everything, don't you?

It wasn't so much a voice he heard as an impression, a feeling that was so strong that he almost mistook it as his own. After all, he sent Angela upstairs, let Zach hang with his friends.

Such sloth. And what's he doing with that girl in the barn? It doesn't look good, does it? The boy and his lustful heart. The Lord would be displeased.

He took a drink of his soda and sat on the old couch. He always prided himself on being open-minded, progressive in his attitude toward his family. His own father's heavy-handed approach forced him into basketball at an early age. All those practices, all the pain and sweat, but all he really wanted to do was read. To his father, a boy that didn't bring home trophies wasn't worth having. And his attitude toward his mother was no better. Dinner had to be on the table by six, the house had to be clean. He did everything he could to ensure that she had no life outside of the home. But Gary watched and learned. As he grew up under the old ogre's eye, he promised himself that he wouldn't force his own son to do anything he didn't want to do, that he'd let his wife follow her passions.

"Well," said the appraiser from the kitchen doorway. "I think I've got good news for you."

After Hours poured through the speakers, every note a pinprick on her skin. Her hands didn't hurt anymore, didn't burn with fatigue or need, but felt glorious as they smoothed the clay. There he was, hidden beneath lumps and imperfect gray. With every stroke of her thumb, every drag of her finger, he came more into sharp focus. As she worked, it was almost as if hands guided hers, showed her where his cheek should end and where the cleft in his chin should be. When the hands moved up her arms, she almost didn't notice until their soft touch raised goosebumps on her skin. It was the music, of course, but as the phantom hands moved up along her shoulders and down her back, she felt a chill of pleasure race through her body. She closed her eyes and let her head fall back and imagined the preacher's hands on her body, a gentle massage, more intimate. It felt almost like a lover's embrace. She wanted to give into it, to let his hands explore every inch of her.

"Angela!" Gary threw the door open with a bang. She shot

upright in her chair, as if she'd been caught doing something, but she was the only one in the room.

"What?" she said. It came out a little too loud, a little too anxious.

"You're never going to belive how much he's appraised the furniture at!"

The smile on his face let her know that the amount wasn't small. He handed her a form on the appraiser's letterhead. At the bottom was the number.

"That's a lot of zeroes," she laughed. "Is he serious?"

"He's coming with a truck tomorrow. They're taking it all to auction next week. He gets ten percent commission, and we get the rest!"

"That's great," she said. She still felt caught, though she couldn't fathom why. It wasn't like there was another man in the room. Just Dizzy and her. And the little preacher's head, but it wasn't quite finished yet.

"That's different," said Gary. He indicated the preacher's head. "Really well done, but it's a bit more serious than your usual stuff, isn't it?"

"What's that supposed to mean?" All her work was serious. So what if she liked to sculpt fairies and fantasy figures. That didn't mean they were frivolous.

"Nothing!" he said. "Just, he looks like he might really exist, that's all."

"I thought I'd try something new." She covered the head with her dishtowel and pushed out of the room past Gary. "That's okay, isn't it?"

"Hey!" he shouted as he followed her down the stairs. "I didn't mean anything by that! Why're you being so pissy?"

She turned and glared. In truth, she didn't know why she was so angry at being disturbed. By all rights, his news should've made her happy. But even his presence in her space grated her nerves, that he had the audacity to comment on her sculpture when he'd never shown so much as a creative bone enraged her.

Thump.

The sound startled them both. At first, she didn't register what it was, only that there was the sound, that it was loud enough for them both to hear, that she felt it through the soles of her feet and into her legs. They stared at each other, her anger and his confusion like a storm between them.

Thump.

It was coming from beneath the house, the same noise as before, strong enough that it felt like something wanted to punch a hole through the floor.

"What the hell...?" Gary took a few tentative steps toward the center of the room. Angela crossed her arms and watched him.

"I heard that yesterday," she said. He couldn't dismiss it this time. He couldn't write it off as her imagination. This time, she was too angry to be afraid.

Thump.

"When? Why didn't you tell me?" He knelt to look under the couch.

"Why? So you could tell me it was my imagination?"

He stood and stared at her, his expression a mixture of exasperation and confusion.

"No, because that kind of noise could mean something's wrong with the house."

"Oh, I see. So *now* you want me to tell you when something scares me."

He didn't say anything for a moment, like he wanted to choose his words carefully.

"I think maybe you need to get out of the house for a little while," he said at last. "Take Zach with you, get some air. You're snapping at me for no reason."

"I..." But he was right. Gary was never anything but supportive of her art. It wasn't like her to fly off the handle at him. But the anger was so real, so hot. Maybe it was cabin fever.

"I'm sorry," she said. "I think maybe an hour or two out of the house might do me some good."

She hugged him, then went to their room to change her clothes. As she traded her sweat pants for jeans and put on a bra, she glanced around the room. There was no one else there, but she still imagined the eyes of the preacher watching her, tracing the line of her hips. When she finished dressing, she stepped into her sandals, grabbed her purse, and hurried out through the kitchen.

The contrast of the dim house and the bright yard washed the colors out until she put on her sunglasses. The truck in front of the barn let her know Zach probably wouldn't be interested in leaving, at least not with her, but she decided to ask anyway.

"Hey Zach," she said as she came around the corner. All four of them stood bolt-upright and stared, as if they'd been caught doing something. "You want to come into town with me?"

"No thanks," he said, a little too quickly. "We're busy."

The others nodded, except for the blond boy who wouldn't meet her eyes and instead stared at his shoes.

"Hello Cindy," she said. "Who are your friends?"

"This is Toby and her brother Chris," said Zach. "They came to help with the truck."

"I see." They were up to something, that much was clear. "And how's it coming?"

They erupted into a chorus of "fine" and more nodding. She got the message. They wanted her to leave them to their privacy. She took a deep breath. A sweet smell tickled her nose, faint, but unmistakable.

"Who's holding," she demanded. All four of their faces melted into horrified expressions, but none of them said anything.

"Come on," she said. "I know that smell. I'm not stupid, you know. Give it up."

Still nothing. She fixed her eyes on her son.

"Zach?" His red-rimmed eyes met hers. "Who?"

"Not me," he said. "I swear."

She focused on the other three. Of course it couldn't have been her son. He was a good boy. But the others, at least one of them had it. She stepped closer and sniffed the air. The scent was light, but fresh.

"Chris?" She glared at him until he looked up at her. His eyes were clear, no sign of being stoned. "Who?"

Chris licked his lips and glanced to the others. He seemed like he was about to blab, when...

"Okay," said Toby. "It's me. I've got it."

"Give." She stuck out her hand. The boy pulled a mint tin from his back pocket and slapped it into her palm. Inside, a full joint sat beside the remains of another. She took the half-burnt one, closed the tin, and handed it back to him.

"Next time," she said. "Share."

Zach's face went from terror to disbelief. She winked at him and turned to leave.

"Don't let your father know," she said as she walked around to the front of the house. Inside, she screamed with laughter. Of course he wouldn't know. She'd not smoked pot since before he was born, but that didn't mean she'd lost her taste for it. Or that she didn't remember its calming effect. It might be just what she needed in the creepy house, with its banging pipes and weird feelings. The last thing she wanted was to start another fight with Gary. Her nerves were already shot.

Angela drove into Shy Grove with no real agenda. She didn't need anything as much as she wanted to get away from the house. Maybe there was a place she could get a cup of coffee and a doughnut. That would be nice, if the people there didn't treat her like a pariah. A quick loop through town showed her what passed for a "busy" Friday in Shy Grove. There were a few cars parked on the street, but no more than the last time she came through town. In fact, she couldn't be certain, but they looked like the same cars. There had to be more of the town, she reasoned. There just had to be. For starters, there wasn't a bank, a doctor's office, or even a decent grocery store. The only thing she could figure was that people drove all the way to Luling for their needs.

As she made the loop through the center of town, she spotted a police car parked at the market. She pulled up beside it and got out. The officer wasn't behind the wheel, which meant he had to be inside. Perfect. Another encounter with the hags in the market wasn't what she wanted, but maybe with the policeman there they might mind their manners.

An old bell chimed as she pushed the door open. It was as if she'd just left, with the same four faces that stared at her. Only this time there was a fifth, this one chubby with mustache.

"Hi," she said to the officer. "I'm Angela Carter."

"Milt Weston." He stuck his hand out and shook hers. "What can I do for you, ma'am?"

"I'm new to the area," she said. "I was hoping someone might be friendly enough to tell me where I could get a cup of coffee? Maybe a bite to eat?"

"Closest place for that would be Luling," he said. "But these ladies here make a fine cup of coffee."

"Oh," she said. "I don't think so. I guess I'll just head on into Luling."

The officer smiled and turned toward the woman behind the meat counter.

"Ida, what'd you say to this young lady?"

"Nothin' that weren't proper," shot back the old woman. "Why do I have to be nice to every stranger that comes into town?"

"Because it's polite, that's why." He turned back to Angela. "You have to excuse them. These old biddies don't know from good manners. Have a seat and I'll get you a coffee and a cruller."

If nothing else, it was worth it to see the looks on the old women's faces. It was also nice for a local to be nice to her. She took a seat at one of the cafe tables near the window. A moment later, the old officer appeared with two mugs of coffee and two pastries on white plates lined with lacy paper doilies.

"So," he said as he sat down. "Miss Ida back there tells me you and your family just moved to town."

"My husband just inherited a house out here." She sipped her coffee. It was strong and hot, just how she liked it. "We haven't decided yet if we're staying."

The officer's smile faded. He took a sip of his coffee and looked up at her.

"He inherited Old Ester's place, eh?"

"Yes, he did," she said. "How did you know?"

"Small town," he said. "I know pretty much everyone around here. And I know who died recently. It's not too big of a stretch to figure it out."

"I see."

"Can I give you some friendly advice?" She nodded. "I'd just let the place sit empty. Don't try to sell it, don't try to live there, just let it rot."

"Ought to burn it down!"

"Hush up, Ida."

"But why?"

"Don't you know anything about Ester?"

"Well, no. I don't." In fact, up until a few weeks ago, she didn't know Gary even *had* and Aunt Ester. Not until the lawyer showed up with the last will and testament. Even then, he wasn't keen to talk about her. The woman was crazy, he said, and his last surviving relative.

"She yours?"

"My husband's," she replied. "His aunt."

He considered for a moment, then stood, his cruller untouched.

"You might want to talk to your husband," he said. "I ain't the right person to tell you about his family."

"Why? What's wrong with Gary's family?" Curiosity burned inside her. Whatever it was sounded important, enough so that almost everyone seemed wary of the house.

"Nothing," he said. "Ester was a peach of a woman. Just… well…you better talk to him." He took his wide-brimmed hat off the counter, nodded to the ladies behind the counters, and walked out into the street.

"I don't understand," she said. The other women busied themselves with counting items on the shelves or dusting. "What's he not telling me?" None of them answered. Enough was enough. She stood and stormed to the meat counter where Ida busied herself with a large knife and a slab of beef.

"If there's something to tell, then God damn it, tell me!"

"There ain't no call for that kind of language," said Ida. "You want to know? Fine, I'll tell you. You know how she died? Ester?"

She shook her head.

"Drowned. In the bathtub. Took 'em a while to find her too. She didn't never come out of that house 'less she really needed something."

"She was very old," said Angela. "It was an accident."

"Weren't no accident!" spat Ida. She slammed her carving knife onto the counter. "Ain't but two ways it could'a happened. She either killed herself or someone did it for her. My money's on the second one."

"That's ridiculous. Who would want to kill an old woman?"

"It's that house," said the woman at the dry goods counter. "It ain't never been right. Not since it was built!"

"Hush your mouth!" said Ida. "You listen to me, and you listen good. Ain't no good to come of that house, you hear? No good! And that's all I'm gonna say on the subject."

She threw a challenging look to the other women, who snapped back to their duties. Angela took the hint, frustrated, and walked back to the counter.

"How much do I owe you?" she said.

"Just go," said the woman at the register. "Least we can do."

Angela thanked her and walked back out to her car.

8

He thought they were busted for sure. Cindy and the guys left right after Mom did, despite his protestations. He couldn't blame them, but he wished Cindy'd stayed, if for no other reason that so she could tell him more about the house. The more he looked at the stones in the floor, the more they did resemble headstones. But they couldn't be. Not in *his* barn.

He made his way back to the ladder and climbed back up to the loft. The work light's rays didn't reach the second floor, but there was still enough daylight that the loft wasn't in total darkness. He looked down over the rail at the stones in the floor again. There wasn't a pattern to how they laid. If they were grave stones, they might've been moved. But they couldn't be. It was a stupid urban legend, one made up to scare kids. Just like the old hook-man, or that one about the girl whose boyfriend they found hanging over his car. That's all the story was, the proverbial poodle in the microwave.

He turned his attention to one of the alcoves. There was that sound again, breathy whispers of wind sneaking through spaces in the boards. Headstones and whispers in the darkness. If he didn't know better, he might be scared. The trouble was, somewhere between what he knew and what he heard, there was that little spark of doubt, that place where the darkness still held monsters.

He crept deeper into the shadowy alcove, toward the whispers and more amorphous shapes. The tarps gave no indication as to what was under them, but he knew they couldn't be nearly as exciting as the one that hid the truck. For starters, they were too small, and there was no way anyone could get another truck up into the loft. But there were so many other things they could've hidden that he had to find out. If there was a motorcycle under one, he wasn't even going to tell Dad, he was just going to claim it.

Under the first tarp, he found yet another dusty, scratched and warped headboard, one that looked made for a queen-sized bed. One more thing for Dad to sell off. The whispers were louder the deeper he went. The second covered a long table, ornately carved from dark wood. There were scratches on the top, plus a ring where something must've sat for a long time. He ran his fingers over the finish and they came up sticky. He pulled on the edge of it to move it away from another tarp and found it almost too heavy to move. How the old woman got it up to the loft, he couldn't begin to guess, but it didn't matter. It stood between him and whatever was under the third tarp. He hunkered down low, grabbed the edge, and gave a yank. For a moment, he was weightless as a piece of it slid outward. He staggered backward until he hit the rail, which creaked and shifted under his body weight. On instinct, he flapped his arms and threw himself forward, landing flat on his stomach on the floor. It took him a few moments to stand back up, for his stomach to stop rolling and his heart to slow down. When he did stand, he looked back down over the rail. It was a long way down, and while it might not kill him, a fall from that height would certainly hurt like hell.

He turned back toward the table and saw a drawer lying on the floor, its paper contents scattered. So that was what he grabbed. He was lucky the rail held, otherwise...

The whispers were louder now, so much so that he almost imagined they were real words.

The yellow papers crinkled as he picked them up. A few disintegrated at his touch, but most stayed intact. Music staffs marked the pages, with lyrics that ranged from "Onward Christian Soldiers" to "The Old Rugged Cross." Church music, left in an old table. He stepped back and took a good look at the thing. It wasn't an old table after all, but an altar. It struck him that the voices ebbed and flowed, as if they were singing.

Cindy's story about the old church came back to him and sent a chill down his back. But it couldn't be. The old church burned, according to her. Struck by lightning from God or whatever. So if it burned, why would the altar be here?

Whatever, it wasn't an altar anymore. Now it was just a hunk of heavy wood that was in his way. He climbed over it to the space where the third tarp concealed another shape. Probably not a motorcycle, but it might be something just as cool. He gave the tarp a yank. A dozen gleaming eyes glared back at him and hissed. Zach let out a yelp as the rats scattered. A few ran straight for him. He stomped and flailed and screamed before finally hopping back up on the table.

"Zach!" He looked down from the loft to see his father, a baseball bat in his hand. "Zach!"

"Up here!" he called.

"I heard a scream!"

"Rats!" Stupid fuzzy disease ridden monsters. They scared the hell out of him, and now he was going to hear about it for days. Was that what he heard, their chattering and scrachting? "It's okay. They just startled me."

"What're you doing up there?"

"I found some more stuff," he called. "You'd better come take a look."

Gary put the bat in the back of the Stepside and made his way up the ladder. When he reached the top, he stopped and caught his breath, then grinned.

"Why are you standing on that table?"

"Rats," said Zach. "Duh. There were a bunch of them, and they were trying to run up my pants leg."

Dad let out a long laugh. "That happened to my grandpa once," he said. "You've never seen an old man strip down to his skivvies faster in your life! So what's up here?"

"Take a look," he said. "More furniture. That appraiser might like some of it. And this old thing."

"Wow," said Gary. "That looks like an old church altar."

"Yeah, and this was in one of the drawers." He passed the sheet music to his father. Gary flipped through the pages until one caught his eye.

"What kind of church did this come from?"

He passed the sheet music back to Zach.

Let our pleasures be thy pleasures, let us share in all your pain, let us sing unto your praises, beneath the blooded rain...

"Never heard that one before," said Gary. "Must've been Pentecostal or something." He turned back toward the ladder. When he was right in front of it, he stopped, without turning.

"You and that girl," he said. "You haven't been misbehaving up here, have you?"

Zach's blood chilled and he went rigid. Mom wouldn't have told, but he might've smelled it.

"No," he said. "Of course not."

"Good boy," said Gary as he descended the stairs.

It wasn't the way he walked, or that he made any threatening gesture. It wasn't even *what* he said, but *how* he said it. His voice. The way he said "good boy." It filled Zach with dread.

Strange, that song. The words all sounded so familiar, but he was sure he'd never heard them before. He could almost hear the melody in his head, but then, most religious dirges sounded the same. Still, it was strange for the boy to find them, and then to hear them in his head.

He shook the feeling off. There was still work to be done, and not nearly enough time in which to do it. Noon tomorrow, and all his aunt's stuff would be gone. From the living room, anyway. Then they could continue with the rest of the house, clear out all that crazy old woman's junk and start to make it feel like a real home. Their home. That was, of course, if Angela and Zach decided to stay. That girl, Cindy, would sure make it hard for Zach to leave, then Angela would be outnumbered, and they could live here. Happily ever after in their country home.

First thing, however, was first. He had to get the furniture shifted so the movers could get it out of the house without damaging it. Most if it he would have no trouble lifting, but a few were going to take two backs. Maybe even three. He shifted what pieces he could until he was satisfied, then turned his attention to the heavier pieces. The couches he could probably move by himself, but the warped and cracked floor might do damage to their spindly legs. The sideboard and hall tree were far too heavy to even attempt. The sideboard in particular might take all three of them. Exhausted, he got a cold soda from the refrigerator, then sat at the kitchen table.

The song was still there, still looping in his head, as if he'd grown up with it, forgotten for a while, but still there, a part of him, when called. He was sure he'd never heard it before, but there it was, all the same.

Tires crunched the gravel driveway outside. The windows didn't rumble as they did with Cindy's truck's powerful engine. Angela must be home. He sipped his soda until she came in through the front door.

"Gary?"

"Kitchen!"

She bustled through the kitchen door and stopped, a quizzical look on her face.

"That's pretty," she said. "What was it?"

"What?"

"That song. What was it?"

"What song?"

She put on hand on her hip and faced him.

"The one you were just humming. Jesus, if you don't want to tell me, just say so."

The sound of the Lord Savior's name rankled him, though he couldn't imagine why. They weren't a particularly religious family, but that she took His blessed name in vain chewed at the back of his mind.

"Sorry," he said. "I don't know. I wasn't aware I was humming anything."

"I do that all the time," she said with a laugh. "It'll catch up to you, probably tonight when you're asleep."

She put her purse on the counter and sat down at the table next to him.

"Tell me about your aunt," she said.

"Why?"

"I just want to know. It just occurred to me that I don't know anything about that side of your family, and I want to know."

She was lying. Her smile twitched a little and something in her eyes didn't quite ring of curiosity. It looked almost like fear. Still, there was no harm in telling her.

"Aunt Ester was crazy," he said. "End of story. She was my mom's sister. Moved here when she was about twenty-ish, and never left. That's about it."

"Why'd she move here, of all places?"

"Why else?" he laughed. "A man. Only this one wasn't just any man. He was a preacher."

Her smile twitched again. "Really?"

"Oh, yeah. My family's from Austin originally. According to my mom, one day this traveling tent-revival thing came blowing through town. She got swept up in the guy's act and followed him out here. He had a whole bunch of 'em."

"Did you ever meet her?"

"Sure, once or twice. But whenever she showed up, the whole family got quiet, like the wrong word would set her off. I think I was twelve the last time I saw her. Now really, why all the sudden interest?"

"It's just..." Something was bothering her. Something scared her, and she didn't want to say what. Like she couldn't trust him, didn't need him. "We're living in her house, going through her things, it just seems a little ghoulish."

"She's dead," he said. "I don't even know why she left me the place. I mean, yeah, I was the only living relative, but why not just leave it to charity or something? She didn't even know me."

"How'd she die?" The question hit him like a slap in the face. He expected her to apologize or to at least look contrite, but she did neither, just sat and stared and expected an answer.

"I don't know," he said. "The lawyer didn't volunteer any information and I didn't ask."

"In town, they say she drowned. In the bathtub."

"'They' who?"

"The women at the general store. They seemed to know a lot about her."

"Why don't you go ask them about her, then?"

"I did." She looked down at the table. "They told me it wasn't their place to tell. Said I should ask you."

"Well, they were right," he roared. "It's not their fucking place to talk about my family!"

She pulled away from him with horror in her eyes. It took him a moment to realize he was standing over her, arm raised as if he would ever strike her. The fear on her face was the same as he felt, and toward the same person.

"I'm sorry," he said. "I'm...I don't know what..."

She got up without a word, snatched up her purse, and ran out the back door, her choked sobs saying more than any words she could've said. He slumped back into the chair with his head in his hands. He could follow her out, try to explain that he didn't realize, would never, but he didn't. She might think he was following her out to hurt her, and he didn't want to frighten her more. He'd just sit and wait for her to calm down, then he'd try to talk to her, tell her how sorry he was.

He took a sip of his soda and began to hum another verse of his comfortable song.

That son of a bitch!

Angela stormed out the back door. He wouldn't follow her, not if he knew what was good for him. Throughout their marriage, through all the arguments, he'd never raised his voice to her unprovoked, and never threatened her. Hot angry tears stung her cheeks as she crossed the yard into the barn.

"Mom?" Zach peered down from the hay loft. "You okay? What's wrong?"

"How did you get up there?" she demanded.

"There's a ladder." He pointed. She made for the ladder and climbed it without a thought to how rickety the thing was or how high up. When she reached the landing, she threw her purse down and sat on a rotted hay bale, face in her hands, and let out jarring sobs.

"Mom?" There was panic in his voice. He wasn't used to seeing her so emotionally out of control. "What happened?"

"It's your father!" she sniffled. "I don't know what I said or what I did, but I've never seen him that angry."

Zach sat next to his mother and put his arm around her. For all the times she comforted him, cleaned his skinned knees, listened when the other children were mean, and was the buffer between him and his father's obvious disappointment, now it was he who comforted her.

"It's this house," she said. Zach stiffened at the phrase.

"What makes you say that?"

"You've got the barn and your truck, I've gotten out for a little while, but your dad's just been here, inside the whole time. I think he needs a break."

"Are you kidding?" Zach pulled away and gaped at her. "I don't care how bad a case of cabin fever he has, he still doesn't get to be an asshole."

"Zachary!" He'd never spoken like that before, not in front of her.

"Sorry." He looked at his shoes.

"I know," she said after a moment. "And he never has before, right?" Sure, there'd been fights, arguments, but Gary was more the type to reason things out, debate in circles and beat the issue into the ground with words, never his fists. He had a knack for making a person feel guilty with a glance, enraging them with a single word, but violence was never his way.

"I guess."

Angela leaned over and reached for her purse. When she'd pulled it to her, she fished inside until she found the half-burnt joint and held it up in front of her son.

"You want to tell me about this?"

"I...we..."

"How long?"

He shrugged.

"Your friends get it for you?"

"Sometimes."

He wouldn't meet her eyes. She stared at the top of his head and remembered when she could make him feel better with a cookie, and mommy-hugs were the best medicine no doctor could prescribe.

"Tell you what," she said. "No more secrets. Not between us. I mean it. Okay?"

"Whatever."

"Don't *whatever* me, promise."

He lifted his head and his eyes met hers.

"I promise."

"Good." She fished a lighter out of her purse, lit the joint, and took a deep drag. The sweet smoke burned on its way down and caught in her lungs. She coughed hard, but fought to keep the smoke down.

"Geez, Mom, you're going to barf."

"Haven't done this in a while," she said after another toke, then she passed the joint to him.

"No secrets," he said. "Right?"

She nodded. Her head felt light, more relaxed. She'd forgotten how good it could be.

"Cindy told me something about the house. I don't know if it's true, but it's weird."

"What'd she tell you?"

She'd come back inside in a minute. She had to know he'd never hurt her. Now that the rage was gone, he couldn't remember why it flared anyway. It was a small town, and there were bound to be stories about Ester. Hell, her exploits were grist for the family mill for most of his life, until his parents died. It might even be good to get some perspective from the people who actually *knew* her, seeing how she was a stranger to him. He needed to tell her how sorry he was, to explain that he didn't mean what he said or did. But he didn't want to chase her. Let her be out of the house. Let her cool off enough to want to come back inside and then they would talk. He would apologize, ask her to forgive him. If he was lucky, she might.

And why should I need her forgiveness? She should be begging for me to forgive her. No. That wasn't right. He needed to clear his head, but there wasn't time.

In the meantime, he decided to try to move the rest of the furniture. It didn't seem right to ask for her help, or Zach's. They were probably talking about what a bastard he was, and they were right. He deserved it.

He decided to see just how heavy the hall tree was. He wouldn't be able to move everything, but some of the smaller heavy items, he could get out of the way before they came back in.

It was solid, that much was obvious, but the seat lifted to a hollow space inside, which made him think he might be able to lift it on his own. He got a hand on either side and pulled. It didn't budge. A second pull and he felt it give. Not much, but enough to make him think he might be able to move it himself. On the third try, it gave and moved toward him, but his hand was caught between the heavy back and the wall. It scraped along his knuckles and squished his fingers between the wall. Before his brain interpreted the pain, he gave it one more yank and properly ground his hand into the rough plaster.

Hot fire shot down his nerves as the skin ripped, so much so that he didn't have time to scream. Instead he sucked air in sharp, stood with his face twisted like a cartoon cat, and flailed his good hand against the side of the box. When he shoved it with his shoulder, it tilted forward just enough to free his hand. Crimson dripped from his knuckles and fingers onto the warped wooden floor. The first aid kit. He needed the first aid kit. Angela knew where it was. She had to. She was the one that packed it.

The sight of his own blood made Gary shudder as he walked across the living room to the kitchen. At the sink, he ran cool water over his injuries, hissing against the sting. As the blood washed down the drain, he saw the injuries more clearly. Most of the hide was pulled off from the wrist to the fingertips. A tough guy like his father might have shrugged it off and gone about his business, but his body shook as shock took firm hold. Angela. He needed Angela. She'd know what to do. He wrapped the mangled hand in a dishtowel and went to the back door.

"Honey?" he called. From the barn, he heard first her giggle, then Zach's. They didn't hear him, probably too busy laughing at something that was his fault. Here he was, working the flesh from his bones, literally, and they were in the barn playing. Mangled hand or no, he'd teach them a thing or two.

He stepped through the back door and across the porch. As his feet touched the ground, all his anger evaporated, left him bewildered. His body quaked and his legs went rubbery. He slumped to the ground.

"Angela…" he tried to shout, but his voice came out as a hoarse whisper. His hand no longer hurt, not a good sign, but throbbed like a bass drum in time with his heart. Shivers raced through his body.

His thoughts grew muddy, forgetful of why he was outside or what happened to his hand. More than pain or fatigue, he was afraid. He licked his lips, took as deep a breath as he was able, and tried one more time, the only word he could think.

"Help!" The effort threw him forward, face down onto the dirt path. He lay there panting as a shriek echoed in his ears and fast footsteps approached. Angela's panic-stricken face was ringed in a growing iris of darkness.

9

The doctor said he'd be right back, but that was forty-five minutes ago. It took both of them to get Gary into the back of the car, and then another hour to reach Seton Medical Center's emergency room. The whole way, Zach dabbed his father's sweat-slicked forehead with a cold cloth, and tried not to look worried. Angela saw no need for a brave face. Her husband's hand bled terribly, and the whole way to the hospital, he hummed a strange song through his delirium. If a cop *dared* try to pull them over, she would've let him chase her all the way to the God-damned emergency room door.

The triage nurse took one look at Gary and ushered him to one of the stalls. She also was kind enough to bring Angela a cup of coffee.

The coffee was cold now, the doctors busy with other patients. Gary lay on the gurney with an oxygen mask over his face and an IV tube protruding from his good hand. The other didn't even look like a hand anymore, but a large ball of gauze and tape.

Zach stood in the corner, his eyes locked on his father's inert form. He looked scared, and Angela couldn't blame him.

The curtain whipped aside with a metallic swish and a plump nurse in lavender scrubs bustled in.

"We just need to do a few more tests," she said. "I have to take more blood."

"He lost a lot," said Angela. "Is that a good idea?"

"I won't take much," said the nurse with a practiced smile.

"He'll never even miss it."

"What's wrong with my dad?" Zach's voice shook as he spoke. "Is he gonna be alright?"

"He's going to be fine," said the nurse. "We've got a hospital full of good doctors here. We'll take care of him."

"But what's *wrong* with him?"

The nurse's smiling facade cracked, just a bit, and confusion clouded her image.

"We don't really know," she said. "The doctor will be by in a minute talk to you."

Before either of them could protest or press for answers, she turned and was gone, the curtain slung back to closed behind her.

"What was he doing?" asked Zach. "I mean...his hand..."

"I think he was trying to move the heavy stuff by himself," she sighed. "There was a bloody smear on the wall, but that's all I could find. None on the floor or anything."

"But how..?"

"I swear, I'll never do that again," slurred Gary. Angela turned to see his eyes half open. "Hi honey. What's up, Tiger?"

Relieved tears rolled down her cheeks.

"Dad!" Zach ran to his father's side and hugged him as gently as he could. Gary smiled through his oxygen mask.

The curtain slid aside again and a tall, balding old man in a long white coat slipped inside.

"You're awake," he said. "That's a good sign."

"What happened?"

"As best we can tell, shock combined with exhaustion. You're lucky. People die from that, you know."

"When can I leave?" Gary's eyes drifted closed in an extended lazy blink.

"You're not going anywhere," said the doctor. "At least not for a couple of days. Your body was trying to tell you that it needed rest. How long have you gone without sleeping?"

"Gary sleeps every night," said Angela. "He's usually in bed by around ten o'clock."

"He's been sleepwalking," said Zach. "I've seen him."

"I have?"

"Hmmmm." The doctor wrote a few notes on Gary's chart. "And how long has this been going on?"

"About a week," said Zach. "Every night, I think."

"We'll have to run a few more tests. We're going to go on and admit you. You'll need to be here for a minimum of forty-eight hours. If the tests come back clean, you'll be able to leave then."

"But the house... The movers..." He tried to sit up in spite of his exhaustion. Angela laid a gentle hand on his chest and eased him back down onto the pillow.

"Zach and I can cover it," she said. "No problem. We'll get everything ready for tomorrow. After the movers leave, we'll come back. Okay?"

He looked unsure, but nodded.

They waited around until he got settled into his room, then Angela kissed his cheek while Zach watched from the doorway. When his medication made him sleep, they took that as their cue to leave.

Neither spoke on the drive home, the bump of the road the only soundtrack. They stopped at a Whataburger on the way for dinner, then headed back to Shy Grove. As the car pulled up in front of the house, the sun dipped below the treetops.

"Okay," said Angela as she killed the engine. "We've got a lot to do, and not a lot of time to do it."

"Yeah," said Zach. She was used to his silence, but the quiet on the drive home was different somehow. He looked worried, which was something to which she was not accustomed. His usual put-out attitude was replaced with something like brooding, but more honest.

"He's going to be fine," she said. "The doctors will take good care of him." She wished she really felt as confident as her words.

"I know," he said. "It's just...I don't know about being alone here. In the house, I mean."

Her stomach fluttered. The prospect of being alone in the house was not one she enjoyed. Of course, there were only strange noises, and Gary explained them all away. The hallucinations were just fits from her subconscious. The house was just a house, nothing evil about it. But in the back of her mind, fear sent out a small tickle that grew to an itch.

"Nothing to worry about," she said. "You'll see."

There were seven large pieces that needed moving. The first five were no problem with both Angela and Zach lifting. By the time they reached the sixth, the air in the living room hung heavy with sweat and Zach's hair was plastered to his forehead. The sixth, while no heavier than the rest, was a different sort of problem. The eight-foot-tall mirrored china cabinet scared the hell out Angela. The panes in the front were set with antique carved glass, all original, all irreplaceable. The mirrors in the back were old fashioned, backed with real silver. A wrong step on the warped floor or a careless handhold and the thing would be worthless. Its gargantuan weight combined with their tired arms made them take special care when moving it.

"Why are we doing this again?" grunted Zach.

"Because," said Angela through clenched teeth. "Your father said we needed to."

They set it down ten feet from its original position, then stood back panting and stretching their backs.

"Your father said the moving guys wanted everything put in one area so they didn't miss anything."

"That's dumb," said Zach. "They're the movers. Aren't they supposed to... you know... *move* stuff?"

"Yeah," she sighed. "They are."

The last piece, the grand side board, seemed too heavy for even an army to move.

"What do you say we leave this one?" Angela gave it one last heave, then gave up with a smile.

"Fine by me. What about that thing by the door?"

"It's a hall-tree," said Angela. "I kind of like it."

"Isn't that the thing Dad busted his hand on?"

"Yeah, but I think maybe it'll look good by our front door. Don't you?"

"Whatever," he snorted. "But you get to tell Dad."

She turned and surveyed the room. Now, with all the furniture off to one side, the room seemed lonely, like the inside of a storage shed. The warped and scratched floor gave the place an abandoned look.

"Hey," said Zach. She looked to see him bent over at the waist staring at something on the floor. "What's this?"

The scratches were pale, surrounded by more scuffs and

wear. At a glance they looked like nothing. In fact, it wasn't until she paid real attention to them that she began to make out shapes in the scratches. A few looked like it might be a knot of some sort, though with so much damage and the wood buckled, she couldn't be sure. But there was one pattern she felt certain about. In no other place on the disfigured floor were there so many symmetrical curves, so many straight lines and points. There was no mistaking the eye in the scratches.

"That's weird," she said. "I wonder what it means..."

Thump.

Zach jumped at the first beat while Angela let out a momentary squeak of terror, her heart pounding in her ribs.

"What the hell was that?" shouted Zach.

Thump.

"It's nothing," she said, though her skin crawled and her breaths seized in her chest.

Thump.

Just the banging pipes, nothing more. Or maybe a raccoon or some other animal under the house. Nothing to worry about.

Thump.

It wasn't as if horror movies were real. There were no monsters in the spooky old house.

Thump.

"Mom?" His voice shook and his eyes were wide, his whole body tensed as if he were ready to scamper from the room. "What's under there?"

"Pipes," she said, though inside she fought to keep from screaming. Every echoing bump drove a nail into her courage, struck her nerves with a hammer, but she couldn't let Zach see her fear. "Or an animal."

Thump.

"It'll stop in a second." *Please let it stop, oh please let it stop, oh please oh please ohpleaseohpleaseohplease...*

Then it was quiet, the only sound, the hum of the air conditioners. She stared at the eye on the floor as if it might blink, the great pounding bumps made by its wooden eyelids. But it didn't come.

"There," she said as she let out a heavy breath. "See? It's stopped. Nothing to worry about."

"You heard that before?"

"Twice," she said. "This makes a third."

"Why didn't you tell me?" His voice was still full of fear, but now with anger thrown in for a kick.

"It didn't seem important," she lied. The truth was, after Gary explained it all away, she didn't want to seem stupid in front of her son. They were just noises, after all.

"Whatever," he said. "I'm going to bed."

"Get a shower first. You're all sweaty."

He groaned and made his way to the bathroom, leaving Angela alone to stare at the rough-carved eye in the floor.

She lied. Mom said no more lies, then she stood there like nothing was wrong. But she couldn't fool him. He saw fear in her eyes. Whatever was under that floor was no animal. Pipes, maybe, but even so, why would she lie to him?

Zach lay in bed, the cool air from the air conditioner blowing off his damp body. He couldn't decide if he was more hurt or angry. Or scared. If it were just the banging pipes, that would be one thing. But Dad walked in his sleep. He still felt eyes on him whenever he was in the house. And then there were the gravestones in the barn.

Of course, those weren't really gravestones. They couldn't be. Who would build a floor out of gravestones? But if they were, it would really amp up the spooky vibe in the house.

He was being stupid. Mom was just trying to protect him, that's all. She had to put on a brave face, right? He snuggled into his pillow.

Yeah. Right.

The cool shower felt incredible over her sore muscles and aching joints. As the water ran down her body, it stripped away the sweat and fear and frustration of the day. Gary was going to be fine. There was nothing but pipes under the house. It was just a house.

She leaned back to rinse the shampoo out of her hair, the water jets like fingers on her scalp. She wasn't much for cool showers. Showers should be hot, almost scalding, but after lifting furniture, and the rest of her day, she didn't want more sweat. She wanted to cool off, to feel the sensual prickle of cold against her naked flesh.

When she was sure all the soap was out of her hair and away from her face, she opened her eyes. Through the shower curtain, in the middle of the bathroom, there stood a shadow, a dark shape, a person.

"Zach! What the hell are you doing in here?"

The shape didn't move, didn't so much as twitch or sway. Though she couldn't make out a face through the curtain, she felt its eyes. It watched her through the curtain, traced her naked form like a predator, hungry for her flesh. It was then that she realized it was too tall to be Zach. Too wide too. In fact, it seemed to resemble Gary's build. But that was impossible, which meant...

With a shriek, she threw the curtain aside. The bathroom was empty. Angela yanked her towel off the rack and hurried to wrap it around her body. The door was still closed. She would have heard it if someone (or some*thing*, she tried not to add) walked in or ran out. But there was nothing. No wavering form, no leering pervert, just an empty bathroom with dirty clothes in a pile on the floor.

She stepped out of the tub, mindful not to let her wet feet slip in the puddle that gathered around her. The bathroom wasn't large. There was nowhere someone could hide. Which meant no one could've been there. She imagined it. Again. She felt her heart slow as she tried to convince herself that everything was fine. She needed sleep, that was all.

As she turned to look at herself in the mirror, her stomach clenched and rolled. In the center of the mirror was a handprint.

"But..."

Klang!

Her foot slipped in the puddle as she jumped and fell against the door.

Klang!

The sound came from the tub! The old cast-iron claw-foot tub rang light an iron bell.

Klang!

"It's the pipes," she whispered.

Klang!

"Just the pipes."

Klang!

"Just the fucking pipes!" The words came out somewhere between a scream and a sob. She sat on the floor panting, tearful eyes locked on the tub. Her hands hurt. She looked down to see that she'd driven her nails into the skin of her palms.

From the tub came a strange noise. It took her a moment to recognize it as gurgling. But the drain was open, there was no water in the tub to drain. Then the gurgling stopped. One last bubble popped, then the bathroom was silent again.

She stayed on the floor until she was certain no more sounds would come from the tub, then she pushed herself to her feet and hurried out of the bathroom and slammed the door behind her.

The bedroom was quiet but for the noise of the air conditioner. The sounds could've been the water pipes, banging as water rushed through them. But it sounded closer than that, as if someone hammered the side of the tub. She backed away from the bathroom door. If the sounds were pipes, then what was the shadow? The handprint?

She continued backward until the backs of her knees touched the bed. For a moment, the image of hands reaching from under the frame, grabbing her by the ankles, snapped into her mind. She scooted to the center of the bed and pulled her feet up underneath her. As she stared, the events in the bathroom replayed through her mind. The shadow was the same size and build as Gary. The handprint was large, like his. She missed him, that was a fact. She never liked sleeping without him. The nightmares were terrible. It wasn't him, or anyone. It was a shadow, just a trick of the light. She missed her husband so much that her mind tricked her. That had to be the explanation.

The handprint was easy to discredit. It was the same size as Gary's. He must've touched the mirror earlier. The steam from the shower made it visible. Except that the water was cool, it made sense. But there was no other rational explanation.

She inched her way off the bed until she stood in front of the bathroom door again, chiding herself. A few house noises, a couple of tricks by an overactive imagination, and here she was, acting like a ten year-old. Sopping wet, wrapped in only a towel, hiding in the center of her bed so the boogey-man wouldn't get her. It was silly. She loved her husband, but was perfectly capable of surviving without him for a couple of nights. There was nothing to be afraid of. She repeated the phrase to herself as she gripped the doorknob and turned. When she tossed the door open, the bathroom was as she knew it would be. Disheveled, perhaps, but otherwise perfectly normal.

"See?" she said. "Nothing there. Stupid girl."

Her clothes hung on the other towel rack beside the tub. She dropped the towel and put on fresh panties and a long t-shirt. Other nights, she might have dried her hair in the nude while Gary watched, but he was injured, and the quiet of the house gave her the shivers even more than the loud bangs from the living room. She dressed quickly, as if someone might be peeking, then put her hair up in a loose bun, because the thought of the dryer's noise unnerved her.

It had to be her imagination. The house was old, quirky, just like Gary said. All the same, she couldn't wait to be done with it, to be back in their little two-bedroom house in San Antonio. The quicker they were done, the quicker they could leave.

She turned on the bedside lamp before turning off the main light. Imagination or no, her nerves were still on edge, and total darkness wasn't something she was prepared to deal with. As she lay in the half light, she scolded herself again. A grown woman, reduced to needing a night-light.

Zach's eyes drifted open in a brief respite from sleep. Something woke him, but his tired brain couldn't process what. His muscles ached and his head felt thick, stuffed with cotton. Whatever woke him up, he didn't care. It would just have to come back later. For now, sleep was all he wanted. His body craved it.

He rolled over and dug his head into his pillow, then let his eyes glide open once more before drifting closed and back to his wonderful state of unconsciousness. The shadow in the doorway seemed perfectly normal, just Dad on his nightly round of sleepwalking.

But Dad was in the hospital.

An electric wave washed through him as the realization hit.

His mind snapped into focus and his bleary eyes shot open wide. With a start, he scrambled to sitting up, a terrified shriek caught in his throat.

But there was no shadow. No one stood in his doorway. The door stood open, but only the darkened hallway waited outside.

Mom!

He scrambled out of bed. If someone was in the house, he needed to tell his mother, had to get her out, protect her. Dad was gone, so he was... what... the man of the house? Maybe not, but if someone was in the house...

He picked up the old Stepside's tire iron from beside his bed.

...they'd sure know they'd been in a fight.

He crept to his door and listened for whispers, footsteps, even the sound of breathing that wasn't his own. The hall was quiet. He held his breath and listened for a moment more. A creak down the hallway set him in motion. He leaped out into the hall, the tire iron brandished like a Viking hammer. The hallway was empty. If there was someone in the house, maybe he already got down the stairs.

Zach hurried down to the first floor, as fast as he dared in the dark. Lights would've been nice, but if there was someone, he wanted the element of surprise.

Pale vestiges of moonlight filtered through the trees and into the windows. It allowed him to see well enough to navigate the living room before he stopped cold. Light from under his mother's door. Mom slept with the light off. Something was wrong.

Fear exploded in him as horrible visions of his mother as a victim flashed through his head. He ran to the door, gave his best war-scream, and gave the door a savage kick. The frame splintered and the door flew open.

For an instant, the span of a blink, he thought he saw a dark figure next to his mother's bed, but in the next heartbeat it was gone. His mother shot out of bed, screaming, and cowered wild-eyed in the corner.

"Mom! Mom it's me! Are you alright?"

His mother's face hardened from fear into exasperated anger.

"What the hell are you doing?" she screamed. "You scared the shit out of me!"

"I'm sorry! I thought I saw..." He scanned the room as he

spoke, tire iron held high.

"Saw what?" she demanded.

Aside from them, the room was empty. He turned and ran to the doorway and flipped on the main light. The shadows retreated to their hiding places, but the room was still empty.

"Saw. What?" she said again.

"I don't know." He lowered the club. "I was in my room, and I thought I saw..."

"Your father." Zach nodded. Angela wobbled to her feet and put her arms around her son. "I miss him too," she sighed. "He'll be home in a couple of days. It was just a dream."

"It wasn't," he said. "It seemed so real."

"*Seemed*. Doesn't mean it was."

"Yeah... But..." He was so sure, it seemed so real.

"Honey, I appreciate you came down here to save me." She kissed his forehead. "But I need you to go back to bed. I'm fine."

But she wasn't. There was fear there, worry, right behind her eyes, as if her face might crack and the wreck of her emotions might come rushing through and drown him. And she'd never admit it. Something was wrong, had her spooked, but she still treated him like a child who needed to be protected from the dark. Fine. If that was the way she wanted it, let whoever was in the house show up again. He'd be ready.

L ight streamed through the windows and warmed the comforter. Angela yawned and stretched beneath it, kicked her feet against persistent consciousness, and reached in half-asleep forgetfulness for Gary's side of the bed. She opened her eyes when her fingers touched his cool pillow. She looked toward the clock and felt her chest hitch. It was already ten-thirty, an hour and a half before the movers were to come. She groaned and threw the blanket off and made her way toward the door. Zach would surely be asleep still. He'd taken to sleeping later and later ever since "teen" became affixed to his age.

"Zach!" she called as she emerged from her room. "Time to get up!"

"I am up."

He sat in a chair in the living room. Not one of the antiques, but one of the kitchen chairs he'd pulled out. Across his lap sat the tire iron. He looked up at her when she came in, his long hair hung in his face. Through his locks, his eyes were red around the edges, watery.

"Why didn't you wake me?"

"I figured you'd be up soon."

"How long have you been awake?"

"A while."

"Did you sleep at all?"

He didn't answer but went into the kitchen and poured himself a glass of orange juice.

"Sweetheart?"

"There was someone in the house last night," he said. "I know it. I saw him. He stood in the doorway to my room, just like Dad when he sleepwalks."

The hairs on the back of her neck prickled. Was it possible, that someone was in the house while she slept, and the only thing that stood between her and him was her fourteen year-old son?

"Come on," she said. "Let's look."

"He's gone by now."

"Let's look anyway."

She led him to the front door. Both deadbolts and the knob were still locked.

"Did you lock those?" He shook his head. "So he couldn't have left that way, right?"

Next she checked the windows, all locked with screens in place. Then he followed her to the kitchen where she checked the back door and windows, all locked.

"He couldn't have left and locked them behind him," she said. "One of those locks is a privacy, so it doesn't even have a key. No one got in last night."

"Or he's still here."

The thought hadn't occurred to her, but now that Zach gave it voice, every instinct she had told her to get the hell out, and fast. But it was light outside, not night, and the sunlight was bracing. She was not afraid of shadows, not when the sunlight filtered in through the windows.

"Fine, then." She went to her bedroom, got Gary's bat from beside the bed, and came back out to find Zach, tire-iron in hand, waiting. "If he's here, let's find him."

She didn't expect to find anyone – imaginary boogey-men didn't stick around in the daytime – but she kept the bat cocked in one hand while she searched first the upstairs, rooms and closets, then down. The house, as she hoped, was empty except for them.

"Satisfied?"

"Whatever," he said. "I know what I saw."

A rumbling engine and crunching gravel cut off her reply. She looked out the window to see Cindy close the door of her truck and walk up the path to the door. When she knocked, Angela opened the door with a smile on her face.

"Hi, Mrs. Carter." The girl still seemed nervous, probably

about being busted. "I brought some stuff for Zach's truck. Is he busy?"

"Come on in," she replied.

Cindy passed through the door and eyed the bat and Zach's tire iron warily.

"Long night," shrugged Angela.

"Oh... kay... I brought the new battery and spark plugs for the truck," she said. "I thought we might see if it'll turn over."

"Sounds good," said Zach. "Let me get my shoes."

As soon as he was out of earshot, Cindy turned to Angela.

"Is everything okay?" There was genuine concern in her voice and eyes. "Is this about yesterday, because we..."

"Everything's fine," said Angela as she set the bat by the door. "We thought we had a prowler last night, that's all. And as for yesterday... After the night we had..."

Cindy pulled a small mint tin from her pocket and handed it to Angela.

"What's this?" Angela opened the tiny metal case and found it full of weed with a pack of rolling papers on top.

"You said to share next time," said Cindy. "If I'd have known you'd be cool about it, I'd have brought you some before. And besides, you look like you could use some relaxation. Anyway, thanks for not being pissed or calling the cops."

Angela laughed as she tucked the tin into her pocket. "What cops? All I saw was one sheriff, and I bet he'd just confiscate it and bake brownies."

"Yeah... Sheriff Weston's my uncle," she said. "Small town. If he caught me, I'd have worse than jail to look forward to."

"Ah."

Zach came down the stairs. He'd changed his clothes to something more appropriate for working on a car and brushed his hair. He still looked tired, but at least he looked clean.

"We'll be in the barn," he said as he disappeared through the kitchen and out the door. Cindy gave a weak smile and waved as she followed.

When they were gone, Angela let out a long breath and went to get dressed. He saw the same figure. If she imagined it, he did too. She was so wrapped in her own thoughts that when the movers pounded on the door, she jumped and let out a tiny shriek of terror.

"Are you guys okay?"

It was the third time she'd asked, and he answered the same as he had the previous two.

"Fine. Just tired."

It was early enough that the barn was still cool from the night before. Sunlight from the hayloft pressed puddles of warmth down on the stone floor. Still, he couldn't get the shadow-man from last night out of his tired mind. At least the barn was quiet, without the whispers from the day before. He felt jumpy enough to really believe they were voices, if he heard them again. But Cindy was with him, and she made it easy to think about things other than phantoms.

There was no telling how old the battery was, so Zach figured it would be best to replace it. The cables had to go as well. It was Cindy that suggested pulling the spark plugs and wires.

"Good thing this thing is so old," she said. "New cars you can't touch without a computer."

The ratchet in his hand clicked with every turn. It fascinated him, how the parts went together, but today it was more work than fun, a distraction from the imaginations of last night. Still, it was worth it to be with Cindy, even if she did pester with the same question over and over again.

He turned the ratchet one more time and the bolt came to a snug stop.

"That's got it," he said. "Now what?" So far, they'd changed the oil, checked the brakes, flushed the radiator and fluids. There were no leaks that he could see, and, if they did everything right, it might be time.

"Battery," she said.

They pulled the battery out of the compartment and marveled at the level of corrosion on the terminals. They looked as if they were made of fuzzy granite, and the casing bulged.

"That thing's an accident waiting to happen," she said.

It took the both of them to lift the battery into the high engine compartment.

"Where are the keys?" asked Cindy.

"In my pocket," he said as he attached the positive terminal. "Why?" He almost hit his head on the hood strut when he felt her hand go into his pocket and fish for them. A few awkward seconds later, during which he held completely still with his eyes closed and a huge nervous smile on his face, she withdrew her hand and jingled them in front of his eyes with an impish grin. Then she jogged around and slid into the driver's seat.

"Hey! I get to start it first!"

"Then hurry up and finish and get over here!"

He grinned as he hurried to tighten the cable and hoped she wouldn't notice the bulge in the front of his pants. No girl ever touched him, especially not down there. He'd never even been kissed by any girl but his mother. It was exciting, and something he couldn't wait to try.

Cindy slid over the bench seat as he climbed in. He took the keys from her and put it in the ignition, then he turned to her with an excited smile. She put one hand on his leg and squeezed, then he took a deep breath and turned the key.

The old engine sputtered and whined, gurgled for a moment, then gave up. He tried again with the same result. One more time, this time while pumping the gas pedal, but the thing just wouldn't cough to life. He slumped back in the seat with his head back.

"Now what?"

"Now," she said as she pulled a baggie and rolling papers from her pocket, "we take a break."

He grinned and helped her out of the truck. They ran to the ladder and climbed to the hayloft, which Zach thought of as "their place." It was quiet and private, shielded from immediate view from down below. It felt good, secret, to be up above looking down, and better to share it with her.

She rolled a joint and lit it, took a long hit, then passed it over to Zach. The sweet smoke burned as it went down his throat into his lungs.

"We'll get it," she said. "No problem. It's just going to take some more time."

"Yeah... What do you think next? Carburetor?"

"Maybe," she said. "It was made before the catalytic converter, so we may have to modify the engine so it'll run good on today's gas."

He stared at her for a moment.

"What?"

"You don't talk like any girl I ever met."

"What's that supposed to mean?" She grinned when she said it, but he could tell that the wrong phrase would cut her to the bone.

"Just that...well...At my school, girls are all about hair and nail polish and stuff. But you, you're pretty and you know about cars. It's cool."

It seemed to satisfy her. At least she didn't slap him and storm out of the loft.

"You want to see something really cool?" He nodded. "Ever shotgun before?"

"What's that?"

"Breathe in when I tell you." She took the joint back and sucked in a long toke, then grabbed him by the shirt and pulled him to her. When her lips were less than an inch away, so close he could smell her skin, almost feel the softness of her lips, she nodded. He opened his mouth and inhaled as she blew smoke in. When he'd sucked in all he could, she pulled him closer and sealed her lips over his.

His first kiss, and it was better than he ever dreamed.

When she pulled away, he let the smoke out slow, his eyes never leaving hers or the devil-may-care look in them.

"How was that?" she asked.

"Nice."

"Just 'nice?'"

He leaned forward and kissed her again. It was awkward, sloppy and wet, clumsy, but she tasted of pot and cherries and smelled sweet. Her lips were soft and her silken hair felt good in his hands. Now he could see what all the fuss was about.

"Zach!" Mom called from down below. They pushed apart quickly and Zach wiped his mouth and smoothed his hair.

"Yeah Mom?" If she caught them, what would she say? Would this be like catching them with pot? Don't tell Dad? Or would she be pissed?

"Where are you two?" Her tone was amused if impatient. She hadn't seen them. Good.

"Up here," yelled Cindy. She stood up and waved over the

rail. "We've found some more antiques!"

"Well, come inside! The movers are gone! I'm making sandwiches! Anybody hungry?"

Now that she'd mentioned it, he realized he hadn't eaten all day, though his stomach was too full of butterflies for him to consider eating. All he could think about was the next kiss. And the one after that, too.

"Starving! We'll be right in!"

He peeked over the rail and watched until he was sure his mother was gone.

"That was close," he muttered.

Cindy giggled, and it was the most beautiful sound he could imagine.

"You're too cute," she said as she headed for the ladder.

Up in the hayloft with Cindy. First weed, then the truck, now girls. He was growing up too fast for her liking. It wasn't as if she expected him to stay a child forever, but just a little longer would've been nice. Part of her hoped they really were just looking through more piles of antiques up there. But when Cindy came in grinning, and Zach followed with an embarrassed look on his face and his ears practically glowing red, that hope was dashed to bits.

As they ate their cold-cut sandwiches, Cindy and Zach regaled her with their plans for the truck, all of which sounded expensive and fantastic.

"So Zach tells me you know a little bit about this house," she said. The table went silent.

"I guess so," she said. "What do you want to know?"

"Mom, we need to..."

"We don't know anything about the woman who lived here or the house, or even the town for that matter. What do you know?"

"Well..." She took a drink of her soda. The subject seemed to make her nervous, but Angela needed to know. "My dad told me that there used to be a church here, maybe about sixty years ago."

"What happened to it?"

"There's all kinds of stories about it." She shifted in her chair. "My dad says the church got struck by lightning and burned down before he was born. My grandma said the preacher was wicked or something, so God punished them."

"Wicked how?"

"I don't know," she said. "But that's what they say. The barn's over part of the old cemetery. They used some of the headstones to make the floor."

Angela shot a look to Zach.

"It's just a story," he said. "I mean, some of the stones in the floor are kinda shaped like headstones, but they wouldn't do that, would they?"

"What about the woman who lived here? Did you know her?"

"Seen her around some," said Cindy. "Thing is, she didn't come around much. When she did, everyone just sorta stepped out of her way. Everyone thought she was crazy."

"How so?" *Crazy Aunt Ester* was how Gary described her. It seemed the whole town thought of her that way.

"Well, she called my uncle a bunch of times. Kept telling him there was someone in her house. It didn't matter how many times he'd come out, there was never anyone there. After a while, she just quit calling, but she still talked about it. Like the house was haunted or something."

"Haunted by what?" Angela leaned in closer.

"I don't know," laughed Cindy. "She just kept getting crazier as the years passed."

"But what about..?"

"Mom," Zach cut in. "We've got stuff to do." He took Cindy by the arm and took her toward the back door.

"We're going to visit your father in a few minutes," she said.

"Aw, can't I stay here? We almost got the truck to start!"

She just bet that wasn't the only reason he wanted to stay. She was afraid the truck's wasn't the only engine he wanted to rev. Still, she needed to give him freedom, needed to let him do his own thing. She nodded.

"Just be careful," she said. "Anything difficult, you wait until I get home."

"Why?" he laughed. "What're you going to do?"

"Administer first aid," she said with a wry smile.

"Don't worry Mrs. Carter," said Cindy as they went outside. "I got my truck. I'll take good care of him."

She just bet she would. Angela sat at the table for a moment, her mind on fire with possibilities and fear. She didn't believe in ghosts, that kind of thing was for uneducated superstitious people. Something was happening, something she couldn't explain, but she was certain ghosts were not at the root of it.

11

Zach watched as his mom's car rolled down the dirt and gravel driveway and out of sight. When he could no longer see her taillights, he let out a relieved breath. Mom was acting weird, no getting around it. She needed to get out of the house for a while, and he needed to be out from under her eye.

"So," said Cindy. "Your mom's gone, no one else is around... what do you want to do?"

"I don't know," he said. It was a lie. He *did* know what he wanted to do, but he couldn't figure out how to say it without sounding crass or disgusting. All he *really* wanted to do was go back up to the hayloft and pick up where they'd left off.

"Come on," she said, flashing her keys in front of him. "Let's go for a drive. Getting out of the barn will do you some good."

Without a word, she turned and made her way to the truck. He followed at a brisk jog. Her truck, unlike his, started on the first try. The radio blared to life, with Led Zepplin's *Kashmir* pouring from the speakers.

"Nice choice," he yelled over Jimmy Paige's wailing guitar. "Where are we going?"

"I don't know," she said as she turned down the radio. "Around. What do you want to do?"

"What *is* there to do around here?"

"Nothing," she said. "But you haven't left the house since..."

"Since taking my dad to the hospital."

"Okay, but that doesn't count," she said. "I have an idea. You want to see the rest of the property?"

"Whose?"

"Yours, stupid!" She laughed. "The old woman owned a pretty good chunk of land out here."

Alone with her, just a truck on an open stretch of land with no one around to see or interrupt?

"Sure!" he said, a little too quickly.

She grinned and put the truck into four-wheel-drive.

"Hold on," she said as the truck bounced along one of the trails that lead off into the unknown.

"I feel better," said Gary. "Not nearly as tired. My hand still hurts, but what are you gonna do?"

"I'm glad." He looked better too, happier and less manic. When Angela left yesterday, it broke her heart. But she couldn't leave Zach to take care of everything himself.

"The movers came today. They picked up everything but the hall tree. The living room is empty."

"How's Zach?"

"I think I caught him making out with Cindy in the hayloft."

"Good for him!"

"Yeah, well, I left the two of them back at the house."

"Brave woman." He smiled. "The doctor says I'm out of here tomorrow. Tests came back clean."

"Good." She couldn't wait to have him back in the house. She felt safer with him around.

"Something wrong?" His eyes narrowed, as if he knew the answer already.

"No," she said. She couldn't tell him about the strange events and stress him out again. He'd insist on leaving, and that could put him at risk. She'd tell him, eventually. But for now, better to let him rest in ignorance. "Everything's fine. You know how much I hate being alone."

"You're not alone. You've got Zach with you."

"It's not the same," she said with a raised eyebrow and a grin. "You can bring me home tomorrow."

Since when was the house in Shy Grove home? They thought about keeping the place, sure, but it wasn't "home." San Antonio was still home as far as she was concerned.

An acre turned out to be not nearly as large as Zach thought. Twelve and a half acres seemed like a lot of land, but it turned out to be less than a mile across. Still, there was plenty to look at. The property was surrounded by barbed wire and scrub grass. Mesquite bushes poked up through the dry areas, pecans in others. To Zach, it was the ugliest piece of land he'd ever seen.

"I love it out here," said Cindy.

"Me too," he lied.

"You hate it, don't you." It wasn't a question. The smirk on her face told him that she knew he was lying.

"Yeah. I grew up in San Antonio. All this looks like a whole lot of nothing to me."

"Depends on where you look," she said, and pointed.

Up ahead, a large grove of trees created a shady grotto. As they got closer, the unmistakable sparkle of water shone through them.

"You knew this was here, didn't you?"

"Of course I did," she laughed. "I told you, there's a lot more to this place than you think."

She pulled up at the edge of the treeline and killed the engine, then got out and walked toward the pond.

"It's spring-fed," she said. "These things are all over the place out here. At night, the one on our property has deer all over it. My daddy said that back when the church was here, they used it for baptisms."

"So I've got my own fishing hole?"

"I doubt there's fish in there," she said. "But it sure is nice on a summer day. Want to go for a swim?"

He froze, terror racing through his body. Was she asking what he thought she was asking?

"We, uh... don't have suits."

Cindy rolled her eyes and giggled.

"Swim in your underpants, if you want," she said. Then she peeled off her shirt and threw it at him. At sixteen, her body was as perfect as he could've hoped for. The thought of swimming in a baptismal pool seemed somehow sacrilegious, but as she shimmied out of her jeans and stood in just a bra and panties, he couldn't possibly say no. His t-shirt came off with such speed that he almost tore it, then his pants. It took him a second to realize he had to remove his sneakers first, all the while Cindy giggled and laughed. When at last he was down to his shorts, she gave him an appraising look. He hoped she wouldn't be disappointed. His body was a little doughy around the middle with wire-thin arms and no chest to speak of. Not to mention his chicken-legs. He was a far cry from the muscled farm-boys from around Shy Grove. She didn't seem to mind as her eyes gave a quick look from his ankles to his neck, then back down.

"Getting a little ahead of yourself, aren't you?"

He followed her gaze and felt his ears flush crimson as he cupped his hands around his crotch. His embarrassment brought more peals of laughter from Cindy.

"C'mon!" she shouted as she ran to the edge of the pond. When she reached the bank, she did not hesitate, but launched herself, arms forward, into the crystal green pool. Not to be outdone, Zach followed.

The water hit his skin like icy barbs and stole the breath from his lungs. He shot back to the surface and tried to let out a shriek of horror at how cold the water was, but all he could do was gasp for air and try to stay afloat.

"Feels good, don't it?" shouted Cindy.

The two of them swam the entirety of the pond, played chase under water and splashed each other. Zach tried to get close to her several times, but she was faster in the water than he, and swam away, only to come up giggling and taunting him again.

The sun hung lower in the sky. He didn't know how long they'd been in the pond, but his shoulders felt tight and the skin was pink. Cindy's tan body wasn't as affected by the sun, but Zach was more used to the glow of a computer screen than real outdoor light.

He turned to suggest they go back in. Cindy bobbed in the center of the pond, her beautiful smile still affixed to her lips.

"You gonna come get me?"

His heart beat faster, harder. This was it. No more games, no more dodging him, he'd finally get to put his hands on her semi-nude body. He dove under and made his way toward her.

Beneath the surface, he dared not open his eyes. Apart from

the fear of the water stinging, he also didn't know what sort of bacteria lived in the pond. When he came up for a breath, Cindy was nowhere to be seen.

"Cindy?" He treaded water as he turned in a circle. If it was a joke, it was getting old fast.

A rapid jet of bubbles startled him. Cindy came up from below the surface fast, her face a mask of panic and pain. She flailed out to him, her fingers curling in his hair and pulling him under the water with her. Beneath the surface, pale and decaying arms reached and clutched, grabbed her by the ankles. She pulled and fought as bubbles of screams flooded forth from her open mouth.

He wrenched his head and felt the hair give, but he didn't give a thought to the pain. Not yet. Then he dove down deeper and got behind her, snagged her around the waist, and pulled. The arms let go of her legs and he was able to pull her struggling form to the surface. She screamed as she broke into the open air, and continued to flail. It was all he could do to get her to the banks and onto the dry ground. When at last they were out of the water, she lay on her side, sobbing and quaking. Her legs were bloody and burned around the ankles, as if every one of those bone-white hands dripped acid from their fingers.

"What the fuck was that?!" he panted. Her only answers were more sobs. He sat beside her until he caught his breath, then he scooped her up and carried her to the bed of her pickup truck. After setting her on the tailgate, he ran back to the pond, his eyes never leaving it, to pick up her clothes. Zach helped her get dressed before he put on his own pants and shirt again.

"Let's get out of here," he said.

"You have to drive," she sniffed. "My legs hurt too bad to work the pedals."

Any other time, Zach might've protested. The truck was a standard, and the only thing he'd ever driven was his father's automatic. And even then, he'd only backed it out of the garage or pulled it forward through an empty parking lot. But Cindy's cries gave him panicked clarity. If she needed him to drive, then he'd give it his best shot.

He helped her into the passenger's seat, took her keys, and ran to the other side.

"Push the clutch and the brake," she whimpered.

The engine started without protest. When he put it in gear, the truck lurched and chugged, but did not die. Cindy shouted instructions while he feverishly tried to stay on the road. The gears ground, but the truck kept moving until they got back to the house, where it chugged, sputtered and lurched to a halt. He hurried around to the passenger door and helped her limp inside and sat her in the uncomfortable wooden kitchen chair. Another chair propped up her legs while he gently pulled her pants legs up to survey the damage.

The burns looked nasty, with several layers of skin gone, but he could not see muscle or bone beneath, for which he was thankful. He ran to get the first aid kit from his parents' room.

"What was that?" His voice was quiet as he dabbed antiseptic ointment on the burns. She winced and sucked air through her teeth at even the lightest touch.

"I don't know." She shook all over, more from pain and shock than fear, he thought. "One minute I was floating there, trying to get you to come out to get me, and the next thing I knew, it felt like something grabbed me and pulled me under."

"There were hands," he said without looking up. "I saw them under the water. Boney white hands. They had you by the ankles."

"That's not possible," she said. "Maybe there was weeds or snakes or something."

"I saw hands," he said. This time he looked right in her frightened eyes so there could be no mistake. No matter what she thought, he saw hands, not weeds. And nothing could convince him otherwise.

"But... how?"

"I don't know," he said. The wounds were coming clean. The bleeding stopped, revealing pink raw flesh gouged in her tan skin. Five strips on each leg, five fingers on each ethereal hand. They would scar, a permanent reminder to mar her beautiful legs. "Didn't you say the old church used the pond as a baptismal?"

"They're just stories," she said, eyes wide. "I was only telling you to give you the willies. I don't know if any of them are true or not.

"I wonder what else about this house is true."

Thump.

They both jumped, he backward onto his backside, she in her chair.

"What the hell..?" Her voice shook and fresh tears streamed down her face.

Thump.

He knew the noise. It was the one that scared his mother, that his father explained away. But after what they'd just seen, he wasn't so sure about banging pipes.

Thump.

"It's coming from the living room," he said. "It always comes from the living room."

He took a tentative step toward the door.

Thump.

"Please," whispered Cindy through tears. "Don't leave me here alone."

"Dad says it's the pipes."

Thump.

"It's the pipes."

Thump.

"IT'S THE PIPES!" His fear turned to a primal scream against the noise, bloodying his throat as it left his body. He screamed until he had no more air left in his lungs, but pushed harder until it seemed he would never draw breath again. A heartbeat later, he sucked back in a greedy breath of air and waited, his wiry frame tensed and ready to run or fight.

The house was silent. Not even the air conditioners hummed, but the air grew cooler as the seconds passed. Somehow, the silence was more terrifying than the banging from beneath the floor.

"I need to be out of here." Cindy's eyes darted back and forth, searching the room for some hidden danger.

"Yeah," said Zach. "Me too."

He backed toward Cindy, his eyes on the living room should the banging start again. Then he stooped and draped her arm around his shoulder and helped her stand. She winced against the pain, but limped alongside him to the door. When they were out of the house again, they both breathed a little easier.

12

Angela knew something was up the moment she pulled up in front of the house. Zach and Cindy weren't in the barn, for one thing. For another, they sat in the bed of her pickup with her legs in Zach's lap. But the thing that really set her on high alert was their hair. Zach's wasn't particularly neat anyway, but Cindy's was always brushed and tidy. Now both of them looked like they'd been swimming. Cindy looked like she'd been crying, and Zach looked terrified and angry.

"Hi guys," she said as she got out of the car. "What's up?"

"It, uh... got too hot in the barn," said Zach. Cindy wouldn't look at her.

"What have you two been up to?"

"Nothing."

Zach was a sweet kid, but a rotten liar. Those two were up to something. Or worse, already did something. But she knew better than to press for answers. All that would accomplish would be Zach turning to stone, and she couldn't bear the thought. When he was ready to talk, he'd come out with whatever it was. And no matter how painful or awkward it might be, she'd still love him and try to understand. She just hoped, whatever it was, they were careful.

"Okay," she said and turned to go into the house.

"Mrs. Carter!" Cindy looked terrified, panicked even. "Don't go in there!"

"What's wrong?" Angela looked back toward the house. It didn't look menacing as it had before, but there was real fear in

Cindy's eyes.

Zach let out a long breath.

"We went inside," he said. "And the banging started again. We just got freaked out, that's all."

She turned back toward the house and stared. Her short time with Gary lifted her spirits enough to realize that she was tired of being afraid of noises and shadows. If there was something in the house, she wanted to know about it and flush it out.

"Zach," she barked. "Come on."

Zach cast a worried glance to Cindy, then helped her down off the truck. She limped a bit, and Angela saw pain in every step, but she wasn't about to let on. Something hurt her, and if it was in Angela's house, she was going to flush it out.

The air inside the kitchen was cool. On the table sat the first aid kit.

"What happened," asked Angela.

"Nothing," said Zach. "Just a little accident."

"We're going to have a talk later," she said. "No secrets, remember?"

They moved from one room to the next, searching corners and shadows, inside closets and under beds, until Angela was satisfied that there was nothing, human or animal, hiding in the house.

"When your father gets home tomorrow, we'll figure out how to get into the crawlspace and flush out whatever's under there."

"But..."

"I think it's time for Cindy to go home."

They looked at each other and Cindy dropped her eyes.

"Yes ma'am."

Zach walked her out to her truck. As soon as they thought they were out of eyesight, Cindy's limp became more pronounced. Maybe she twisted her ankle or cut herself on something. The half-empty tube of antiseptic cream on the table seemed to support the latter. She watched as Zach helped her into the truck, then he fished in his pocket and handed her something shiny, kissed her, then closed the door. He stood in the drive until the rumble of her engine faded, then he turned and trudged back into the house.

"What was that?" she demanded. "What were you two

doing?"

"Nothing."

"Don't lie to me, young man. What did you give her before she left?"

"Her keys."

"Why did you have her keys?"

"She...was teaching me how to drive a standard."

As lies went, it was a good one, but a lie nonetheless. She could tell by the way his ears turned pink and his eyebrows twitched.

"So why do you two look like you've been swimming?"

Got him. His ears flashed scarlet and his eyes took a downward turn.

"Where?"

"There's a pond," he said quietly. "On the far end of the property. It got hot outside and we thought..."

"Were you wearing suits?"

"We weren't skinny dipping, Mom." There was the Zach she was used to, the one who was usually exasperated and just wanted the conversation over.

"And how'd she get hurt?"

His eyes went wide and he looked up at her, mouth agape.

"Please, do you think I'm stupid? You left the first aid kit on the table and she was limping. What was it, twisted ankle?"

"She...cut herself," he said. "On a rock."

"And she let you drive her back here so you could take care of it. Is that about right?"

He nodded.

"Why didn't you just say that in the first place?" She kissed his forehead. "Sometimes, I swear, you make things so much harder than they need to be. "

She moved over to the pantry and began making dinner.

"So where's this pond? I might like to go swimming myself."

"I don't think it's safe," he said. Before she could ask what he meant, he left the kitchen and went upstairs to his room.

Zach didn't like lying to her, but he didn't know what else to do. Bad enough that she put together what they were doing out there in her head, but if he told her what he saw she'd never believe it. Just like the weird pounding noise, she write it off as his imagination, like he was a dumb kid who didn't know the difference between plants and arms.

The memory of the bone-white hands dragging Cindy brought with it a shiver and made his flesh creep. She said it was just a story, but they seemed real enough to him. If he just had Internet access, he could look up the town records or find old news reports, *something* to either disprove or verify the stories. Then, at least, he'd know what he was dealing with. One thing was for sure, the pond wasn't safe. And he wasn't crazy about staying in the house either, which left the barn and its possibly-tombstone floors and the breathy whispers from between the boards.

He dug around through his satchel until he found his cell phone and clicked it on, just for the hell of it. The battery read full, but there was still no signal. Time to face facts, unless he got Mom to drive him somewhere or Cindy came back, and he wouldn't blame her if she never did, he was stuck, still dependant on his mother to shuttle him around like a child. And there was nowhere to go, anyway, not in this armpit of a town.

He picked up the tire iron from beside his bed and headed back downstairs. On the way out, he passed by the room Mom designated as her studio. Jazz and the scent of burning weed filtered from under the door which meant she was working on something. Good. He still couldn't quite wrap his mind around his mom smoking pot, but maybe she'd get good and baked and leave him alone for a little while.

When he reached the bottom of the stairs, he couldn't stop his gaze from falling in the center of the living room and the scratched floorboards. The more he thought about it, the more certain he was that the pattern on the floor was no accident. Dad's crazy aunt put it there, but why? And what did it mean?

He made a wide circle around the symbol on his way out the back door. Outside, the dry heat of the Texas summer beat down on the cracked ground, baked it into bricks. By the time he crossed the fifty or so feet to the barn, his shirt was already soaked in sweat. By all rights, the barn should've been a hot house, but no matter the time of day, it always seemed cooler inside.

The old truck stared at him with plaintive eyes. "Fix me," it seemed to say. But there wasn't much he could do without the right parts. In truth, he wished for Toby and Chris to come back to teach him more about automechanics. Maybe there was a class on the subject that he could take in the fall.

He tucked the tire iron into his belt and made his way over to the stall that was stacked high with old papers and magazines. The ones near the bottom were tied in neat little parcels with twine, but close to the top of the pile it looked like Ester gave up on any hope of neatness. The piles of unbound paper lay toppled and scattered throughout the bottom of the stall.

He wasn't sure what he was looking for, only that he'd know it when he found it. Many of the papers on top were recent, only going back a month or two. "The Shy Grove Gazette" was emblazoned across the top in fancy letters, like dressing it up could make it more than just a small-town dirt-sheet.

The headlines weren't interesting. "Calf Gives Birth" read one, "Drought Worsens" read another. It wasn't until he pushed away all the papers from the past ten years that he started to find more interesting fare.

The parcels seemed to be organized by year, with the earliest of them close to the bottom. He sat down on a tied stack and popped the twine off another with his pocket knife. The headlines told a sad tale in reverse, with the prosper and hope of Shy Grove lost before it was even borne.

Zach stayed in the barn and sifted through papers until the light started to fade and his mother called him inside. The last set of papers he read was from 1971, when the town's decay really started to take hold. One photo he recognized as downtown, when the buildings were still relatively new, but they already showed signs of the slow death that ate away Shy Grove.

He put the stack aside and went back to the house for dinner.

Hot water beat down on her head and ran down her back in a delicious waterfall. Combined with the relaxing effects of the last joint she smoked, she felt much better. The head was nearly finished, and the more she worked on it, the more she wanted it to be perfect. Her little man, the man from her dream. It wasn't cheating on Gary, she told herself. The little man wasn't even real, as far as she knew. But when she worked on him, worked her fingers through the clay, it awakened old feelings in her. Gary was a good lover, but the want, the animal lust burned out a long time ago. Now, for whatever reason, this older man, this priest if her dream was to be believed, gave her the urge to explore her body again like she hadn't done since she was in her twenties.

She closed her eyes as she rubbed soap over her skin. It was silly, stupid even, to fantasize about a man she'd seen once in a dream, one who'd delivered her to a weird orgy no less, but as soap slid around her breasts and backside, she imagined his rough and calloused hands guiding it, cleaning her in preparation. It wasn't like her, but damn it, it felt so *good*.

The water turned cold before she was done, so she rinsed and toweled off. Instead of putting her hair up or drying it, she brushed it and left it wet and hanging, the sensation somehow adding to her mood. Still naked, she went back into her room, shut off the light, and slid beneath the sheets. There was no need to be afraid of the dark tonight. If anything were there to watch her, it was *him*. Somehow, it seemed right that the man from her dreams would watch.

She laid back on her pillow, closed her eyes, and breathed a great sigh of pleasure.

Zach knew he was dreaming. He had to be. No way he'd be out at the pond in the middle of the night, with or without Cindy. But the pond glowed in front of him with reflected moonlight, and Cindy walked ahead, dressed in a sheer white gown. With the light behind her, he could tell she was naked underneath, which suited him just fine. A dream it may be, but it was one he liked.

Off in the distance, growing closer, voices sang out a familiar tune. He couldn't place it at first, but as it grew louder he shuddered. It was the same song his father hummed, the one they found together in the old church altar, the one the wind seemed to sing as it whispered through the boards of the barn. From the opposite direction, twenty lights flickered, torches, carried by people whose faces he couldn't see for their dark hoods. In front of them walked an older man, tall and broad chested, in what looked like a priest's frock.

He followed Cindy to the edge of the pond.

"Don't go in," his dream-self said, but her face remained blank, as if she didn't hear him. When the priest reached the far edge of the pond, he continued straight in, walked as if he thought he might walk across the top of the water. When he reached a point where the water was up to his waist, he gestured.

Cindy lifted the gown over her head and tossed it aside. The moonlight revealed scars across her back and legs, scars he knew weren't there earlier. She stepped nude into the water. Where she touched, the water rippled away from her in large swirls of red until the pond looked like one giant puddle of blood. He wanted to run away, to wake up, to scream and pull her out of the crimson pond, but instead he stood and stared, transfixed.

"A sacrifice must be made," said the priest as Cindy swam to him. "Our Lord must be honored for the bounty he gives, for the pleasure we take. As it has always been, so shall it always be."

Cindy turned with her back to the priest and faced Zach. There was no emotion on her face, but the blood that dripped from her hair looked like tears as it streaked from her eyes. From behind his back, the priest drew a short blade. Zach could do nothing but watch as he drew it across her throat and let her blood mingle with the rest in the pond. As her body slid under the surface, hands came from underwater to welcome her to her new family of the dead.

Zach woke up with a scream stuck in his throat, bathed in sweat. If his cell phone worked, he'd have called her right then, to hell with the hour, just to make sure she was alright. As the smell of copper and cedar faded from his nostrils and his breathing slowed, he glanced over to see the dark shadow in his door again.

"Stay away from her." He tried to snarl, but it came out more as a terrified whimper.

The figure shuddered, as if it were laughing, then turned and glided down the hallway. Zach scrambled out of bed after it, tire iron in hand. When he cleared the door, moonlight on the landing brought out more of the shadow's details. He recognized the broad chest. It was the preacher from his dream. On the landing, it stopped and turned. It seemed almost to wink at him before the darkness that made up its shadowy body fell like ash to the ground and was gone.

Zach backed into his room and closed the door. In his lifetime, he could only recall going to church for his grandma's funeral, but as he sat cross-legged on his bed with the old tire iron clutched to his chest, he begged whatever god might be listening to protect him.

13

Zach insisted on going to the hospital to pick up Gary. At first, Angela was glad that he showed some concern for his father, but as they pulled out of the driveway, she realized there was more to it than that. Sure, he was happy Gary got a clean bill of health and the all-clear to leave, but there was something else, like he was afraid to stay in the house alone. When she went to wake him up, she found him asleep sitting up with his back to a corner and that filthy old tire iron clutched to his chest. When she spoke his name, he awoke with a start and almost swung it at her.

It was just a bad dream, he told her, brought on by Cindy's injury at the pond combined with all the creepy stories. More lies, but she didn't want to press him. Gary was coming home, and she didn't want anything to spoil her good mood.

No, not *home*. Gary might think of the strange house, not their house in San Antonio, home, but not her. San Antonio was *home*. Shy Grove was just a house, a place for them to pick clean and then sell, if they could.

For the full hour's drive to Luling, Zach said nothing. Alhough, even in silence, it was apparent the further away from the house they got, the more he seemed to relax.

Gary was in good spirits, and Zach's presence brightened his mood. He even hugged the kid. More amazing to Angela was that Zach hugged him back.

On the way home, they stopped for burgers. Gary had to eat one-handed because of his bandages, but he managed well enough for a double cheeseburger with extra bacon. Halfway through the meal, Angela spoke up.

"Zach and Cindy found a pond at the far end of the property."

Gary paused in mid chew.

"Oh?" He cocked one eyebrow up at Zach. The boy's ears turned pink.

"Yeah," he said through a mouthful of fries.

"And?" Gary wasn't going to let it go, just like Angela knew he wouldn't.

"And nothing," said Zach. "We went for a swim. That's all."

"Swimming, huh?" Gary's eyes sparkled like they always did when he knew he was making Zach uncomfortable. "What kind of swimming?"

"Geez," said Zach. His ears looked painfully red as he got up to throw his trash away, then he hurried to the restroom. When he was out of sight, Gary let out a shrill giggle.

"That was mean," he said. "You could've at least waited until we got home."

There it was again, the strange house as *home*. She felt herself bristle at the word, but let it slide.

"Cindy got hurt out there," said Angela. "And he won't talk to me about it. In fact, since you've been gone, there's a lot he won't talk to me about."

"I'm home now," he said with a smile and a kiss on the forehead. "We'll get it sorted."

Gary felt rested, more so than he'd felt in days. The doctor said he needed to take better care of himself. Bags of fluids and lots of antibiotics later, and he felt like a new man. More, he couldn't wait to get back to the house. There was so much more to be done. He wouldn't be able to lift with his bum hand, but Angela would pull her weight and Zach would help, whether he felt like it or not. Hard work built character, and the Lord smiled on men with character. He wondered why such a thought would occur to him as they pulled into the long driveway.

When the house came into view, he smiled. To anyone else, it looked like another old house, but the windows seemed to welcome him back home. He got out of the car and breathed in deep the smell of the dirt and cedar trees.

"Okay," he said. "Where're we at?"

"I'm cleaning out the stalls in the barn," said Zach. "I can't do much more with the truck until I get some more parts. Cindy's looking into them to see what I need."

"Good boy," said Gary. Then he turned to Angela.

"I've got my studio almost cleaned out," she said. "Then I'll move to another room."

"You're taking too long," said Gary with a smile. "That room should've only taken you a day. Two tops. Don't worry, though. I'll get us back on track." He pretended not to notice Angela's narrowed eyes burning into the back of his skull as he bounded up the steps to the porch.

Zach went the other way around toward the barn.

"Zach! I want those stalls cleaned out. I need to see at least one a day until that barn is empty. Get me?"

"Yessir," said Zach as he trudged away, sneakers kicking up dirt as he walked.

One a day. Zach guessed that was doable. Not exactly fair, considering he was the only one working in the barn, but doable. Anything was preferable to being stuck in that house. It was good to have Dad back, but he seemed far too happy, like he'd forgotten everything about their lives in San Antonio. He hoped it would pass.

He made his way toward the first stall, the one stacked high with old furniture, and pulled the clipboard off the hood of the truck. Make a list, mark it down, leave nothing unaccounted for.

Two headboards and a stack of chairs later, Zach's arms ached and his face dripped with sweat. He peeled his soaked shirt off and hung it on a nail outside the stall to dry. Maybe Cindy would come. He wouldn't mind if she saw him without his shirt on. Maybe she wouldn't mind either. She certainly didn't seem to mind at the pond.

The thought of the pond made his stomach flip. She might not come back. He glanced into the next stall where the old papers waited for him. If he could finish up the first stall before too long, he might have more time to read. If Dad wanted to know, he would just tell him he was sorting them for recycling.

Some people paid big money for antique newspapers, if there was important news in them. If they went back as far as he thought, he bet he might find one with news of the moon landing on it, or something of equal importance. It was a good excuse to just sit and read through the history of Shy Grove.

By the time he was done with the first stall, he had six pages worth of furniture, knick-knacks, cooking utensils, and one ugly broken jewelry box. The gaudy thing might have been beautiful when it was new, but now divots of old dried glue marked where plastic jewels once sat, and the brass hinges no longer shone. Much of the face of the thing bore deep scratches and marks where rodents chewed. He picked it up to throw it into a garbage bin, but it was heavier than he expected. There was something inside it.

In his mind's eye, he pictured the box filled with pearls, gold coins and jewelry. After all, what did people usually keep in jewelry boxes but valuables?

On its front, an old lock that looked every bit as corroded and immovable as the hinges hung. It was a cheap lock, and he could break it open easily, but later. It was more of a curiosity to him at the moment.

He set the box aside and did not mark it on the list. Whatever was in there, if it was worth anything, he wanted to be the first to see it.

With the stall empty, and still enough light left to read, he stepped back into the second stall to the stacks of newspapers. The next stack, from 1970, showed nothing but headline after headline of problems and town despair. There was the occasional hopeful mention of industry coming back, or of a bumper crop, but for the most part it was a chronicle of the beginnings of Shy Grove's death rattle. It occurred to him as he flipped through the stacks that the older piles had more papers in them. A quick glance at the dates on the 1970 stack showed why, only fifty-two newspapers. Things got so bad that the newspaper went weekly instead of daily.

The next stack was full of interesting stories, from the nuclear test that Russia did to the murderer of Robert Kennedy being sentenced to death. The copies with the most important events, like the July moon landing, he put aside in a pile for his father to try to sell. Others with headlines only important to him, like the one that told of Jim Morrison's arrest for exposing himself, he set in a separate pile. Still, for all the news, good and bad, there was an undertow of despair when it came to local news.

At 1965, the light was too dim to read anymore. He thought about turning on the work lights, but decided against it. All it would do was delay the inevitable. He was tired, and eventually he had to go back into the house. Mom and Dad weren't the problem anymore. It was the house itself. He was almost used to the feeling of being watched, but that shadow on the landing last night still gave him the shivers. But now Dad was home, well rested and things could get back to normal. If something were in the house, Dad could handle it.

He gathered the stack of important headlines and his clipboard and made his way to the house. Inside, Mom and Dad sat at the kitchen table, smiling and talking like they did when he was younger.

"Hey, Dad," he said as he closed the door behind him. "Look what I found. These might be worth some cash, right?"

Gary took the stack and flipped through the headlines.

"Might be," he said with a smile. "Good find. How's it going with the truck?"

"Not working yet, but it'll get there."

"Good." He nodded, then looked up at Zach. Something in his eyes, the way they didn't twitch or the way they seemed to drill into his skull, made Zach nervous. "Your mom tells me that there have been a few issues in the past two days."

"Yeah," he said. "Lots of weird stuff going on."

"So I hear. What's this about you busting in on your mom waving a tire iron around?"

Zach didn't know quite what to say. It wasn't like that, not at all. Sure, it might've *seemed* that way to her, but he explained everything. She understood. At least he thought she did.

"I didn't bust in on her," he said. "I thought there was someone in the house. I was trying to protect her."

"And who did you think was in the house?" His tone was patronizing, like he didn't believe him at all. Like he still thought of Zach as a kid who needed to be coddled.

"It was a guy," insisted Zach. "An old guy who looked like

he was made of shadow." As he said it, he wished he could suck it back into his mouth so it would never be heard. His ears got warmer.

"Made out of shadow, you say," mocked Dad. "And how exactly is that possible?"

"It's not, but that's what I saw."

"Zach. Buddy. People aren't made of shadows, are they?"

"No, but..."

"And you didn't find anyone in the house, did you?"

"Well, no, but..."

"So do you think, maybe, you might have been dreaming?"

"I really did see him!" shouted Zach. Bad enough that Dad didn't believe him, but he didn't have to make fun of him too. "He was standing in my doorway just like you've done every night! And I followed him to the stairs, and when he turned around and saw me he just kinda fell apart, like the dark just let go."

"That's just not possible in the real world," said Dad, the infuriating smile never leaving his face. "The only way you saw that is if you were dreaming. End of story."

"But..."

"Hey! It's okay. Old houses do that to people. But you'll get used to it."

Zach's stomach clenched and the muscles in the back of his neck knotted.

"What's that mean?"

"You know, if we decide to stay," said Gary. "I'm really starting to like it here."

Mom smiled and nodded, though he could tell she didn't mean it. She hated the house just as much as he did. It scared her, made her act strange.

"I don't..." he said, then stormed up the stairs to his room. He slammed the door hard. It felt good, if a little childish. It distracted him from the feeling of being trapped. They couldn't stay. They just couldn't. He had a life back home, not here, and so did Mom, whether she wanted to admit it or not. It wasn't right for them to force him to live in this little shithole of a town.

The bed creaked and groaned as he threw himself down on it. Had there been a telephone in the house, he might call his buddies back home, but there was only one person whose voice he really wanted to hear. She didn't come by today. He knew he looked forward to seeing her, but he wasn't prepared for how much he felt her absence, how much he thought about her when she wasn't around. If this was what love felt like, everyone else could have it. It was great when she was around, but when she wasn't it made him feel awful.

He glanced up at the door. It was closed, but for how long? Dad was back, sure, but it was Dad who first walked into his room in the middle of the night. Now the shadow did the same thing. There wasn't a lock on the doorknob, otherwise he'd make good use of it. Instead, he got up and propped several boxes in front of the door. When he stepped away, it didn't look strong enough to keep out a toddler, much less a full-grown man. Even if that man was made of darkness. *Especially* if he were made of darkness.

He looked around the room for anything else to secure his door. Apart from a few pieces of heavy furniture, nothing seemed useful. The tire iron was his only weapon, but the flat end of it might do just the trick. He stuck it between the door and jamb at floor level, then kicked it until it was wedged tight. When he was satisfied, Zach undressed and climbed into bed, pulled the blanket up to his chin, and stared at the door until his eyes were too heavy to stay awake.

14

Morning came long before Zach awoke. Sunlight streamed through the tattered curtains of his room, but his body refused to let go of rest. When at last his eyes did open, he yawned and stretched. It was the first night since they'd come to Shy Grove that he'd slept the night through. No one opened his door last night, no terrible dreams, just wonderful unconsciousness.

He rolled over to see the boxes still in front of the door and the tire-iron just where he left it. No sign of anyone even trying to get in. Dad might've been right. He was, after all, very tired, and the house was old. Maybe his imagination, combined with fatigue, blew things out of proportion.

He rolled out of bed, pulled on his pants and a fresh t-shirt, then moved the boxes aside. It took him a couple of yanks to dislodge the tire-iron, but once it was free of the door, he tossed it onto his bed and made his way downstairs.

"'Bout time you got up." Dad stood in the living room surrounded by boxes. "I was starting to think the boogey-man got you."

Zach groaned. Bad enough his lack of sleep did a number on his imagination, but now he was going to have to hear about it for at least a few weeks until Dad beat it into the ground and humiliated him.

"Leave him alone," said Mom as she came in from the kitchen. For the two days Dad was gone, she wore only sweat pants and t-shirts. Now, however, she looked like the model housewife from a 50's homemaker magazine. She wore Capri pants and a shirt tied at the waist with white sneakers and a scarf around her hair. And the way she moved, less walking and more dancing. It was as if he woke up in some alternate reality, a world in which the *Saturday Evening Post* covers came to life.

"Mind your mouth," snarled Dad, then smiled at Zach.

"Um... okay..."

He made his way to the kitchen, poured himself a glass of orange juice, and drank it all in greedy gulps, then went back to the living room. Mom sat on the floor with her legs curled beneath her, a position he'd never seen her in, as she wrapped plates in newspapers from the waste bin outside. Dad wore an eerie smile as he folded clothes and placed them into other boxes.

"I'm going out to the barn," he said. Something about the scene unsettled him. "Got more stalls to go through."

"Good for you," boomed Dad. "The Lord does not look kindly on sloth or shirking duties!"

"Um... whatever."

He took the stairs two at a time to his room, put on his shoes and grabbed the tire iron, and headed back out as quick as he could. On the way out, he made a conscious effort not to look at his parents.

Outside in the barn, he moved on to the third stall. What appeared to be a whole lot of junk turned out to be piles of tools. As he set to work pulling them out piece at a time, he marked them on his clipboard. In one pile he found a hammer, old saw blades, screwdrivers and five or six antique planers. In another he found spades, rakes, two shovels and several trowels. As he made his way to the back of the stall, he glanced over to the wall. On the other side were more newspapers, more of Shy Grove's history that begged to be read. First this stall, then more reading.

The back of the stall held larger pieces of equipment, all with long rusted blades and worm-eaten handles. On the wall hung a giant scythe, the kind he'd only seen in drawings of the Grim Reaper. He pulled it off the wall and stepped back out of the stall.

The scythe was heavy, awkward to his young arms. Even rusty, the blade still looked dangerous and cool. The worn handle felt good in his hands, as if he were meant to have it. He wondered if Dad would let him keep it. He gave it a few practice swings, then set it in the bed of his truck. It was as good a place as any, and it wasn't small enough to hide like the jewelry box.

The thought of the box hit him with an idea. Hidden in the stall was not the right place for it. It was, after all, his, and whatever was in it, he wanted to see first. If someone else found it, they'd doubtless open it first. He jogged over to its hiding place and removed it. Curiosity nicked at his brain for a moment before he slid it under the passenger seat of the truck and closed the door, then he went back to work.

After an hour and a half, he had several organized piles of garbage and sellable items to show his father. The barn was oppressively hot, but it was still better than being inside with Mom and Dad and their freaky behavior. He peeled his shirt off and hung it on a nail, and went back to cleaning out the stall.

After another hour, he stopped when he heard a familiar rumble coming up the driveway. The feeling of happiness that washed over him was a balm for all the angst and anger he felt yesterday. Cindy got out of the truck and limped over to the barn. He met her halfway between her truck and his and hugged her.

"Ew," she giggled. "You're all sweaty."

"I thought you country girls like that."

"Think again."

He smiled. "I'm glad you came back."

"Of course I did," she said. "I like you. You didn't think I was going to let a little thing like almost drowning keep me away, did you? You saved me, remember?"

The memory of her burned legs, of the white arms rising from the dark bottom of the pond, of her terrified face brought his fear racing back. How could he have thought he'd imagined it?

He pressed his lips to hers and let them linger for a moment before pulling away. She smiled and limped with him back into the barn.

"So how come you didn't come by yesterday?"

"Sunday," she said. "I was in church. I don't like going, but I mainly go for my daddy. Mom died a while back, and I'm all he's got, so I go with him."

He wanted to ask how her mom died, but thought the question too awkward.

"How're your legs?"

"They hurt," she said. "But I'll survive. I've had worse." She looked around at the piles. "You've been busy."

"Yeah. Dad wants me to clean out one a day until the whole barn's done."

"Find anything good?"

He grinned and jogged to the bed of the truck, pulled out the scythe, and struck a pose.

"What do you think?"

"That thing's bigger than you are," she laughed. "And almost as skinny!"

"Yeah? Well look at these." He took her to his piles of newspapers. "It's the whole history of the town. And check out the headlines on these."

"Wow." He could tell by the look on her face that she wasn't just being kind, she genuinely was interested. "This is pretty cool. What else did you find?"

"There is one more thing," he said. He left her sitting on a stack of newspapers while he retrieved the box from the cab of the truck. On the way back, he stooped and picked up a flat-head screwdriver.

"What's in it?"

"I don't know," he said, then offered her the screwdriver. "Wanna find out?"

"You do it," she smiled. "If there's jewelry in it, pick out the prettiest piece for me."

Zach wedged the screwdriver between the latch and lid and gave it a twist. Wood splintered and creaked, but the lock stayed put. He tried again on the other side with similar results.

"Hang on," he said, and jogged to get the hammer from the pile. With the screwdriver in one hand and the hammer in the other, he forced the lock until it came away.

The hinges protested as he pushed the lid open. From inside, a peculiar smell, metallic and acrid, floated up. Inside lay a large bundle of cloth that stank.

"That's not jewelry," said Cindy.

He picked up the bundle. It was too heavy to be jewlery. With trembling hands, he unrolled it. Inside was a small revolver.

"Holy shit," he said. "Who keeps a gun in a jewelry box?" It didn't matter, though. No way his parents would let him keep a gun. Even if Dad wanted to, Mom would veto the idea. Of course, if they didn't *know* about the gun, they couldn't keep it away from him. He rolled the revolver back up into the cloth.

In the bottom of the box was an old photograph, yellowed with age and gun oil and torn on the edges. He took it out for a better look. In it was a group of people, more than a dozen of them, smiling bright in front of a simple white building with a cross on the front. He scanned the faces, looking for some trace of someone he might recognize, but soon realized that there was no chance that he knew any of them. Even if one had been his grandmother or Dad's crazy aunt, they looked too young. In the background of he photo stood a lone figure that he couldn't quite make out. He took the photo out of the stall to where the light was better.

"Oh God," he said.

"What?"

He took the photo back to Cindy and pointed to the figure, the one that made his heart race with fear. It was a bad image, and the man was out of focus, but his shining bald head, the barrel chest, made him certain there was no mistake.

"See that guy?"

"What about him?"

"That," said Zach, "Is the guy I think I saw in the house."

He turned the photo over. On the back in faded ink were the words "Blessed Blood of the Lamb, 1949."

"That's impossible," said Cindy. "If that's the church that was here, that guy's been dead for a long time."

"Yeah, but that's not all. When I saw him, he looked just like that. The same age. It was like he stepped out of this picture and into my house."

She shivered and rubbed her arms.

"Do your parents know?"

"They don't believe me." He put the picture and the gun back in the box, then took it to the truck and stuffed it under the seat. When he turned back, Cindy stood and limped toward him. She took his hands in hers and looked into his eyes.

"I believe you," she said, and kissed him.

"Ahem."

They pulled away from each other. Mom stood in the barn doorway with a tray in her hands. On it was a pitcher with two glasses filled with ice.

"I thought you two might like some lemonade." The smile she wore seemed somehow false, as if it might crack and turn into a scream.

"Sure," said Zach.

"Thanks Mrs. Carter," said Cindy.

Mom took the tray around to the back of the Stepside and set it down in the bed. Her eyebrows raised when she saw the scythe.

"Where'd you find this?"

"It was in the stall," said Zach. "I thought it looked kinda cool."

"Hmmm." She clicked her tongue on the roof of her mouth and shook her head. "Boys." Then she shrugged, smiled again, and went back toward the house.

"Tell me that wasn't weird," said Zach as soon as she was out of earshot.

Cindy nodded, her eyes still wide and brows together.

"They're both like that," he said.

Dad came out of the house before Mom got through the back door. He said something to her, then they both turned toward the barn.

"Kids!" he said. "Mom and I have to go into town for a little while. Will you two be alright by yourselves?"

"Yeah," said Zach. He hated being called a kid, and Dad knew it. Especially in front of his friends, and Cindy qualified as more than a friend.

"You two behave yourselves now," said Dad with a wave of his bandaged hand. Then he slipped his other arm around Mom's waist as they walked to the car. Zach and Cindy stood and watched them go until the car pulled out of view.

It was good to be out again. And to think, he worried. So much stress, so much uncertainty, but now things were beginning to come clear. Shy Grove was where they belonged. If he could just bring Zach into line, everything would be fine.

Gary glanced over to Angela, who sat with a placid smile on her face. She wasn't completely sold on the idea of leaving San Antonio behind, but like a good little wife, she followed his lead.

Strange that he'd never considered taking the hard line before, never considered putting his foot down. But the longer she stayed, the more she would come to see how right everything felt. A new beginning. And if she didn't learn her place, then, by God, he'd *teach* her.

They drove into town and parked in front of the general store. Gary gave Angela's hand a reassuring squeeze, then shut off the engine.

"You'll see," he said. "Everything's going to be better."

Her smile was timid, unsure, unlike her usual fierce expressions. Too many of her own ideas, too many wild thoughts. It was time for her to do as the Lord intended, and let the man take the lead. After all, man was made in His image, was he not?

They got out of the car. He waited on the sidewalk for her to catch up, then he took her hand and they walked together into the store.

The old women were still there. If he didn't know any better, he'd swear they lived in the shop, each sleeping behind her station.

"I'm afraid we got off on the wrong foot," he announced as the jingling bell died. "I'm Gary Carter, and this is my wife, Angela."

The old women said nothing, but stared with narrow eyes and suspicious minds. He couldn't blame them, but that's what this trip into town was all about: Building relationships.

"I inherited Ester Carter's house, and we'd like to invite you all over for a housewarming. Isn't that right, Angel?"

Angela nodded and gave the weak smile again.

"Wednesday night. Around seven? We'll be serving finger sandwiches and coffee. Please tell your friends."

"Planning on staying, are you?" The woman behind the butcher's counter folded her arms across her sagging bosom.

"We're even thinking of joining your church," said Gary with a smile. Of course, he never dreamed of such a thing before coming to Shy Grove. In fact, he didn't know if there even *was* a church in town. Church just wasn't the type of thing a man like him cared for. But now it seemed right, necessary even. "You'll come, yes?"

The old woman's mouth twisted in a wry smile.

"Oh yeah," she said. "We'll be there."

"Good! Now, we'll need supplies. Angel?"

Angela fished a list out of her pocketbook and handed it to the butcher, who set to work filling the order. Cold cuts of chicken, turkey and ham, pickles, and pumpernickel bread seemed just the right thing for a gathering of new friends. Plus an extra pound of coffee. Friends never let friends go without. And that was the purpose of bringing the community together, to help each other.

When the order stood ready on the counter, Gary took as many bags as he could with his good hand, and waved with the other. He allowed Angela to take his wallet and pay for the order.

"Wednesday night," he sang as they left the store.

Outside, he waited while Angela opened the trunk and placed the groceries inside.

"See?" he said. "That wasn't so bad, was it? Before long, they'll come to love us like family."

"Are you sure about this?" Her voice was quiet, as if she were afraid to question his decisions. And well she should be.

"Of course I'm certain," he laughed. "Silly girl, always afraid people won't like you. You trust me, don't you?"

She nodded.

"Good. Now let's get home and see what that son of yours is up to."

It was weird to watch them walk into the store. Mom hated it in there, said the old biddies that ran the place were rude to her. Weirder still to sit in Cindy's truck like a couple of cops on stake-out. When they came out, a chill raced through his tailbone. It wasn't the way they walked, and he couldn't hear their conversation. But that smile, that weird Norman-Rockwell grin that dad wore gave him the creeps.

"What d'you think they're doing?" Cindy stared over the steering wheel as if she might be able to read their lips if she just looked hard enough.

"I don't know," said Zach. "But they're not acting right. That's not... *them.*"

"C'mon," said Cindy. "Let's pick up that starter."

Cindy waited until their car pulled out before she let her truck idle past the general store. When they pulled up in front of the auto parts store, Zach was surprised to find it closed.

"No one's working today?"

"Nah," she said. "Business has been slow. Hell, you've been our only customer for about a week now."

He shrugged and got out of the truck. Cindy unlocked the door and let him in, then locked it again behind her. As they made their way to the back, he couldn't help the feeling of excitement that came along with being there when it was supposed to be closed. Of course, he wasn't doing anything wrong, but somehow it seemed mischievous to be there with the door locked behind them and only the dim safety lights on.

The shop was quiet, too much so for the middle of the day. He never noticed things like piped in music or the chattering radio that every shop played, but without it, the silence was almost overwhelming. Every step seemed to echo, every item brushed a cacophony. The scent of cleaning solution did little to mask the smell of motor oil and metal. He wasn't supposed to be there, and it felt good.

He followed Cindy behind the counter, where she went to work finding his order. With her back turned, he was free to trace her figure from top to bottom. Sure, he'd seen her nearly naked, but her jeans hugged her in all the right places, and her black t-shirt was almost too small. She reached up to a high shelf, stood on her toes to find the box. He couldn't help himself. He put his arms around her waist and hugged her close.

She didn't resist, only giggled as his awkward hands explored her body. When they found their way up to her breasts, she didn't pull away or protest, but put her hands over his, guiding him to how she liked to be touched.

"What're you doing?" she purred.

He didn't answer because he didn't know what to say that wouldn't sound stupid or over-eager. He'd never touched a girl before, and he didn't want his inexperience to show.

She turned in his embrace and draped her arms around his neck. Part of him expected her to slap him, like women in old movies did when guys went too far. But another part remembered other movies, where teens alone in places they shouldn't be wound up naked and covered in sweat.

She kissed him and ground her hips against his. When she pulled away, he felt light-headed. His heart raced and his stomach wriggled. He hoped she felt his hard-on through his pants, and that she wanted it.

"I like you," she said. "But I'm not ready to go all the way. Not yet."

His disappointment must've registered on his face because her smile faltered a bit. Then she slid her hand across the front of his pants.

"But when I am," she said. "You'll be the first to know.

When Zach and Cindy pulled up at the house, his parents were in the barn waiting for them. Even though they'd done nothing wrong, not really, he still couldn't fight away the feeling of being caught. His stomach wriggled and he didn't want to look his mother in the eyes.

"Where've you two been?" asked Dad.

"We needed to pick up a new starter," said Cindy. "I think we've almost got the Stepside running."

"You could've left a note or something, young man." Mom's stern tone wasn't something he was used to from her.

"Sorry," he said. "It won't happen again."

"Well, see that it doesn't." Something about the way his father looked at Zach unsettled him, like he was a wild dog on a short leash. Dad never hit him, hardly even raised his voice, but there was an odd intensity to his words that threatened. Worse, the way he looked at Cindy, or rather did *not* look at her. It seemed he looked everywhere *but* her.

"We're going to install the part," said Zach as he took Cindy's hand and moved toward the door.

"Okay," said Dad. "But hurry up. We've got a housewarming party to get ready for."

Zach stopped in his tracks and turned.

"What housewarming party?"

"We invited several of our new neighbors over so they'd get to know us. You know, introduce ourselves to the community."

"Why?" Zach couldn't believe what he heard. "It's not like

we're staying..."

Cindy let go of his hand and walked deeper into the barn, her head down.

"Oh, now you did it," said Dad. "And we *might* be staying. We've kind of grown to like the place."

"But..."

"But what?" said Dad. "It's not your decision. Where we live is up to the grown-ups. Get me?"

"Nothing's definite yet, sweetheart," said Mom. Her voice shook and her eyes darted from Dad and back. "We'll talk about it. Okay? Now, I think you hurt her feelings." She turned and walked back toward the house.

Cindy stood with her back to him, her upper body under the hood of the Stepside.

"Hey," he said. She didn't answer. "Are you okay?"

"Fine." Her voice was hard, edged. She was anything but.

"Look, I'm sorry, okay? It's just..."

"It's fine," she said as she stood up and slammed the hood. "It's not like I expected you to stay or anything. I just thought..." Her shoulders jerked as she lowered her head. Zach stood stunned, unsure what to do.

"I didn't mean to upset you."

"Why would I be upset?" She wiped her eyes with her wrists and glared at him. Though her chin quivered, her eyes burned with pain. "Just because I really like you. What did you think? That I fool around with every guy I meet?"

"No, I just..."

"Nevermind." She threw a crescent wrench down and stormed out of the barn. Zach stood and watched her get into her truck and drive away. If there were anything in Shy Grove worth staying for, it was her. But, of course, now he'd blown his chance. He sat down on the Stepside's bumper and ran his hands through his hair.

The floor seemed to pitch and wave as Gary fell to his hands and knees. Bile climbed up his throat as his stomach spasmed. His head felt muddy and his eyes wouldn't focus, then his arms went weak and he hit the floor hard with his face.

"Gary!" Angela knelt by his side and cradled his head.

So many thoughts passed through his mind, clouded by fog. There was anger, but at what or whom he could not be certain. Stranger still that the anger brought with it a sense of glee that felt oily and diseased. As the fog in his head cleared, his stomach settled, his eyes focused. Strength crept back into his arms and legs. He sat up slowly, fearful that any quick movement would send him back down to the warped and twisted floor.

"What the hell was that?" It was more a question to himself than Angela.

"Honey? Are you okay? What happened?"

"I don't know," he said. "I just got woozy all the sudden."

"I hope you're not having a relapse," said Angela. "We've got too much to do and I can't do it all myself."

"What're you talking about?"

Angela stared at him, brows knit and questioning.

"You invited the whole damned town over, remember?"

Gary pushed himself to sitting up. Had he? Why would he do such a thing? As far as he was concerned, the town was full of rednecks and narrow-minded suspicious yokels. And besides, it wasn't as if they were staying.

"When did I do that?" he demanded.

"What is wrong with you? You drove me into town and made me go with you to invite them."

A fleeting image of the inside of the general store and that old butcher-woman – what was her name? – but it was gone too fast, like he'd seen the scene in a snapshot. Bad enough that he couldn't remember what he said, but he couldn't even remember the drive into town. Worse, he had a terrible feeling deep inside, but didn't know about what, only whom.

"Where's Zach?"

"In the barn, where he usually is."

"Is Cindy with him?"

"I heard her drive off a little while ago," she said, the puzzled look never leaving her face. "All his talk about leaving when we were done..."

He scrambled to his feet, leaving Angela sitting in the floor looking confused, and hurried to the back door.

"Zach!" He went from hurried walk to jog as he passed

through the back door and made his way to the barn. The boy sat on the bumper of his truck, looking miserable. He looked up as Gary went into the barn.

"Yeah, Dad?" His tone was one Gary knew all too well, flat and emotionless. Zach was angry about something, and it was more than likely something he'd done.

"Is everything okay?"

"Fine," he said. He sounded like his mother.

"Son, if something's wrong, you can tell me, okay? I can't do anything about it if you don't tell me what *it* is."

"Whatever," said Zach. He stood abruptly and stalked around to the bed of the truck. Just like always, the kid didn't feel like talking. But it was important to Gary to know. Something inside pushed him to find out, told him that he needed to know. He followed Zach around the truck. In the bed, the old scythe sat waiting for a reaper.

"Wow," said Gary. "That's kinda cool. Where'd you find it?"

Zach gave a slight nod in the direction of the stalls.

"What're you going to do with it?"

"Don't know," said Zach without looking up. "I want to keep it, but..."

"Well, why don't you?"

"'Cause I figured you wouldn't let me." He still wouldn't look at him.

"You didn't even ask," said Gary. He pulled the old blade from the truck bed and tested its weight. The work-worn handle felt good in his hands. "Come on. Tell me what's bugging you."

"You've been acting weird." The boy looked at his shoes. "You get mad at Mom and you sound different... mean. Like you're not you. I didn't want to ask because..."

Gary stared at him hard and tried to remember any cross words. None came to mind, though through his cloudy mind, he couldn't be sure. The urge struck him to swing the scythe, to show him just how weird and mean things could get, but he let the feeling pass and dropped the blade back into the pickup bed.

"I'm sorry," he said. "I'm under a lot of stress, and..."

"Whatever," said Zach. His eyes darted from Gary's face to the scythe and back again. "The point is, I don't want to stay here. My whole life's back home, and you keep acting like we're moving in for good. It isn't fair to me. Or Mom."

He didn't know what to say. Sure, he'd toyed with the idea of staying, living out in the country away from every modern device and distraction, but that's all it was. Daydreaming. Truth be told, he'd have just as hard a time trying to live without e-mail as Zach. But there was something else, something Zach wasn't saying.

"Is that it?"

Zach didn't answer.

"Is it Cindy?"

"I don't want to be here," he said. "But I don't want to leave her here either. And the more I talk about leaving, the more upset she gets."

"Well, I can't blame her for that," said Gary. "She likes you."

"It bugs me, too. She's the only thing that makes me want to stay here."

Alarm bells went off in Gary's head. Something about the girl, about Zach's wanting to be with her, he found unsettling. Maybe it was just parental instinct kicking in. They *were* awfully close, and Gary remembered what *he* was like at Zach's age. In fact, he was right around Zach's age when he lost his virginity. The thought sent a cold chill down his spine.

"We're not staying," said Gary. "That's pretty much a given. How you handle Cindy is up to you, but I'd suggest having fun while you have time together."

Zach looked up at him as if it was the dumbest thing he'd ever heard.

"Just not *too* much fun."

Zach's ears turned pink and his eyes went wide.

"Jeez, Dad!"

He grinned, though inside he still worried, a nagging kind of itch in the back of his brain that Zach was in danger.

"So... what else have you found out here? A truck and a scythe, you find all the good stuff."

Zach grinned a little.

"I found all this," he said as he walked to the second stall. "It's more of the old newspapers from way back. Tells the whole history of Shy Grove."

Gary squatted in the stall and picked up one of the yellowed copies. The headline read of drought and dead crops.

"Sounds cheery," said Gary.

"It gets better the farther back you go. Like every year, if you go backward, lightens up just a little bit."

"Huh. Well, keep reading. And keep your eyes peeled for an antique stack of *Playboy*s, willya?"

Zach groaned as Gary walked back to the house. The boy was fine. Nothing to worry about. Just parental nerves, nothing more.

Inside, Angela still sat on the floor, an odd expression on her face. It was the same one she got after a severe headache, what she called a "migraine hangover," with eyebrows knit and her mouth turned to a frown.

"You okay?"

"Yeah," she said. "I think so. I was actually going to ask you the same thing. You've been acting weird since you got back."

In truth, he didn't feel entirely right. Since he walked through the door, something felt off, a slight pressure in his head that tightened the further into the house he went. It didn't hurt, exactly, but felt more like he wore an ill-fitting hat. The further into the house he got, the tighter the hat became. And then there was the question of the last few hours, and where they went.

"Yeah," he said. "About that."

"It's like you're another person sometimes."

"I'm fine," he lied. "Just distracted. I've got a lot on my mind."

"It's this house," she nodded. "There's too much to do. Maybe we should get away. Go back home for a couple of days. We've got enough money to hire someone to go through all this junk."

The pressure in his head tightened to pain. They couldn't leave, not until the job was done. Not until everything was put in order. Not ever.

"No," he said. "I think it'll be better if we just tough it out and get it done. That way we won't have to come back."

"Okay," she said. "But I need a break from the boxes."

Angela got up and walked toward the stairs. He stopped her on the way and kissed her.

"I love you. Things'll get better. You'll see."

"I know," she said with a faint smile. "I just want to relax. I'll be up in my studio."

She closed the door behind her and leaned against it as she let out a heavy breath she wasn't even aware she was holding. Gary wasn't all right, that was easy to see. One moment he was himself, the awkward teacher she'd fallen in love with, rough around the edges and opinionated, and the next, he stood with an eerie smile and cocksure attitude that bordered on fanaticism. And what was with all the talk of "the Lord?"

She sat down on the stool by her sculpting table. The dishtowel-covered lump in the middle made her giddy, but she couldn't figure why. It was a lump of clay, shaped by her hands, but a lump of clay nonetheless. Still, she caught herself thinking on it several times, imagining her thumbs and fingers working grooves and creases until the face came out just right. It was as if touching the clay figure brought the man from her dreams to life in front of her so he could touch her the way he did in her dreams. Every time she thought about the little clay bust, she felt hungry with sexual desire.

She removed the cloth and felt a tingle in her tailbone. The little man looked almost perfect, but not quite. There was still a ways to go, and she knew she would enjoy every moment of it.

She picked a CD out of her case and put it in the player. Bye-bye Dizzy, hello Jimi. She hit the button and, after a moment, the distorted scratch and warble of "Voodoo Chile" poured from the speakers. After the first few bars, she moved to the window and slid it open, then pulled the little tin from Cindy out of her tool box. Time to relax.

The little clay pipe was one she sculpted and fired herself, though she was careful to not let Gary see it. She knew his opinion on weed, and it was an argument she didn't want to have. Besides, she could always quit when they went back to San Antonio. She pinched a bit into the bowl and lit it, sucked in hard and didn't choke this time. Two long hits and the bowl was empty, but it was enough. Her skin tingled with the familiar buzz that made her wonder why she ever gave it up.

Angela sat back down on the stool with her eyes closed as the drums and bass kicked in and let it pour into her. Every thump of the drum she felt in her heartbeat, every bass scale tickled her skin as if she were the one being played. She reached out and touched the clay head as Jimi began to sing. The clay was soft and warm, not cold and hard as she'd expected. The feeling of it sliding through her fingers was strange, erotic.

"*Well I stand up next to the mountain; I chop it down with the edge of my hand...*"

She felt the urge to swing her head in time with the music, to run her clay-stained fingers across her body, to pull her shirt open and let the clay taste her breasts.

In the dark theater behind her eyelids, snippits of the dream, all that she could remember, played out. The strange man, his strong hands, her naked flesh, the others around her. Never in her life did she think of scenarios like the one she dreamed about, but now it tantalized her, awakened some primal part of her biology she never knew existed.

She blinked her eyes open. The statue sat in front of her, somehow changed. Its expression was wrong, different. The cold sneer on its face wasn't there before, nor was the look of blatant lust. Why would she, did she, change his expression from serenity to...this? Not that it mattered. The look suited him. It just struck her as strange.

But no more strange was her discovery that she sat at her table with her shirt open and bra lifted above her breasts. Muddy-brown splotches of clay marked her skin and streaked her nipples. A shudder drilled down her legs as she stood abruptly and made for the door, adjusting her bra and buttoning her shirt as she moved. It was ridiculous, uncomfortable even, for such thoughts to be in her head. They weren't hers, couldn't be.

As she reached the door and put her hand on the knob, a tiny voice in the back of her mind stopped her.

But they were your thoughts. It's what you want, isn't it? Didn't it feel good?

She stopped and turned back toward the table where the little man sat awaiting completion. It did feel good. She bit her lip against the thoughts that raced through her mind. What if someone were to walk in? They wouldn't, of course. They never disturbed her when she worked. And if they did? What would Gary say?

She pushed the lock button on the doorknob, then turned back toward her table and the little man on it. Another voice, different from the first, tiny and afraid, asked if she knew what she was doing. She didn't, but she didn't care. She unbuttoned her shirt and hung it on a hook on the back of the door.

Zach kicked at one of the stacks of newspaper in the second stall. Dad found the scythe, but at least he didn't know about the gun. No way he would let him keep that, no matter how cool he wanted to be.

He lifted one of the old stacks and thumbed through the edges with the dates. So long ago. He didn't feel like going through them. They were about people who were probably dead before he was born, and he didn't care anymore. He tossed the stack into the recycle bin and reached for the next. As his hands grabbed the twine that bound it, he froze. The photo on the front page wasn't someone he recognized, but the name below it he knew. Ester Carter. The girl in the photo was young, maybe in her late twenties, with dark hair and suspicious angry eyes. The headline above read "Churchgoer Suspected in Fire."

As the words sunk in, a chill raced through Zach's body. The wind blew through the boards again. But it sounded more like voices than usual. In fact, he could make out individual tones, if not words.

Zach cut the twine and pulled the paper free. The story on the front page told of his father's aunt, of the destruction of the church in a blaze. All inside the church were burned to death, it said, though several church members were not in the building at the time. Among those listed as missing was the reverend Horatio McBride, who lived in the church. His body was never found.

It was as Cindy said, more or less, that the church burned, but there was no vengeful God that threw bolts of lightning, just his father's aunt with a lit match. He stared at the photo, looking for some explanation, but found none in her cold dark eyes. Dad would want to know. It might explain why the people around Shy Grove didn't like the house, didn't like his aunt.

He took the paper and hurried out of the barn, pausing just long enough to give the odd-shaped stones in the floor a fretful glance. If the stories were true, it might also be true that they were headstones. But that was stupid. No one would build a barn over a cemetery. Still, the sight of them was eerie, as if he could still smell the smoke and burnt flesh after all of this time.

He hurried across the yard and into the house.

"Dad!"

"Yeah," came his father's voice from across the living room. He followed it until he found his father laying in bed with his pillow over his head.

"You okay?"

"Yeah, just a headache. What's up?"

"I found something you're gonna want to see."

Dad moved the pillow and sat up slowly. The way he scrunched his eyes showed the pain involved. Zach held out the newspaper like a holy artifact.

"That's your aunt, isn't it?"

Dad scanned the page and frowned.

"It's her," he said. "But I never heard about this. This must've been when she was about thirty. Wow, so they thought she burned the church down."

"Yeah, but why would she do that?"

"Hold on, there. It says 'suspected.' If they thought she did it, she was never convicted."

"It might be why the people here didn't like her."

Dad nodded before he handed the paper back.

"Keep looking," he said as he lay back down and pulled the pillow over his eyes. "Let me know what you find out. If there really was a church where the house was, that might explain some of the stuff we found."

"Sure. One more thing," said Zach. "What if those stones in the barn really are grave markers?"

"I don't know," said Dad from under the pillow. "Even if they are, so what? We're not staying. Now let me try to fight this headache off, huh?"

Zach closed the door behind him as he left the room. He thought about going upstairs to talk to his mother, but the door to her "studio" was closed, and he could hear Hendrix leaking from under the door. She didn't like to be disturbed when she was working.

He hurried back out to the barn and the stacks of old papers. Maybe he could find a cause, or at least more about the church. As he walked, he scanned the rest of the article. There'd been troubles, though the paper didn't say what they were. Only that the church was embroiled in controversy, accusations and secrets. The more he read, the more he got the impression that whoever wrote the article did so with a breath of relief that the church was gone. It also listed the names of those killed in the blaze.

When he reached the barn, he headed for the second stall. The papers were out of order, but he could sort them into some sort of time line. He sat down on one of the newer stacks and began to go through them.

The whispers began almost as soon as he sat, though quiet enough that he didn't notice at first. As he worked, they grew louder, and he found his attention drifting to the stones in the floor of the barn. More than once, he caught himself staring at one of the stones, the one that looked most like a grave marker, with the yellowed newspaper dangling unread from his hand, and garbled words playing in his ears. The third time he caught himself, he stood, went to the third stall and found a shovel. If it was, it was, and then he'd know Cindy's wild story was true. If it wasn't, he could lay his worries to rest.

It took him the better part of an hour to chip away the grout and dirt and mortar from around the stone, with the voices gaining subtle crescendo. When it was clear, he wedged the tip of the shovel under one of its edges and pushed down. It didn't budge. His skinny body didn't have enough weight for the task. Urged by the now screaming voices, hurried back to the third stall and found small block of steel, one that resembled a cartoon anvil, that was just small enough that he could lift it. He muscled the block over and wedged it under the metal part of the shovel, where the blade met the wooden handle. A lever, his father once told him, was more powerful than brute strength, and all he needed was a fulcrum. With the block in place, he leaned on the shovel's handle until he heard it creak, and the stone shifted. Not much, but enough so he could wedge the shovel blade further beneath it. The voices grew to fever pitch with his efforts as he pushed again, reset the fulcrum, and applied his weight again. When the stone came free, the voices stopped, the eerie silence an oppressive blanket. He thought at first that the handle snapped, as he went toppling to the ground and landed hard on his shoulder. When he sat up, the stone stood at an angle, the dirt-encrusted bottom of it clearly visible.

Zach scrambled to his feet and crept to the stone. It was far heavier than he could lift by himself, and the dirt on the bottom was compacted and thick. It would take a chisel to get through it, or at least a powerful water jet. He rushed to the third stall again, his heartbeat pounding in his ears, and dug through the ancient tools until he found an old hammer and a paint scraper. It would have to do.

The dirt came away in clumps at times, but mostly as dusty clouds that wafted through the air. As he worked, the whispers began again, a breathy rhythm that beat in time with his heart and the hammer. A lucky hit caused a tiny avalanche of clods, but not enough to see the other side. As he brought the hammer down on the paint-scraper handle again and again, he wished Cindy were there to share his discovery. He hoped she was wrong, that the stories were just that and nothing more, but with every cloud of dirt that poofed into the air, every syllable breathed and hissed on the air, the more solid the feeling of dread in his stomach became.

After what seemed like hours, he struck a blow hard enough to cut through the hard dirt to the stone beneath. He twisted the scraper until a section of dirt came away, and the voices were once again silent. He stared at what lay beneath. Letters, rough-carved into the stone, stared back at him. A "Q," "u" and "i," with the rest obscured by more dirt. He grabbed the newspaper from the Stepside's bumper where he left it and scanned the article. Quillin. Ellen Quillin. Perished in the fire that reduced her church to ashes. It had to be her. And if she was here, then the rest of the stones might well be...

It was then that he realized what the voices were saying.

Help us! It burns! It burns!

The cavernous barn seemed claustrophobic, not enough space for himself and the dead. He stood and ran out into the open air. He might not be able to tell them about the voices, but wait'll Dad saw the stone. Wait'll *Mom* saw it. She'd have a heart attack! He glanced up to the window of her studio and froze. There stood his mother, her head swaying to Hendrix, her eyes closed in ecstasy, naked and running her hands over her breasts. It took a moment for his brain to process what he saw, then, without thinking, he barked "Mom!"

She jerked at his voice and her eyes snapped open. She stared out the window and saw him, then seemed to notice for the first time that she was naked, and yanked the lace curtains shut.

16

What was she thinking? One moment, she felt the clay slide through her fingers, the next she stood nude in the window, practically masturbating for the world to see. Worse, for her son to see. At the time, it felt so good, so delicious, to work the clay around her nipples and slide wet mud across her tender flesh. But his voice snapped her out of it, broke whatever spell the combination of pot-smoke, Hendrix, and the statue wove, and she was herself again, naked and ashamed.

She didn't bother getting dressed, but hurried down the stairs with her clothes in her hands. When she reached the bedroom, she gently pushed the door open so there would be no sound. Gary lay on the bed, victim of one of his headaches, with the pillow over his face. Good. She didn't feel up to the task of answering the hundred awkward questions he would surely ask.

She hustled across the room to the bathroom, breathing silent thanks that she didn't encounter Zach on the way. She couldn't imagine the questions he would ask, or how she would even begin to answer them.

With the bathroom door closed behind her, she dropped her clothes and turned on the water as hot as it would go. Then she turned and looked at her reflection in the mirror. Clay caked her face, smeared around her mouth as if she'd been eating it. Long finger-wide streaks traced the line of her neck and encircled her breasts, then continued downward, across her hip bones and across her thighs. Clay caked her pubic hair, and streaked her buttocks.

She sat down on the edge of the bathtub while the shower steamed the room, and sobbed. The strange thoughts, the little man on her sculpting table, Gary's weird mood swings, it was all too much. Though she'd never admit it to anyone, she was terrified. And what would Zach think? If she lied, tried to formulate some flimsy explanation for what he saw, would he believe it? Probably not. He'd see through it in a heartbeat, know she'd lied to him, and lose what little remained of his respect for her. And that was what truly scared her, the thought of losing her baby boy.

She stepped into the scalding jet of water and flinched as it burned her skin. She had to get the clay off, had to remove the filth from her body and the filthy thoughts from her mind.

But they felt so good. Every imagined caress, each flick and stroke made her hungry for more. And it terrified her.

She took the rough loofah and scrubbed her skin pink while the hot water carried away the alien thoughts.

But they weren't alien, were they? Is it so wrong to want pleasure? To desire sensation?

The door to the bathroom opened with the shrill sound of old hinges. She froze in place, sweat mixing with the hot water. Gary pulled the curtain aside. He wore that smile, the eerie grin that did not seem at home on his face, but melted her legs like butter. He didn't speak a word, but slowly climbed into the shower with her, his desire evident. She reached to embrace him, but he took her arms and gave her a rough turn, then bent her over. As he took a handful of her wet hair, she almost resisted, but then he took her hard. And it was what she wanted.

It was hours before Zach screwed up his courage to go back into the house. It wasn't the oppressive feeling of being watched that bothered him now. He knew what waited for him. Awkward silence, or worse, an even more awkward attempt at an explanation. Neither one was a welcome possibility, but if it had to be anything, let it be the first. He stayed outside, though not in the barn. He couldn't stand to be in it, now that he knew he was essentially walking over a mass grave. What he took to be the wind were their voices. They had to be. And it made the barn feel less safe, no longer like his private sanctuary. He did, however, drag a couple of stacks of old newspapers outside to read while he waited for his stomach to quit rolling. The graves were real enough, as was the connection to his father's aunt. And the cries of agony he heard made his stomach knot. But he kept returning to the real question of why.

The next paper in the stack told part of the story, of Ester Carter accusing Horatio McBride of unspeakable acts, at least by the standards of the 1940's. Zach snorted as he wondered what the people of Shy Grove would've thought of today's headlines, where it seemed every day brought new accusations against priests. So she had a real mad-on for the church. He scanned the article until he found a paragraph that detailed her accusations. Imprisonment, sexual abuse, even murder was among the crimes. The more he read, the more she sounded like a crackpot to him. Things like that just didn't happen in polite society the 1940's. But what if they had?

He tossed the paper aside and flipped through the next few issues. Headlines told of prosperity, of healthy crops and herds, of booming businesses. But below them, in smaller print, he noticed an underlying current of something dark that moved in Shy Grove, a shadow that the rest of the town either didn't see or turned a blind eye to. In almost every issue, the victorious headlines drew attention away from smaller print in which something tragic occurred. A missing child, a prized goat found slaughtered, a woman found dead in a ditch outside of town. Yet for all these things, the town prospered and everyone appeared happy in the photos.

He continued skimming the issues until he found a headline that seemed more important than the rest. "New Preacher Comes to Shy Grove," said the front page. It wasn't so much the headline that caught his attention, but the image that accompanied it. Although the man in the photo was a stranger to him, he knew certain pieces of the man's face. His eyes held the same expression his father's had lately, full of energy and just a hair off maniacal. But the thing that chilled him to the bone was the smile, the same malignant grin that at once seemed inviting and threatening. It was the same smile his father wore.

Angela hummed as she cooked dinner. She hurt all over, and not just from the aggressive scrubbing. Gary was rough, harder on her than ever, but it seemed right to her, and she bore her pains with satisfied pride. He let her exorcise her most animalistic lusts, and gave her back more, and it wasn't wrong because he was her husband. No matter what he wanted, all he had to do was flash that smile and take command of her, and she would give it to him without question.

Zach came through the back door and paused when he saw her. Her stomach fluttered, but she looked back to the pot of noodles on the stove as if nothing had happened. She was thankful when he didn't speak before leaving the room.

Gary was in the living room, packing more boxes with his aunt's things. If Zach told him what he saw, what would Gary think? But Zach wouldn't tell. He just...wouldn't. She knew him well enough to know he got uncomfortable if someone said the word "boob" around him. For him to tell what he saw was unimaginable. But what if he did?

They ate dinner in relative silence. Gary sat grinning at one end of the table while she did her best to act as if nothing were wrong. For his part, Zach stared at his plate and ate little.

"I need to go into town tomorrow," he said between bites. "I want to hit the auto parts store."

"Going to see Cindy, are you?" The way Gary stared at him while he spoke made her uncomfortable, the leering smile, and the fact that he never seemed to blink.

"Maybe," muttered Zach.

"Why don't you drive him?" He turned his unblinking eyes on Angela.

"We've still got a lot to do..."

"Yeah, and we'll never get finished if you keep taking forever to clean out that one room," he chuckled. "C'mon, the kid's been working like a Turk. A break might do him some good, and I can get plenty done with what we've already brought down. While you're at it, you can stop in at the grocery, maybe make nice with the locals."

Her stomach fluttered at the suggestion. The way he said it, the way he grinned, it sounded like a dare, as if he knew what Zach saw and wanted nothing more than to put her in the worst possible position. Alone in the car with him.

"Sure," she said. "No problem."

Zach stared at her for a moment, then stood abruptly and snatched his plate from the table. He hurried to the sink, rinsed, and stacked his dish in the washer, then stormed out of the room and up the stairs. Angela jumped when he slammed the door.

"What the fuck?!"

Zack slammed the door behind him and kicked the bed frame. First Dad said they were staying, then that they weren't. Now he acted like they were again. Whether they were or weren't, something was seriously wrong with Dad. And Mom.

That weirdo smile Dad wore, the way he stared and laughed, it wasn't him. It was like someone else wearing his skin, someone greasy and slick. And the changes happened so fast. One moment, Dad was normal, bookish and happy. The next...

He thought about the headlines, about Crazy Aunt Ester. Maybe insanity ran in the family. The thought that he might be watching his father have a nervous breakdown filled him with dread. Did she act like Dad before she flipped out and burned the church down?

Help us! It burns! All those people, burned alive. Maybe that's what was wrong with Dad. Insanity, he heard, was hereditary.

And Mom...

He shuddered at the thought. She'd always been strong, self assured and the first to disagree with Dad whenever she thought he was wrong. She got onto him about his drinking, weathered the storm when he got angry, and even pushed him into AA. But now, she seemed like a different person. Subservient, almost. As if she craved Dad's approval, and he could do no wrong just because he was a man. That wasn't the Angela Carter he knew, wasn't the woman he called Mom.

It was the house. It had to be. All their bizarre behavior started when they came into the house, with its weird banging noises and whispers and graves in the barn and family secrets. But that was dumb. It was, after all, just a house, just a pile of wood and brick. He remembered reading somewhere about mold spores that caused hallucinations. Maybe the walls were full of them. But then, why didn't they affect him as well? Or maybe they *did*, and he just couldn't see it. Maybe that was what made him hear screaming victims.

He wedged the tire-iron into the doorframe, then slumped down onto his bed. Cindy might know something, might be able to help. Of course, she wouldn't know any more than he. How could she? But still, he wanted to see her. He felt her absence more than he thought he would. Sure, she was just some girl in a shithole town, but she was more than that to him. She was more than just swimming in her underwear, more than fixing his truck. He missed her laugh, her voice, her smell. He missed her kisses.

He leaned forward and looked out his window at the barn, and watched for shadows darting in and out. He knew now that one of them that first night was her, and he wished just to see her shadow again.

After an hour, his eyes drooped and he slumped back onto his bed. He stared at the ceiling until sleep claimed him.

Thump.

Gary awoke with a start, his body slick with sweat. He still smelled smoke from his dream, felt the heat from the flames, heard the laughter over the fire's roar.

Thump.

"Did you hear that?" Angela's disembodied voice hissed through the darkness, accompanied by a shaking grip on his thigh.

Thump.

That noise again. It beat in time with the pounding in his head.

Thump.

Enough was enough. It had to stop. Pipes, wild animal, or leprechaun, whatever was under that floor had to go.

Thump.

Gary threw the sheet aside and swung himself to standing. The sudden movement combined with his already aching head made his stomach lurch. He staggered to keep his feet.

Thump.

"I hear it," he growled. "God damn it, I hear it."

He didn't bother putting on pants or a shirt, but tottered out into the living room.

Thump.

"Really?" He glared at the space where the couch once sat.

Thump.

"Oh yeah?" He stormed to the back door and out toward the barn. Inside, he fumbled for the switch on the work light. White lightning ignited from the bulbs when he found it. After a moment, his vision cleared and he strode to the third stall and rummaged through until he found an old axe. With a triumphant laugh, he hurried back into the house to find Angela in the bedroom doorway, her face twisted in fear.

Thump.

"What are you doing?" she whimpered.

Thump.

"What does it look like?" He lifted the axe high above his head and brought it down on the old floor. Wood splintered and gave way to the rusty axe head.

"Have you lost your mind?!" Angela seemed about to rush to his side, but stayed just out of range of the axe blade.

"Dad!" Zach, wearing only a pair of pajama bottoms, stared down from the landing, his face a mix of confusion and fear.

Gary grinned, wide eyed, as he brought the axe down again.

"Had. Enough. Of the. God. Damned! Thumping!" Every word, he punctuated with another swing of the axe until the floor opened like a festered wound. When the hole was big enough, he tossed the axe aside and climbed in up to his waist, and threw debris over his shoulders to get it out of his way. There had to be a source, something under the house that wouldn't let him rest, something that terrified his wife and unnerved his son. Whatever it was, tonight was the night for it to go.

"No pipes," he said. "No animals! So what the hell is making that noise?"

He kicked debris with his bare feet until he felt something solid and rough beneath his heels.

"Zach!" he bellowed as he climbed out of the hole. "Help me!"

He didn't wait for his son as he hurried out the back door into the night air again. By the time he got to the barn, Zach was hot on his heels. He pulled the plug on the work lights and coiled the cord around his arm.

"Grab the other side," he said. Zach obeyed without a word, though the fear in his eyes spoke volumes. It didn't matter. In another few minutes, the mystery would be solved and they could all go back to sleep without thumping to disturb them.

They brought the work lights inside. Angela stood at the edge of the hole, her hands clasped to her bosom as if she were concerned she'd fall out of her t-shirt.

"What is wrong with you?" she hissed.

"You wanted to know what the noise was," he said with exaggerated patience. "*I* wanted to know what the noise was." He pointed at Zach. "Hell, *he* wanted to know what it was. So guess what? Now we're *all* going to find out!"

"It's three in the morning!"

"It woke me up!" he bellowed. "And I'm not getting back to sleep until I know what it was!"

She stood stunned for a moment, her mouth hanging agape. Then she narrowed her eyes into cold stones.

"You could at least put on some pants."

It was his turn to gape. He looked down at his dirt and sweat-stained briefs, then back to his wife and son. The ridiculousness of the situation struck him at once in the form of a giggle that started deep in his belly and grew until it erupted from his mouth in a loud shriek. Angela pulled Zach closer, which made him laugh harder. If they only knew how silly they looked! So terrified, as if they thought...

He looked from the hole to the axe and back to his cowering wife and son.

"I'd never hurt you two," he said. All the humor was gone from his voice. "I'm sorry. I just... I needed to know... I lost my temper. Please..."

He stepped forward to hug them, but Angela flinched. He'd done it this time, scared her until she feared for the safety of them both. It hurt, but he understood. Crazy laugh, swinging an axe, cutting a hole in the floor in his underwear. No wonder she was afraid. He would be too, if the positions were reversed.

He turned and went back to the bedroom, found a pair of shorts in the dresser drawer, and pulled them on. He didn't see the need for a t-shirt, or even shoes. What mattered was seeing what was in that damned hole.

When he came out, he found Zach at the edge of the hole on his hands and knees, peering into the darkness. Angela stood behind him, as if she were ready to pull him out if something nasty reached up and pulled him under. Gary moved the work lights to the edge of the splintered wood, then plugged them in. They blazed to life and bathed what was under the house in light.

"Gimme a hand, boy!" he said as he moved to the edge and dropped down into the hole.

It wasn't deep, only up to his hips if he stood upright. Crouched down, his back and the top of his head still hovered above the edge. But still, there was enough room for what he needed to do. He swept the broken bits of wood away with his hands, oblivious to splinters and rocks that stuck to his bandage. When he found the edge of the large stone, he cleared it away as best he could, then climbed out of the hole and looked down at his handiwork.

The stone wasn't part of a slab or any natural formation.

"It's a grave marker," said Zach.

"Bullshit," snorted Gary. "Who builds a house over a grave?"

"The same people who built the barn over a cemetery," he said. "I dug up one of the stones. There was a name on the back of it."

"So?"

"It was the name of one of the people killed when your aunt burned that church down."

The slab didn't look like a grave marker to Gary. It wasn't polished smooth, intricately carved. It just looked like a flat rectangle of rock. He doubted it was even marble. Over the top of it, instead of a name were symbols, circles and lines, swirls and stars, all in a familiar pattern.

"Those look like the scratches on the floor," he muttered. "Maybe there's a name on the back of this one too."

"No!" shouted Angela. "I've had enough! Thanks to you, we've got the whole town coming over tomorrow...TONIGHT, and you just hacked a hole in the floor! I don't care if it's a grave stone or the cover to a God damned treasure chest, you're not digging it up! Not tonight!"

"But..."

"No!" She stormed out of the room and slammed the bedroom door.

Gary took a long look around the room. It was in shambles. The axe, the pieces of floor scattered about, the distinct lack of furniture. It looked like a bomb went off under the house, and he was the psycho who set it off. No matter how obsessive he got, he'd never been this bad about anything. What the hell was wrong with him?

"Zach, go back to bed." His son stared at him for a moment, then shrugged and trudged up the stairs, leaving Gary alone in the midst of the ruin he'd made.

Angela was asleep, or at least pretending to be so, when he came to bed. He cleaned up the living room as best as could be expected and set the axe outside by the kitchen door. He thought about taking a shower, but decided he'd wash the sheets in the morning. He was tired into his bones. He fell asleep straight away, and wasn't even aware when his consciousness faded and the dreams began.

He stood before a group of people. A congregation of eager eyes and rough hands, country skin and dresses. It was good that they came, believed the *word* as he told it. The others had it wrong, with their Sunday penance, their fine clothes and fat pockets. They knew nothing of sacrifice, of how to truly please the *Lord*. As it was in the old days, so was it now. The *Lord* was vengeful, full of wrath and deserving of a show of obedience.

Make a joyful noise unto the Lord, it was written. His congregation brought forth the noise, through the joy of song, of pleasure. And as *He* gave his only begotten son, so too did they give one of theirs, offer it up to *Him* to glorify *His* name, that he might bestow upon them blessings for the land.

"Let her be brought forth," he heard himself say.

From the back of the tiny church, his deacons led a woman, untouched and draped in white, to the front of the church. When she reached the pulpit, she dropped to her knees and smiled.

"Speak your name, child."

"Ester," she said. She was new to the flock, new to their ways. But she accepted them with an open heart.

"Ester, are you unknown to man?" It was important. Only a firstborn could appease *Him*.

"Yes."

He looked out over the congregation at the hard eyes of the men, the swollen bellies of the women. "Is there anyone here who doubts her word?"

There was not a murmur, not a hand or a shuffling of feet.

"Rise," he said to her. She stood and took his outstretched hand, and he led her to face the congregation.

"As it takes a community to raise a child, so too does it take a community to make one."

He tugged a string at her back and her gown fell to the floor, revealing the glory that *He* created. She did not try to cover her nakedness, but stood proud and bare in *His* sight, and the sight of her brothers and sisters of the *Lord*.

"Come, then, brethren. Let us help her do her part to glorify *Him*, for the good of us all."

"For the good of us all," repeated the congregation.

As one, they rose and filed toward the pulpit. The women guided her to the altar table where she was laid on her back. One woman placed a cotton pillow with a homespun cover under her head. Two others held her arms up high while the rest encircled her and placed one hand on her soft flesh. The men stood back while Gary pulled the front of his robe open to reveal his own nakedness, swollen and proud. When he penetrated her, she winced but did not cry out. Her smile did not falter. He moved with her, thrust until he grunted and deposited his holy seed, then stepped back.

"For the child she bears must be of ours, not of only one man," he heard himself say. The men lined up, old and young, fat and thin, and each took their turn. The women whispered "Glory to God" as each of their men finished, and another took his place. No man could claim parentage of the child that would come, and all could.

At least one of them was due before the next sacrifice, and another after that. When this one was due, it would be time again.

As each man finished, he took his seat again, a look of placid satisfaction at a duty performed on his face. When the last sat down, the women joined their husbands and brothers and smiled at them, proud for doing their share for the community.

Ester lay on the altar, her flesh beaded with sweat and a euphoric smile on her face. She leaked blood and semen.

With the gentleness of a good father, he covered her in her discarded gown and stroked her hair.

"It is done," he said. Then he turned to the crowd and cried out "Hallelujah!" The congregation responded in kind.

17

Zach didn't sleep. Too many images of dark figures and thoughts of his father with an axe and a crazy smile filled his head. He lay there in the darkness until the sun brightened his room and chased away the shadows. When he decided that it was stupid to just lay there, he got up, pulled on his jeans and a t-shirt, and headed down the stairs. In the living room, the hole in the floor still looked like a wound that hadn't scabbed over yet.

He made his way into the kitchen where his mother and father sat at the table with coffee in front of them and their heads in their hands. They both looked hung over, dead tired and irritable. His mother had a list in front of her as well.

"Anything else?"

"I don't think so," mumbled Dad. "Just get what we need to get through tonight and I'll try to cover up the hole."

"With what?" demanded Mom.

"There's some wood and a couple of rugs rolled up in the barn," offered Zach. His parents looked up at him like they only just noticed he'd entered the room.

"Good to know," said Dad as he took another pull on his coffee cup.

"You need me to stay and help?" He hoped the answer was no. He needed to see Cindy again.

"Nah," said Dad with a half-smile. "You go on. Get what you need in town. I'll have it done by the time you get back."

Zach grabbed a mug, filled it with coffee, then went to take a shower. If he were to see Cindy, he wanted to look his best. Half an hour later, he stood in clean clothes and wet, but brushed, hair in the kitchen while Angela tied her sneakers and gathered her list and keys.

"We won't be too long," she said on her way out the door. "Maybe an hour or two."

"Take your time," said Dad. "What time did I tell everyone to show up?"

"Seven."

"Plenty of time."

They headed out the door and to the car. Zach got in and closed the door. When his mother closed hers, the air became stale, oppressive. He felt like he should say something, anything to ease the awkwardness between them. Instead, he said nothing and stared out the window.

When they pulled into the main street, she finally spoke.

"I won't be long. I just need a few things."

That went counter to his plan. He needed to talk to Cindy, wanted to apologize. If her absence showed him anything, it was that he really cared about her. If they did leave, she would be the one person he missed.

"But I wanted to talk to Cindy. I was going to take her to the Dairy Queen for lunch."

Mom looked at him over her sunglasses, let out an exasperated sigh, then nodded.

"Fine. I'll meet you there. Don't worry, I'll sit on the other side of the room so you two can talk."

It wasn't perfect, but it would have to do.

Mom parked the car halfway between the auto parts store and the general store. He got out and hurried down the sidewalk, hopeful that she'd even be there.

Bells chimed as he walked through the door.

"Be right with you!" Her voice sounded the same as it did when he last saw her, beautiful but tinged with sadness. When she came out from the back, she wore a practiced smile that faded when she saw him.

"Hi." It was the only thing he could think to say.

"Hi."

"Look... I wanted to talk to you."

"So?" She grabbed a box of sparkplugs off the counter and walked toward the back. "Talk."

"I'm sorry," he began. "I didn't mean..."

"To what? Leave me here? Treat me like an easy lay? Remind me of how much you can't stand to be here? Which one?"

This wasn't at all going the way he planned. He swallowed hard and stared down at the counter. He couldn't stand to see her face angry at him again.

"All of it," he said. "It was shitty and stupid, and I'm really sorry."

"Fine," she said, the same way his Mom said when nothing was really fine and she was still pissed off. "No problem. Now can I get you some parts or something? I'm on the clock."

"Don't be like that," he said. "Please? I really just want you to not be mad at me. Come on. Can I buy you lunch?"

"You think lunch is going to get you off the hook?"

"It's worth a try." He smiled. She didn't smile back.

"Okay," she said after a moment. "Fine. Lunch. Dairy Queen?"

"Is there anyplace else in town?"

"No," she said. "Dad! I'm going on lunch break."

"Okay," came a deep rumbling voice from the back of the store. The man sounded like a bear.

"Your Dad's here? Can I meet him?"

"I came home from your house crying the other day. Do you really think that's a wise idea?"

She had a point. And if the man's voice was anything to judge by, Cindy's father was among the *last* people he wanted angry with him.

Angela sat on the hard bench seat of the booth and sipped her soda, her mood dark. The women at the general store were nice, at least moreso than the last time she went there. But there was something strange in the way they looked at her, something almost predatory. They were all looking forward to visiting tonight, they said, and wanted to know if they should bring anything. Angela suggested ice and chairs, then left with her purchases as quickly as she could. By the time she got to Dairy Queen, Zach and Cindy were already seated, enjoying burgers and fries like any teen-aged couple.

Couple. The word felt acidic to her mind. As if they would be together forever, or even a little while past the end of the month.

Cindy frowned while Zach looked at her with such sincerity on his face. She couldn't hear what he said, but she could guess. Confessions of love, caring, devotion, all of it worthless if they left. No, not *if*, *when* they were finally done with the weird old house and got to go home to San Antonio.

Cindy smiled. Oh no. It was the oldest trick in a girl's arsenal, the smile-look-down-giggle-hand-grab. Sure enough, Cindy's hand inched forward and took Zach's, and his face lit up with happiness. What did he know about happiness, or love for that matter? He was only fourteen, for Christ's sake! Soon to be fifteen, but still, he'd never even had a real girlfriend before.

They sat for the rest of their lunch nibbling fries, sipping their milkshakes, and making goo-goo eyes at each other. When they leaned forward and kissed, Angela couldn't take anymore. She got up, threw away her trash, and hurried out the door to the car. She didn't make any effort to keep her presence, or discomfort, a secret from the kids, but cleared her throat loudly as she passed their table.

"You brought your *mom*?"

"How else was I supposed to get here?"

She shook her head and laughed. Maybe she was laughing at him, maybe not, but her laugh still made him happy.

"So now what?" she said as she ate another French fry.

"Come over tonight," said Zach. "No truck work, no talking about staying or going. Just you and me."

"I'm already coming over," she said. "Your dad made sure the whole town was coming."

Zach groaned. "Which is how many people?"

"There's only about two hundred people who live here," she said. "But I bet most of them won't come. Maybe twenty? Thirty?"

"This is going to suck. You know, he doesn't even remember doing it? And last night he hacked a hole in the living room floor."

Cindy stared at him, a look of concern on her face. "Why?"

"The banging noise. It woke him up and he went all... I don't know... Nicholson on the floor."

"Did he find out what it was?"

"There was nothing under there," said Zach between fries. "Just a big slab of rock. No pipes, no animals. Nothing."

"What was the rock?"

"I don't know. Might be another grave stone."

Cindy shivered and rubbed her arms.

"You were right, by the way. Those are gravestones in the barn. I dug one up. There's a name on the back of it."

"Whose?"

"Someone who died when crazy Aunt Ester burned the church down. I'm betting the rest are there too."

"Wait," she said, her eyes wide. "Your dad's *aunt* was the one who burned the church down?"

"I think so," he said. "She was a suspect, according to the papers. But they never proved anything."

"And her old house is build over the churchyard?"

He nodded. "And there's more." He told her about the voices in the barn, how their screams got louder when he turned up the stone. It sounded like a weird set-up for a horror movie, but he had to admit, in a weird macabre kind of way, it was sort of cool.

"Wow," she said. Cindy looked down at her watch, then glanced out the window. "I'd better get back to work. And your mom looks ready to go."

"She's been acting weird too," said Zach as he gathered their hamburger wrappers and empty fry-boats, and tried not to picture his mother in the upstairs window. "Wait'll I tell you what I caught *her* doing."

"Tonight," she said. "Maybe we can figure out what's going on together."

She got up and he walked her to the door. Her hand felt good in his, like it belonged there. She leaned in and kissed him before going outside and across the street to the auto parts store. Zach stood and admired the swing of her hips as she walked away.

When she disappeared back into the auto parts store, he turned and made his way back to the parking lot. His mother leaned against the hood of the car, her arms crossed and an impatient look on her face.

"Ready?"

Zach nodded and climbed into the car, his heart light. Sure, he may not be staying, but Cindy wasn't mad at him anymore. If they did wind up residents of Shy Grove, she would make living here not such a bad thing.

Gary wiped sweat from his forehead as he stood back and surveyed his handiwork. It wasn't perfect. Hell, it looked like a band-aid over an axe-wound, but the plywood planks and area rugs would have to do. He'd searched the house for every chair he could find and came up with a pathetic dozen. Maybe their guests would bring their own chairs.

He glanced at his watch. It was just past noon. Angela and Zach had been gone since ten, which meant they'd be home soon. Time to get cleaned up. He turned to head toward the bedroom.

Thump.

Not again. Not now.

Thump.

He turned toward the hole in the floor. There was nothing under there, nothing but a chunk of stone. Nothing that could pound on the floor from beneath.

Thump.

It moved. The plywood, the rugs, he could've sworn he saw them bounce, moved as if something physical underneath punched the board and wanted out.

Thump.

They'd be home soon. What would Angela say if she walked through the door and found the living room in shambles again?

Thump.

He had to know. He could be quick, cover it back up before they got home. But he had to know.

Thump.

Gary dragged the carpets off the planks in the floor as they jumped again and clattered against one another. There *was* something under there. There had to be.

Thump.

The plywood slid away, revealing nothing but the empty hole beneath. But that was impossible. There had to be a reason, some source. Something moved the boards, God damn it, but what?

He lowered himself into the hole and crouched over the stone. Could the stone itself have somehow shifted and hit the floor? As ludicrous as it sounded, he was willing to entertain any number of weird theories, so long as they could make the pounding stop.

He reached down and put one hand the stone. It was warm to the touch, not at all what he expected. And more, it hummed, vibrated even, such that, when he touched it, he felt it in his teeth.

"What the fuck..?"

The thought died in his mind as a wave of nausea swept through and crowded his brain. At once he tried to scream against the pain and suck in breath that its sudden arrival stole from him. His arms went weak and gave way, sending him face down on the slab. As his cheek touched it, the voices started, whispers and laughter, screams and fevered shouts. They flowed into his head and pushed him aside, filling his thoughts with knowledge of what needed to be done.

When he stood up, he felt strong. There was much to do, so much time passed. First, to clean up the mess, then to prepare for the arrival of his new flock.

Angela pulled up in front of the house a little after one. Zach seemed happier, but the sight of the old house dragged her mood back down. Strangers were coming, people she neither knew nor *wanted* to know would be there in six hours, and then they could put it all behind them. They could finish pulling whatever was left out of the house, then go back home. Maybe then, Gary would stop acting strangely and her own odd erotic dreams would stop.

She killed the engine and Zach climbed out and hurried inside with bouncy happy steps. That girl brought out the best in him, that much was plain to see. But still she wondered how long before she'd have to soothe his heart like putting a bandage on a skinned knee.

She followed him to the house and stopped just inside the door. The hole in the living room floor was covered, and all the debris had been cleared. But it wasn't Gary's repair work that stopped Zach or herself. It was Gary himself. He knelt in the center of the room, over the hole in the floor, with an old crucifix in his hand. It looked for all the world to her like he was praying.

"Looks good in here," she said after a moment.

"Better, anyway," he replied with a smile. That same smile that made her want to do whatever he wanted, no matter how vile or innocent. "Did you talk to the women at the store?"

"Yes." He mind clouded. A moment ago, she'd been worried, angry about something. Now she couldn't remember why. "They're coming."

"Good." He turned to Zach. "How 'bout you? Did you talk to Cindy?"

"Yeah," he said. The boy looked confused, a little frightened.

"And?"

"She's coming tonight too," he said. "With her dad."

"Good! Then we'll finally get to meet him!"

"Yeah," said Zach. "Whatever." He made a wide circle around Gary as he made for the stairs and his room.

"Such a good boy," said Gary as he watched him go. "Nothing more could a man ask in his first-born son."

Alarms went off in Angela's head, but she couldn't finger why.

"Have you finished your sculpture?" he said without turning.

"Almost," she said. She wanted to please him, make him proud. After all, she was his wife, and what was she without him?

"I'd like it done by tonight," he said. "I want to show it to our new neighbors."

Inside, a part of her rebelled. There was too much to do, not enough time to finish and fire it before the others arrived. But the part that was in control scolded her disobedience. He wanted it done, and it was her duty to try to please him.

"I'll do my best," she said with a demure smile.

"I know you will," said Gary. His kiss on her forehead tickled and sent electric sparks down her back, then he turned and went about his business.

Angela hurried up the stairs to her studio where the little man sat waiting. He looked more finished than she remembered, but there was still much to do. No time for ridiculous music or pleasurable caresses. It was time to get down to work.

She unrolled her sculpting tools, stainless steel hooks and gouges which she only used when a project was close to done, and set to work with a song in her heart and hunger in her eyes.

18

Zach crept down the stairs and out of the house. Graves or not, Dad was acting too bizarre to deal with. And what the hell was wrong with Mom? She went from sure of herself to spineless in the time it took for Dad to smile. The more he thought about it, the more certain he was that what was wrong with them had to do with whatever was in the floor. There was no way he was going to get to it with Dad prowling the house like a deranged handyman. Better to head out to his sanctuary and try to stay out of their way. If he was lucky, he and Cindy could hide out in the barn until their little party was over.

Under his arm, he carried a bag with a few parts in it. Nothing big, but every little unimportant piece, when put together, made an important whole. If he could get the Stepside running, maybe he and Cindy would go for a drive while Mom and Dad did whatever they were going to do.

An hour of steady work went by before he stopped and peeled his sweat-soaked shirt off, wiped his face with a dry corner, and hung it over the truck's bed. One more piece to go, then he had to figure something else out to occupy his time. He glanced at the newspapers. Maybe there was something in there to explain what was going on, though he doubted it.

The last piece was the ignition switch. Since the truck was so old, there wasn't any chance of finding one that might be original to the model, but Cindy managed to find one that would substitute. It took him half an hour to pull the old piece out and put the new one on, then he stood back and admired his work. On the outside, the old truck looked almost the same as it did when he found it. Less dusty perhaps, and the new tires took a few years off its appearance. But the real work was under the hood, under the body. That was where the aging process seemed to move backward, like the truck was being reborn.

He slid into the driver's seat, pushed in the clutch and stuck the key into the new ignition switch. Then he held his breath as he turned the key.

The old truck sputtered and coughed, protested as it woke up from its long slumber, then the engine kicked over and the thing roared to life. Despite everything going on with his parents and the house, he couldn't help the big toothy smile that landed on his face, or the whoop of joy that erupted from his mouth. He sat, crowing like a lunatic and slapping the steering wheel, and drank his small victory in.

His first instinct was to run inside, tell his parents that the truck was fixed, but he reminded himself of why he was outside in the first place. *Be invisible.* Besides, it wouldn't be right not to share the first ride in the Stepside with Cindy. After all, without her help, he'd have never gotten it started. And she was his girl now, for however long it lasted. If Mom and Dad quit changing their minds and decided to stay, he supposed he could deal with it, so long as Cindy was around.

He killed the engine and pocketed the key, closed the door and gave the panel a loving pat. Not bad for a boy who, up until a week ago, never looked under the hood of a car before in his life.

The newspapers in the second stall beckoned, and he went to them with a spring in his step. Things were going better than he'd hoped for. Maybe there were answers in the old papers after all. He plopped down on his usual stack of papers and picked up a few copies from the older stack. As he flipped through the pages, his euphoria eased a bit, and worry crept back into his mind. Something in the house. Something affecting Mom and Dad.

He passed several copies until his attention snapped to a single photograph that made his gut twist. The yellowed paper showed a middle-aged man with a broad smile and bald head. The headline above the photo read "New Preacher Comes to Town!" with the story below identifying him as Horatio McBride. That the name was one he'd read before wasn't what bothered him, but that the face in the photograph was one he knew quite well. The other photos from more recent papers never did the man justice, as they showed him at a distance or in the background. But now, the photo's focal point, he saw Horatio McBride in all his glory. And he was almost identical to his father.

It didn't take nearly as long as Angela thought it would to finish the bust. A couple of hours spent in earnest work, and the figure was as perfect as she could make it. It didn't occur to her before, when it was still rough and unfinished how much the little man looked like Gary, but now that the cheeks were smooth and the lips sat just right, she saw the resemblance. And why shouldn't she? The little man aroused her desires, and who else could do so but her husband?

She carefully loaded the bust onto a sheet-pan and carried it down the stairs. Gary sat in the kitchen drinking lemonade with a pleased smile on his face.

"Look!" she beamed. "It's done! It'll take days to fire it, so it'll have to go out wet, but the scuplt is done at least."

"I knew you could," he said. "And with time to spare."

"I'm sorry I don't have enough time to fire it properly."

"And what are you going to do while we wait for our guests?"

She thought for a moment. Gary hated sloth, almost as much as *He* did. But she was so tired from her labors. And they were up so late last night with all the silliness in the living room. She almost didn't dare to ask, but spoke the question before she could pull it back into her mouth.

"Would you mind if I took a nap?"

Gary put down his glass with a thoughtful look and slowly stood. It was wrong of her to ask, she knew, and she shouldn't have done it. Whatever punishment he decided to issue, she deserved.

He put his strong hands on her shoulders and she quivered at his touch.

"I think that would be a fine idea," he said. "You've worked hard, and you deserve it. And you want to be rested when our new friends come calling, don't you?"

She nodded gratefully and smiled.

"Go on, now," he said. "Sweet dreams."

She hurried to their bedroom and snuggled into the bed. As she drifted, somewhere in her mind a voice shouted, screamed at her to get up, to get out and away, but she giggled at the little voice. Why would she want to leave? She let her breathing slow until it reached an easy rhythm and her eyes felt heavy. After a while, the darkness thickened and the little voice faded into sweet silence, and she passed into sleep and dreams.

The grass was cool on Angela's bare feet, though the night was warm. Around her, faces she knew, though she didn't know how, walked alongside. They held torches, she her belly, swollen with the gift she'd been given. There was no physical pleasure in the act, but enough came from the knowledge that what she did was for the community, for their faith, for the *Lord*.

That was six months ago. The baby grew stronger every day. When she first felt it kick, she thought it broke something inside her, and couldn't wait to get it out so it could serve the purpose for which it was conceived. But as time went by, she found herself talking to him – she knew it was a boy – and became more protective of the life growing inside her. He wasn't something to be used or given over to a vengeful God. He was her son.

They came upon the pond behind the church, far away from prying eyes where non-believers couldn't see. It was their baptismal, their sacred place where children were given to *Him* and where the penitent came to beg forgiveness. The preacher lead the congregation to the edge of the water.

"Brothers and sisters," he said, arms raised. "There is among us a doubter."

The congregation murmured, punctuated with a muffled whine. A man in torn overalls, his hands bound in baling wire, stumbled to his knees before the preacher. A ragged bloody collar of wire looped around his sweaty neck. His squeals came from behind a filthy cloth jammed into his mouth. The man struggled, his eyes blazing, but while she felt pity for the poor farmer, Angela did nothing to help.

"Brother Geoff," said the preacher as he tugged the knotted rag out of the farmer's mouth. "What do you have to say for yourself?"

Geoff coughed and spat dry burlap, then stared up at McBride.

"It ain't right!" he wheezed. "Y'all ain't doin' the work of the Lord! Y'all's in with the debbil!"

McBride's boot silenced him with a brutal kick to the ribs.

"Lies!" he roared. "These are the words of Satan! Thou shalt not bear false witness unto thy neighbor, sayeth *Lord*, does he not? Such hurtful words, brother Geoff, against your kin!"

McBride drew back again, as if to kick the farmer's head off his shoulders, but seemed to think better of it and stopped. He turned and whispered to another man, then turned back to the farmer. Such hatred and malice dripped from his smile, it made Angela wince.

"You will bear false witness no more," he said as someone handed him a long knife and a pair of pliers.

Angela turned away as two strong men held Geoff by the head and McBride leaned over his open mouth, but she couldn't escape the sounds. Squeals, followed by whimpers, followed by anguished sobs echoed from the rocks and trees. When she turned back, the farmer hung limp in the other men's arms, his chin a river of blood, his eyes slack.

The smiling preacher held aloft in blood-slicked hands his trophy, the blasphemous tongue claimed from the farmer's mouth, for his congregation to see.

"Such is what comes from lies!" Then he threw the piece of ruined flesh into the pond. "Our work tonight shall be the last holy sight his eyes behold!"

Horatio nodded to the men, who raised Geoff's head and held his eyes open, then he waded into the pond up to his waist.

"Neighbors," he said. "Brothers and sisters. We are gathered here to do what we must, to pay tribute to the one true God!"

"Halleluiah" answered the congregation. She herself answered in kind, but her baby shifted, and worry crept into her mind.

"Tonight, our sister Hannah brings forth her first born, for the *Lord* did say unto Moses, 'Consecrate to me all the firstborn; whatever is the first to open the womb among the Israelites, of human beings and animals, is mine!'"

The congregation answered "Hallelujah" again as a young

woman brought forth a screaming child wrapped tight in strips of cloth.

"With this, oh *Lord*, we beg thee forgiveness of our sins, and ask for bountiful crops and prosperity to glorify your name!"

The preacher took the child from his mother and raised the child high above his head, then plunged the struggling infant into the water. Angela's stomach churned and bucked as the baby recoiled against what it couldn't see and her own mind fought to make sense.

The preacher pulled a long curved knife from his belt and held it up high in one hand while the other kept the baby beneath the water.

"The *Lord* demanded blood from the faithful, and so let this blood nourish our souls and this land!"

The dagger came down fast, pierced the water with hardly a splash, and crimson erupted from beneath its surface. A desperate moan poured out of the tongueless farmer as the men who held him took blades of their own to his eyes. Angela awoke screaming.

19

The sun sank low into the trees, its tired beams peeked through the windows of the old house. They would begin to arrive before the sun set, but it would be dark soon after. Angela waited in the kitchen as she sliced bread and made finger sandwiches and coffee. She seemed better, recovered from whatever terrible nightmare awakened her, yet she still looked on him as if she were afraid of something. There was no time to deal with her silliness now. Afterward, there would be words and, if need be, discipline.

The bust sat in the middle of the kitchen table surrounded by wildflowers, Angela's idea. Gary squatted down and took a closer look. The likeness was admirable, near perfect. Angela did a fine job. Even got the crook of his nose just right. It wouldn't make him go any easier on her later, though. To shirk one's duty in punishing the wicked was as bad as the sin itself.

He looked out the kitchen window toward the barn. The boy already had the work lights blazing. Worked like a government mule, that one. With a little discipline, and the fear of God struck into him, he might make an alright fellow. But then, there was that sullen attitude, his smart mouth. As his father, it was his duty to expunge the filth from his vocabulary and the sloth from his bones. But it was his mother's duty to make sure he had the right frame of mind. Another mark against her. Still, plans were in motion. The boy could be useful yet.

Zach paced the barn like a caged animal. When he made a complete circuit of the floor, he climbed the ladder and walked along the beams and into the hay loft before descending again. The image of Horatio McBride burned in his brain, as did everything else the article told him, and the ones after it. The new preacher, the sudden prosperity of the town, the missing children. It made sense in a macabre kind of way. While the papers weren't forthcoming with any details, he knew enough to put the basic story together himself, and it scared the proverbial Hell right out of him. Of course, then came the questions. Like, why did Ester burn the church? And where'd she get the money to buy the land and build a house? But the question that plagued his mind, even as he kicked past piles of junk and tried to keep his balance in the hay loft, was why did the crazy preacher Horatio McBride look so much like his father.

A hundred different explanations popped into his head, each more far-fetched than the last. But more than his insane theories, what bothered him was that he needed to tell someone, needed another voice to tell him that his suspicions weren't paranoia or stupidity. And at the moment, there was no one safe to tell.

He looked out the large door in the loft and realized he could just see the grove of trees that hid the pond in the distance. On the wind came the whispers again, their cadence familiar as the song his father hummed. In his heart, Zach knew what they were, even if he didn't want to admit it. Against the night sky, the branches gave a slight wave, as if throwing the whispers toward the barn. The sight of their dense leaves, and the knowledge of what lay beyond them, made his nerves wriggle like worms under his flesh.

A flash of light from the other direction caught his attention, and he leaned out the door a bit to see its source, an old station wagon bouncing up the long driveway. The guests were starting to arrive.

He turned and made his way back to the ladder and down to the floor of the barn. Another set of lights approached, then another, and another. With every car, his muscles tightened, his nerves stretched until he wanted to scream out or tear something apart just to dispel the energy. One by one, more than a dozen cars arrived, but still no sign of the big black truck he wanted to see. Hers.

She said she'd be here. She promised.

He stalked back to the stall where the important newspapers sat in a special pile. A year of unmatched prosperity, then the church burned, then the town began to die.

It wasn't a quick death either. First there was a dry spell that killed off most of the crops. The cattle died off from disease or starvation. Over the next few years, the papers told an increasingly woeful tale of a town that withered and turned to dust.

A low rumble caught his attention and he ran to the front of the barn and peeked around the door. The huge black truck pulled up behind the rest.

"Finally!"

Both doors opened. Cindy's brother Chris and Toby got out of one side. A man with a curled up gimmie-hat, he assumed her father, got out of the other, followed by Cindy. Toby and Chris headed toward the front of the house. Her father stopped and watched her head for the barn for a moment, then made his way toward the front door as well.

When her father was out of sight, she hurried toward him. He met her halfway and caught her in a tight embrace. When he didn't pull away, he felt her tense.

"What's the matter?" She pulled away and searched his eyes for an answer.

"Everything," he said. "I read the papers, and there was this guy, and my dad looks like him, and..."

"Shhh." She pulled him close and hugged him tight. "Slow down. Whatever it is, we can figure it out, right?"

Her body pushed against his was the balm he needed, the scent of her hair better than wildflowers. No matter what it was, she was right. Between the two of them, they'd get to the bottom of whatever was happening.

"Start at the beginning," she said.

"I got the Stepside running."

Gary waited until he was certain no one else would arrive before he came away from the door. It was important for the host to greet the guests as they walked in. That was just manners. He directed them toward the kitchen where Angela handed out cups of coffee or water and little paper plates for the sandwiches. Everyone took one and smiled with appreciation before returning to the living room where they made polite and nervous conversation. As they passed the table, they all regarded Angela's statue with surprise. A few complemented her on her work. Angela beamed with pride.

The last man to come in was accompanied by two boys he remembered, Cindy's little brother and her friend. When the man walked through the door, he removed his hat in a sign of respect. Gary went to shake his hand, then stared into his familiar face. Though the man was a full head taller than he, Gary recognized the similarities between them.

"You must be Cindy's father," he said. "Gary Carter."

"Trevor," said the man with a warm smile that Gary knew as well as his own.

"Head on into the kitchen," he said. "My wife's outdone herself with refreshments."

The tall version of himself nodded and ambled off, trailed by the two boys. Yes, their meeting was long overdue, but nothing that couldn't be rectified.

When Trevor and the boys reappeared from the kitchen, Gary took his place on the stairs so he could see them all and, more important, they could see him. As he looked out over them, he was overcome with the notion that he knew them already, recognized them even.

"Hello!" he said in a loud clear voice. The conversations stopped as all faces turned toward him. "I'm so glad so many of you could come tonight. My wife and I wanted to take this opportunity to introduce ourselves. I'm Gary Carter. My wife is Angela. My little angel, I call her."

Polite laughter filtered through the crowd.

"I'm sure everyone knows the stories about this house, about the land. About my aunt. Well, we wanted to put those rumors to rest tonight. What happened here so long ago was a tragedy. I'm sure that a few of you remember it, but most of you were too young. Since we've been here, we've experienced an...eye-opening. This place was once sacred ground."

He looked out over the crowd's rapt faces.

"And it can be again."

A murmur filled the room as the younger folk turned to their neighbors. The older ones in the group stared at him. Their mouths twitched as if they wanted to smile. In their eyes he saw hopeful recognition.

"Shy Grove was once a beautiful prosperous town," he said. "I think we can make it so again. I can't undo what was done, but together, we can right an old wrong. We can redeem this house, and put to rest those who lie without peace here."

"How?"

The lone voice came from the back of the room where the old woman from the general store sat in an old rocker. The faces turned to her, regarded her question, then turned back to him for an answer.

"Those of you who remember, look at me. Look at the statue my lovely wife made. Remember that face and see it in me, and in others here." He nodded to Trevor, who smiled up at him. "I want to help this town to come back to life. And to those who want to help, come back Friday night around this same time. Now, I think for those who remember, we ought to have a song."

Several shrugged and looked toward each other, but a few faces lit up at the suggestion. Hope brimmed in their eyes. Gary cleared his throat and began to sing.

Let our pleasures be thy pleasures, let us share in all your pain... A few voices joined in with him, one after another until every face smiled and lifted its voice in song. *Let us sing unto your praises, beneath the blooded rain...*

"That just can't be right." Cindy stared at the paper, eyes wide and jaw agape. Even she could see the resemblance, and she hadn't talked to Dad but, what? A couple of times? "That's just spooky."

"That's not all," said Zach as he handed her another paper. "Take a look. Disappearances during the year the church was built, a few more in the year after. Then check this out. Ester was a member of the church. That's her in front."

"She was pregnant."

"They all were. Look close." He pointed to their bulging tummies, some disguised by dark colors ad the poor quality of the photo in old newsprint, but on others, the evidence was plain to see.

"So? They were a bunch of farmers. Women were always pregnant at that time."

"Ester never married," said Zach. "She didn't have any kids. That's why my dad inherited this place."

Her eyes didn't register what he was trying to get across.

"Okay, look at this."

He flipped through the newspapers until he pulled several issues from the pile.

"No birth announcements. I went through all the papers for nine months, and there were no birth announcements. Funerals, yes, but no birth announcements. So what happened to the babies?"

"You don't think this preacher guy..."

"I don't know what to think. But Ester was pregnant in this photo. Three months later, she burned the church down. It doesn't make sense."

"So what do you think that was your dad found under the house?"

"I'm not sure," said Zach. "But I think it might be Horatio McBride's grave."

"The preacher? Now you're being paranoid."

The back door of the house opened and let loud conversations and laughter out into the yard. Zach and Cindy shifted, as if they didn't want to be caught sitting so close together.

"We can talk more tomorrow," said Cindy.

"You'll come back?"

"Of course I will," she said as she punched his arm. "You're my boyfriend, aren't you?"

He grinned despite the nervousness he felt. To hear her call him her boyfriend was a shot of joy.

"Cindy!" The deep voice carried across the yard and made his nervousness come back. Nothing like a girl's father to turn even the bravest boy, which he wasn't, into a coward. A large man lumbered across the yard toward the barn, flanked by Toby and Chris. When he came into the light of the work lights, he removed his baseball cap. Zach couldn't help but stare up at his face.

"You must be Zach," said Trevor. "I'm Cindy's dad."

"I know," he said. "I mean, yeah. Nice to meet you."

"You two been behaving out here?"

"Nope," said Cindy with a wink. "We've been smoking dope and screwing in the hay loft."

Zach felt his testicles shrink up inside his body. He wished he could melt into one of the cracks in the floor before the giant in front of him snapped and beat him to death in a blind rage for defiling his daughter.

But Trevor didn't look at all perturbed.

"Well, long as you weren't tearing the tags off mattresses or doing anything illegal, I guess that's alright." He turned and walked toward the truck. "Let's get home. Nice to meet you, Zach."

Zach tried to respond, but the only sound that would come out of his mouth was a pathetic dry croak. Cindy giggled and kissed his cheek.

"See you tomorrow."

He watched her go and couldn't decide whether he liked her even more, or he wanted to strangle her for scaring him so bad.

Everything went well. Gary stood by the back door and shook hands with people as they left. Angela made her way to the living room and picked up the discarded paper plates and coffee mugs. The people seemed nice, at least to Gary. At least a few of them said they liked her sculpture. But she couldn't get over that dream. Every time she looked at Gary and his smile, she felt torn between wanting to please him and the overwhelming dread that accompanied his voice. When he started singing, she almost had to leave the house to keep from screaming. It wasn't just the song, or Gary's singing voice, but the *way* he sang it that disturbed her. He sounded too much like one of those television preachers, his voice too similar to the preacher from her dream. But Gary would never try to hurt his own son, his first and only. After Zach was born, the doctor recommended a full hysterectomy because her womb was so damaged, so there would be no more. It upset her that she was no longer able to have children, and for a while she felt like less of a woman, but Zach filled her heart more than she dreamed a child could.

But the way he talked, it was as if it wasn't Gary talking,

but some other man, vibrant and charismatic and wonderful. Lately he both aroused and frightened her, almost as much as she frightened herself.

As the last of the guests left, she pulled the bag from the garbage can and hurried to take it out to the large waste bins. She didn't want to be alone with him at the moment. His excitement was palpable, so much so that he couldn't hold still. And when he spoke to their guests, he bounced from foot to foot like he might leap up in the air and dance. And that song.

She shivered.

The song frightened her more than anything. At the first few words, the song triggered a feeling of dread in her worse than anything she'd felt before in her life. It gave her the impression that something was terribly wrong with Zach, that she had to leave, to take him with her and get as far away from Shy Grove as she could. But that was silly. Gary knew what was best, and whatever it was, she would abide it.

"Angel," he said as she reached the door. "Come back here for a minute. We need to talk."

She let the bag loose in her hand and set it by the door. Then, eyes on her shoes, she turned to face him.

"You've been acting skittish all night. Is there a problem?"

"No." Her voice came out quiet, like the squeak of a mouse. His reprimand made her feel like a child.

"That's good," he said. He cut the distance between them and moved behind her so he could whisper in her ear. "Because you know what has to be done, don't you?"

"Yes." She did. She knew the terrible thing that would bring Shy Grove back, that would sate the *Lord's* wrath. But she couldn't let him. It was wrong, plain wrong, but how could she say no to *Him*? To Gary?

"There will be no betrayal," he hissed. "Not this time. We're going to set things right."

"Yes." Her throat constricted as she tried to fight off tears and keep her fear down in her belly.

"Tend to your chores," he said. "And call the boy in. Then you can tend to my needs."

"I...I will."

"Good girl." He kissed the back of her head and made his

way toward the bedroom. "Hallelujah!" he shouted as he closed the bedroom door.

Outside, the warm night air kissed her face with dry lips. She carried the bag to the bin and threw it in, then went around to the front of the barn. Zach sat on the hood of his truck. At the sight of him, love and pride swelled in her chest. He looked such the man perched up there, like James Dean with more unruly hair. All he needed was the red jacket.

"Your father says it's time to come in," she said.

"Mom? What's wrong with you?"

He didn't say it mean, or with any trace of his usual sarcasm or biting anger. It was an innocent question, one that jarred her. Something *was* wrong, but she didn't know what. She knew something bad was going to happen, something vile and repugnant, but the image wouldn't form in her head.

"Nothing," she lied. "Why?"

"You don't seem... yourself lately."

If it was that obvious to him, maybe there really was something wrong.

"You and Dad... you both are acting weird. Dad's got that smile, and the song, and... well, just his whole *him* isn't right. And you, you're acting more like his servant than like my mom."

"Is it wrong for a wife to want to please her husband?"

"It is when it's you. Since when do you bow down and act like a maid to anyone?"

It was a fair question, one she couldn't answer. Her own father was a bastard, and demanded strict respect that blossomed into hatred. The last time he took his belt to her, she swore she'd never bow down to any man again, and she didn't. But her head felt fuzzy. Pressure built behind her eyes, as if something were trying to push its way out and in at the same time.

"I don't know what you're talking about," she said. "I'm just happy here."

He nodded and looked down at the floor, slid off the hood of the truck and walked toward the house.

"I thought you said no more lies between us, remember?"

A retort formed, biting and perfect, but it died on her tongue. He was right. Her eyes burned with tears that leaked down her cheeks, and the pressure in her head grew stronger. She turned to stop him, to apologize and explain, but it was too late. The back door swung closed and left her alone in the barn.

She glanced around, as if an answer might be spray-painted on one of the walls. Her gaze landed on a single newspaper on the hood of the truck. Zach must've been reading it. She took the yellowed pages in her hand, and almost dropped it when she saw her husband's face staring back at her from the front page.

Horatio McBride.

She put the paper back on the truck's hood and hurried back to the house. She had to tell Gary that they needed to leave. Tonight. Now. The house, Hell, the whole *town* was unhealthy. Better to leave the place for the woods to reclaim than to stay another minute.

As Angela passed through the back door, the pressure in her head doubled. She needed to tell Gary something. Something important. But what? The thought was just there, so vital that it couldn't wait, but it was gone. Inside her head, a voice screamed out, but it faded before she understood what it meant.

Angela smoothed out the front of her skirt and wiped her hands across her face. Why were her cheeks wet? Had she been crying? How silly of her. There was no reason for tears, not after tonight. It wasn't every day when Shy Grove got a new preacher. And what a preacher he was, her husband. She hurried toward the bedroom so she wouldn't keep Gary waiting.

20

"Oh, Christ almighty."

Gary's head hurt worse than any hangover. His drinking days were behind him, but damned if it didn't feel like he went off the wagon last night. Every muscle in his body felt weak, his legs like they were full of sand. His teeth felt like they had a thick coat of something awful on them, and his mouth tasted like he'd eaten a dead animal.

He chanced opening his eyes and regretted it when the sunlight hit him like a sledgehammer. Whatever he did last night, he at least hoped it was worth the pain, though he couldn't imagine anything would be.

Angela's place in the bed was empty, the pillow cool. She'd been up for a while. It was nice of her to let him sleep, but he couldn't help but wonder why. In fact, he couldn't remember much of yesterday.

He pushed the sheets aside and realized he was naked. It didn't matter to him, but it wasn't something he was used to. When they were first married, Angela and he slept nude most nights, but in the past ten years he at least slept in his underwear, she in an oversized t-shirt. He staggered out of bed and turned around to look for his clothes. A dark stain marked the sheets on Angela's side. Alarms went off in his pounding head, and he stumbled to the dresser for a pair of pants before he staggered out of the room to find her.

Angela stood in the kitchen dressed in a bathrobe. Her hair

stood up in shocks as she fried two eggs in a pan.

"Hey," he said.

"Fuck off," she growled.

"Whoa... wait... what's the matter?"

Angela glared at him, then slammed the pan down on the stove with a *bang*.

"Don't tell me you don't remember," she hissed. "I hurt in places I didn't even know I *had*, so the least you can do is remember doing it to me, you psycho!"

Her anger bubbled over, but didn't completely cover her embarrassment. Whatever he did, she felt violated, something he never wanted her to feel. He tried to be a kind lover, gentle and considerate. Being rough in bed wasn't his way. But she stood there, a victim, part of her seething with anger, the other cowering in shame.

"I'm sorry," he said. "I don't know what happened." He felt lost, accused of a crime he surely couldn't commit, but as he moved to hug her, she pushed him away, slid her eggs out of the pan and onto a plate, and limped to the kitchen table. She winced as she sat, slow to touch the hard wooden seat. Beneath the edges of her robe, he saw deep scratches, a bite mark. He dreaded how the rest of her body looked.

He sat down across from her, but she wouldn't look at him.

"Please," he said. "Tell me what happened. I'd never hurt you. You know that."

"I thought I did," she said through tears. "You were rough last night. Too rough. When I told you it hurt, you hit me and did it harder. You got off to me crying."

Gary sat stunned, unable to speak. He'd never done, *would* never do, anything so unspeakable. The strength of their relationship was built on mutual respect, neither holding dominion over the other. For him to force her was unthinkable.

"We're leaving." She didn't look up from her eggs, nor did she say it like a threat. It was a simple fact, a statement of what was about to happen. "I'm taking Zach and we're going home."

The pain in his head doubled, clouded his vision and sent arcs of heat through his temples. It felt as if something were trying to push his eyes out of their sockets, and his eardrums rang and stretched until he was sure they would burst. On his upper lip he felt first a drip, then a trickle. A coppery taste filled his mouth. He didn't need to look in a mirror to see that he was bleeding again.

Angela, to her credit, looked up and her mask of angry resolution cracked into abject terror. Gary tried to hold up either hand, to tell her he was fine, but his arms went rigid, his fingers dug into the table like claws. His jaw locked and though he could breathe, flecks of pink foam shot from his mouth with every breath. He tried to stand, to force his arms away from the table, but his legs kicked and jerked with their own agenda, threw him out of the chair and onto the floor where he lay and twitched until a dark iris closed around his vision.

When he opened his eyes again, he expected to be alone. But Angela sat by his side on the bed, a damp washcloth in her hand, dabbing at his forehead. Zach sat in a chair across the room. His long hair looked disheveled from hands running through it a hundred times with worry.

He tried to speak but his throat felt cut and scarred on the inside. Angela gently lifted his head and put a glass of water to his lips. He drank a few gulps, then licked his lips.

"What happened?"

"You had a seizure," said Angela. "Grand mal. You scared the shit out of me."

"I don't have seizures," he said as he tried to sit up, but the pressure in his head forced him back down to the pillow.

"You do now," said Zach. "Do you remember anything?"

"No."

Zach and Angela shot each other a look he knew well. Worry and confusion.

"Why?"

Neither of them looked like they wanted to be the one to say, but Angela took a deep breath as she put the washcloth over his forehead.

"You were singing."

Gary blinked at them. Singing? While in the middle of a seizure? How was it even possible?

"It was that weirdo song we found in the barn," said Zach.

"I don't even know that song," said Gary.

"Seems like you do."

"We need to get you to a doctor," said Angela. "Your hand

looks better, but you're acting strange. "

"You both are," muttered Zach.

They both stared at the boy.

"Don't you two feel it? You," he said as he nodded to his father, "keep acting like you're some holy-rolling preacher from down south. And you keep turning into this little mousy, I-don't-have-any-opinion woman who can't think for herself and only does what he tells you! What the hell is wrong with you both? Am I the only one who sees it?"

Gary stared, his jaw hanging open. In all their time together, Angela had never once been the submissive type. But then, there were long blank spots in his memory. What did he do last night?

"If you ask me," said Zach as he got up and went to the doorway. "It's this house. I think we ought to leave."

Zach stormed out of the house and let the back door slam in his wake. As he stepped off the porch, he felt it again, the weight that came off his shoulders whenever he was out of the house. Of course, they wouldn't listen. They never did. Not to a stupid teen-ager. There was a distinct difference between the Mom and Dad he grew up with and the two people who sat in that bedroom right now. And while his own parents weren't terribly cool, they were better than Dad when he had that weird Horatio McBride-smile on his face, and Mom when she acted like a dog that was beaten into submission.

The barn smelled of oil and mildew, hay and compost. It was hot outside, but cooler in the barn. Maybe the seizure would make them see that they had to get out. Then he could get back to his life with his friends.

But without Cindy.

He needed to talk to her, to tell her what she meant to him, but he knew how that would end up. Just like last time, she'd end up crying and angry and he would feel alone and stupid. Mom wanted to leave, he could see that when he talked to her when she wasn't under whatever kind of spell Dad had on her. But she wouldn't. Not if Dad had anything to say about it.

"Zach."

His mother stood in the doorway of the barn. The way she

stood, her posture, with her head down and that placid smile on her face, made his skin crawl. It happened again.

"Your father is better now. He wants you to come back inside. We're going to have a family talk."

"I don't want to talk," he said. "I want to go. Now."

"Don't be like that." Her voice was soft, soothing in a way that made him feel grimy. "Just come back inside. We need to make some decisions. As a family."

She turned and walked back toward the house. She didn't even walk like his mother anymore, with confidence in her steps. Now she shuffled, as if she was being pulled by a leash back to her master.

He didn't want to go back into the house. If she was changed, Dad was changed too, and he already knew what that meant. Family meetings and decisions aside, they were back to wanting to stay. At the door, she turned.

"Come on," she said, her voice stern. "Now."

Zach obeyed, though in his mind a plan already began to form.

Inside, his father sat at the kitchen table, his shirt caked with his own blood, that damned eerie smile plastered to his mouth.

"Sit down, son."

Mom stood behind him, hands clasped in front of her lap, while he sipped his coffee.

"Your mom and I have come to a decision."

It was as if nothing had happened. There was no seizure, no blood, no crazy singing. They both looked...pleasant.

"Let me guess," said Zach. "We're staying."

A flash of surprise crossed his father's face, but not so much so that it wiped away the smile.

"Yes," he said. "Yes we are. But I want you to know why."

His father launched into a long speech about community, about building something worthwhile, all the while his mother nodded placidly behind him. Zach didn't listen. He'd heard enough. As crazy as it sounded, even to his ears, he'd managed to piece together what was happening. It wasn't just the house, but the old preacher. The shadow on the stairs, the head his mother sculpted, the pictures in the old papers. Somehow, he realized the man in front of him was no longer Gary Carter. The man who wore his father's face was Horatio McBride.

"Do you understand?"

"Yeah," he lied. "I get it."

"And you're alright with that?"

"Sure."

"Good!" beamed the man who was no longer his father. "Our new friends are coming back over tomorrow. It will be a very special time."

"I bet."

"I'd like to have the barn cleaned out by then," he said. "I'll help you..."

"No," said Zach, a little faster than he intended. "You've just had a seizure. You need to rest. I'll take care of it."

The smile on his father's face grew wider.

"Good boy," said Gary. "A man couldn't ask more in a first-born son."

"I'd better get started," said Zach. He got up from the table and hurried out the door.

Night came fast, but not nearly quick enough for Zach. He did as he said he would, stayed in the barn for the rest of the day cleaning. The whispering voices that floated between the boards were strangely absent, as if they knew something was about to happen. When he was done, it still looked like a barn, just not so messy. He went into the house for dinner, careful not to say or do anything to his parents that might tip them off. After eating, he took a cold shower to wash away the sweat and grime of the day, and to strengthen his resolve. It wasn't a perfect plan, but he didn't know what else to do.

He told his parents that he was going to bed, then made his way to his room and waited. He must've dozed a bit, because his clock read well after midnight when he climbed out of bed again. He quickly stripped and changed into his blue jeans and a t-shirt, then crept to his door and listened for footsteps, voices, or even a breath. But there was nothing. He moved the tire iron and opened his door. The hinges let out a tiny groan, but not enough to wake the whole house, he hoped. The hallway was clear as far as he could see. He stepped out and tip-toed to the landing.

"What'cha doing up, boy?" The voice cut into him and made his innards wriggle. His father stood in the hole in the living room floor. A trick of the moonlight as it filtered in through the windows made it look like the stone in the hole glowed with a strange blue light.

"Nothing," he stammered. "I thought I heard a noise or voices or something down here."

"Woke you up, did I?" said his father, the eerie smile still affixed to his face. "Nothing to worry about. Just me doing the Lord's work. Back to bed with you."

"Yessir," said Zach. He hurried back to his room and jammed the tire iron back in the door.

"Shit!" he hissed. His whole plan was based around being able to get out of the house. He needed another way.

The air conditioner blew cold air at his neck, and Zach got an idea. If he could be quiet about it, he might be able to get out after all. He slipped his sneakers on, then lifted the window and held the unit so it wouldn't fall, then propped the window open with a ruler. Then he gritted his teeth and pulled hard. The window unit came out without much trouble, and even less sound. He placed it on his bed and climbed out through the window, onto the roof.

Light from the almost full moon bathed the yard so that he could see well enough. The barn was only a few yards away. All he needed to do was figure out how to get down without making too much noise, or without breaking his legs in the process. A quick look told him that there was no easy way to get to the ground. What he wouldn't have given for a tree in the right spot. The distance didn't look so high from the ground, but staring down it seemed deadly.

"Zach?" His father's voice came through the door, accompanied by pounding. "What're you doing in there, boy?"

His heart shifted into double time as he swallowed hard and made his decision.

"Zach! Open this door right now!"

One step, two steps, then he jumped. He flapped his arms as if they might bear him aloft into the night sky, then hit the ground hard. Pain shot through his knees and ankles as his weight came down on them, and his butt struck the dirt, but he lived through the fall. He staggered to his feet and limped toward the barn.

When he reached the Stepside, he slid into the driver's seat and said a silent prayer, then turned the key. The old truck roared to life. He pulled the switch for the lights and felt his stomach turn over. Gary stood in the doorway of the barn, the eerie smile replaced by a grimace of fury.

"What do you think you're doing?" he shouted. "Get your ass

back in the house!"

Gears ground as Zach fought to put the old truck in gear, then he gunned the engine and let the emergency brake go. The Stepside growled and rumbled past his father, who shouted and slapped the side. In the rear-view mirror, he watched as his father ran back into the house. He had only seconds before Gary would come after him in the family car. But there was no way Zach was about to let that happen.

He swung the wheel hard and hoped that the old truck's steel frame and panels were more sturdy than the plastic and aluminum of his Dad's Toyota. The resulting crunch sent a wave of nervous laughter through Zach's frame, a real sense of joy in the destruction. Then he hit the gas, ground the gears until he found second, and roared down the long driveway.

At the main road, he almost lost control of the truck, but it fishtailed around until he set it straight again.

"Now what, genius?"

His plan had several parts, the first being to actually get out of the house. That done, he needed to talk to Cindy. But, he realized, he had no idea where she lived, or even how to get hold of her. The only place he knew was the auto parts store, and the chances of her being there after midnight were nonexistent. He had less than a half tank of gas and twenty dollars in his pocket, not enough to fill up. And the way the Stepside sucked down fuel, half a tank wouldn't last long. His best bet was to find some place close by and hide, sleep in the truck, then try to find Cindy tomorrow. Mom and Dad didn't have a phone in the house, and their cell phones didn't work out here either, so chances were good that they wouldn't be able to contact the police. And even if they did, what then? He could tell them... what? That his parents were acting weird because of a dead preacher in the house? Yeah, that would work. If he'd paid attention, he might be able to get back to San Antonio. But, of course, he'd been too wrapped up in his own little world of showing his parents how miserable he was to notice stupid things like how to get back to the interstate. Town it would have to be.

The square in Shy Grove looked strange in the moonlight, more haunted than dead. Every shop looked lonely, plantive. What streetlights there were cast weak blue light on the ground.

No stray dogs or cats, no late-night drivers except for him. Just buildings and black windows like sorrowful eyes that stared out at the street.

He idled along until he came to the auto parts store. As he figured, the windows were dark. And why wouldn't they be? It wasn't like she *lived* there or anything. Across the street, the feed-store parking lot had a drive that went around back. A good place to hide, he decided. As good a place as any until the sheriff found him, and wouldn't that make a good impression on his niece?

He pulled the truck up under a tree in the back and shut off the engine and the lights. It was stupid. What did he hope to accomplish? Come morning, he'd either find Cindy, or the sheriff would find him and take him back to his parents. Either way, it was too late to back out now.

He locked the doors and stretched out on the bench seat, then closed his eyes and drifted off to sleep.

Sunlight woke him first, then a tapping noise by his head. He opened his eyes to find a stern-looking man with a red face and a black ball cap staring in at him. The man was using the handle of a shovel to tap the window.

Zach bolted upright, blinked a few times, then rolled the window down.

"What the hell're you doing in my lot?" demanded the man.

"I'm sorry," stammered Zach. "I just..."

"This ain't no hotel! Get that hunka shit out of here!"

Zach scrambled to comply. When the truck coughed to life, he put it in gear and pulled the truck around in a wide circle until he made it out of the gate. The lights in the auto parts store were on and Cindy's black truck sat out front. He pulled the Stepside across the street and into an empty parking place, then he checked his hair, smelled his breath in his hand, and got out.

That little shit.

Gary wrestled with the tire iron from Zach's room and front wheel well of his car. The boy'd done a real piece of work on it, plowed it in so the car wouldn't turn without shredding the tire. The door was crushed shut too. When he got home, there'd be hell to pay.

Last night, the boy snuck out, ran like his pants were on fire. It wasn't enough that he left though, oh no. He had to damage the family car in the process with that steel monster of his. It was a mistake to let him keep it, he saw that now. But it wouldn't matter after tonight. The truck would be Gary's, and that would be fine.

With no telephone in the house, he couldn't exactly call for the sheriff, either, but that wasn't too much of a problem. The *Lord* provided, when needs arose. After the boy's taillights disappeared down the drive, he and Angela knelt together in the middle of the living room and prayed. Oh they prayed hard, asking *Him* for aid, and *He* would never let one of his most devoted down. Not when the stakes were so high. The Sheriff showed up less than an hour later with sleep still in his eyes.

"I felt the good Lord calling me," he said.

Now there was nothing left to do but wait and get the house ready for tonight. They'd be back, his flock, and Shy Grove could live again.

There might even be time for a little discipline with the wife. She threatened to leave yesterday, and that wasn't going to work at all. A man who couldn't control his woman wasn't much of a man, was he? And she threatened to take the boy with her. That much he couldn't endure. He poured himself back into the weakling with such speed that it damned near killed him, but it worked out fine. That Godless academic didn't even know what hit him, and now he screamed and pounded away, as if he might have a chance of getting out. But the *Lord* saw fit to give him strength, to allow him to hold dominion over Gary. The body was his now, and that was all there was to it.

Angela came out of he house with a glass of lemonade.

Well, *almost* all there was to it. What were women for but to serve the needs of their husbands, after all? And she knew what was coming, and that it was for the good of the community. Things had to be set right, both with the town and in her head. Too much high-society living, that's what did it. It made her willful, and made her son a pain in the ass to boot.

Soon as the sheriff got back with the boy, there'd be a reckoning, that much was certain. They'd see what was what and then get on with the business at hand.

"Is there anything I can do to help?" Angela stood a few feet away and wrung her hands.

He almost laughed.

"No. What would you know about cars anyway? Get yourself back inside. It's almost lunch time."

She didn't answer, but nodded and went back into the house. Yes, a little discipline would be good for her demeanor, good for her soul. She was just as weak as Gary. She needed not just to learn her place, but to *know* it.

Bells chimed over the doorway of the auto parts store.

"Just a second," came Cindy's voice from out of the back. Zach hurried up to the counter. When she came out, her face brightened into a warm smile.

"Hi! What're you doing here?"

"We need to talk," he said. "Somewhere private."

Her expression darkened.

"What's going on?"

"It's my parents. Please, can we go somewhere?"

"Dad! I'm going to lunch!"

"It's nine-thirty in the morning!" came his exasperated reply.

"Breakfast, then," she said.

"Okay, sweetie! Bring me back some pancakes!"

She came from around the counter and took his hand. He lead her out of the store.

"*You* drove here?" she said when she saw the Stepside.

"Yeah," he said. "I had to get out of there."

"How'd you do?"

"Jerked the whole way," he said with a slight smile. "But I think I'll get the hang of it."

"All the same, we'll take mine."

They climbed into the truck and backed out, then headed down the road and out of the main part of town. When they reached a wooded grove with a picnic table on a slab, they stopped and got out. Zach waited until they were seated at the table before he blurted his thoughts.

"I think my parents are possessed," he said. Cindy took a moment before her mouth twitched into a grin. "I'm serious! They're acting really weird, and I don't know what to do. It's the house, I know it is."

"Okay," she said. "Calm down. What's going on?"

"I read about the old preacher, Horatio McBride, right? Remember the photo? Well, Dad's been acting like he's all psycho, and he has this big weird smile. And he's been singing this song a whole lot, one we found in the barn, only he doesn't know it, and it sound's like a religious hymn, and..."

"Woah," she said. "Calm down. You're not making any sense."

"None of it makes sense!" he shouted. "My parents are acting like a couple of nuts, and I know it has something to do with the house and the old church!"

"Okay, so you said you found something under the floorboards. Did you dig it up?"

"No, but I found my dad standing in the hole last night."

"Doing what?"

"I don't—" A shrill whoop caught his attention as the sheriff's car pulled up beside Cindy's truck. "Shit."

Sheriff Weston stepped out of his car and put on a slow easy grin as he ambled up to the table.

"Hello, Zach. Your momma and dad have been looking for you. Hiya, pumpkin." He sauntered over to the table and took a seat beside Cindy.

"Hi, Uncle Milt."

"Now, we got us a whole mess of problems here." Zach felt the bottom fall out of his stomach. "Driving without a license, destruction of property, running away... boy, I could put you in Juvie for a while."

"How 'bout I take him back?" Cindy smiled and the sheriff smiled back. "Someone's gotta drive his truck back, right?"

"Oh yeah," he said. "I forgot trespassing. Earl over at the feed store told me he caught you sleeping in his lot."

"I didn't want to go home," said Zach.

The sheriff seemed to consider for a moment, then pushed his sunglasses up on his face.

"You get him home," he said to Cindy. "His folks are worried. I'll drop by to tell them you're coming. Just make sure to have him home before tonight. You hear me?"

"Sure thing, Sheriff," she said with a salute. "I'll have him home pretty quick."

The sheriff pushed himself to his feet and gave Zach one last steely look, then he grinned at Cindy and ambled over to his cruiser. "Not too late," he said as he got in. He beeped his siren once before he drove away.

"You ran away," said Cindy. "And you thought to come and see me. That's sweet."

"I needed to see you. You know what's going on at the house. You're the one who told me about the bodies in the floor. I just didn't know who else to turn to."

She took his hand and squeezed it tight.

"Come on," she said. "We'll go back together."

"I'm not going back. I'm going home. Back to San Antonio."

"But I thought..."

"Come with me." As soon as he said it, he knew how stupid it sounded. A fourteen, soon to be fifteen-year-old and his sixteen-year-old girlfriend, both runaways, couldn't hope to get far before they were caught. But anything was better than going back to his Mom and Dad. The way they looked at him suggested something like cancer, something that would chew him up and swallow him if he didn't get away.

It wasn't that he didn't love his parents, but he didn't know what else he could do for them. All he knew was he had to get them out of the house. The way they acted, he didn't think that was going to be easy.

"I can't," said Cindy. "I mean, I want to, but..."

"I don't want to do this alone," he said. "You said yourself you want to get out of this shithole town. Come with me. San Antonio's great. We can crash with my friends until we figure something out."

His heart stopped for what felt like forever while he stared into her eyes. *Please please please...* Then she broke into a smile.

"Okay," she said. "Let's go get your truck, then we have to swing by my house."

"Why?"

"Clothes, stupid. Then we can go."

His heart leaped like a frog in his chest. It was the best of both worlds. He could get back to San Antonio and his friends, and still have Cindy. Then he could bring back the cops, or the Army, anyone who would listen and help his parents. He didn't like the thought of abandoning them, but what could he do? As much as he liked to think of himself as grown up, inside he was just a kid, and no one listened to kids. Especially not when they told stories about haunted houses and possessed parents.

That had to be it. The dead people, the shadows, the whispers in the barn, the strange personality shifts of his parents, it all fit. It had to be haunted, and it didn't take him more than one guess to decide by whom.

When they pulled into town, they found the sheriff in his car, parked beside the Stepside. Cindy let him out where the sheriff could see him, and he put on a nervous smile.

"You heading back?" asked the sheriff.

"Yessir," said Zach. "Right now."

"Thought you was going to let her drive."

"C'mon." Zach tried to play it cool. "Would you let anyone else drive if this was your truck?"

His ears went red and his armpits went damp as the sheriff seemed to consider for a moment, then the older man's face broke out into a wide grin.

"I guess not," he said. "Straight home, and no more driving till you're legal, you get me?"

"Yessir," said Zach as he scrambled into the driver's seat. The truck started without protest, but it took him a couple of tries and more gear grinding to get it backed out. When he made it out into the street, he waved to the sheriff, who winced as he ground into first and bucked off behind Cindy.

They agreed to take the back way to her house on account of it being the opposite direction, and they wanted to at least appear to be going back to Zach's mom and dad. When they cleared town square, Cindy hung a right on another country road and took off. Zach did his best to keep up, but the distance between the two cars spread by the second. She was little more than a black speck and taillights when her truck turned right again. When he reached the corner, he stamped the break and clutch.

The sheriff's cruiser was parked across the road in front of what Zach assumed was her house. Standing in front of it was her uncle, along with her father. Cindy was out of the car, yelling at them. They were too far away for him to hear any of the conversation, but she gestured and waved her arms and he knew she was in trouble. As if he needed any more convincing, her father struck her with a vicious backhand across the face and knocked her to the ground.

"No!"

Her father scooped her up and stuck her in the back of the cruiser. In a panic, Zach stomped on the gas and let off the clutch. The old truck lurched, but didn't die on him as it kicked up dirt and gravel behind him. He drove until he was sure they weren't following, then pulled off behind a large patch of scrub. He let his foot off the brake and let the truck grunt into silence.

Hot tears rolled down his cheeks as he banged his fists against the steering wheel. First his parents, now Cindy. There was no one to help him now, and he wished for his mom's comforting touch, his father's hand tussling his hair. He wanted to put his arms around Cindy, but he'd been too late. He sat in the car and sobbed until his chest ached with the strain and his throat was raw from coughing.

Outside, the sun began its slow descent in the sky. Everyone was going to the old house. Cindy's father insisted she be there. But why?

Little snippets of information flooded into his mind, things he saw, things he read over the last few days. The pictures of the pregnant girls. The lack of birth announcements. The hands at the bottom of the pond. The strange tomb, because that's what it had to be, buried under the house. None of it made any sense. And then there was Ester, pregnant as the rest of them and happy one day, crazed and fire-bombing the place the next. What happened to her baby?

The image of his father and the photo of Horatio McBride flashed through his head, then of Cindy's father. Realization grabbed him like a cold skeletal hand at the base of his neck. It was a sick thought, grotesque to him. But his mother always protected him, even from his own father. Just like Ester did for her son.

Let our pleasures be thy pleasures...

Dad wasn't her nephew. And Horatio McBride was his father. Just like he was Cindy's father's. But then, what happened to the other babies?

His stomach churned and his eyes went wide and pieces

began to click into place for him. The arms in the bottom of the pond, their baptismal, the place where they made sacrifices to their God. He felt sick.

Let us sing your praises beneath the blooded rain...

Zach threw the door open and scrambled out of the truck into the cool night air. He heaved onto a mesquite bush until the spasms in his already empty stomach stopped. They killed them. They murdered the babies in that pond. That sick fuck. And if that were the case, he shuddered to think of what they planned to do to Cindy.

And if he was right, it meant that Cindy was his cousin.

A return to the old ways, he heard his father say. *Make Shy Grove great again.* His fear gave way to anger at the thought of something diseased forcing his parents to murder the girl he loved. And, kid or not, he had to do something about it.

Zach climbed back into the truck and fished under the seat for the old jewelry box. It was right where he left it, undisturbed. He opened it and took out the pistol. He'd never shot one before. It seemed simple enough. Point, pull the trigger, pray he hit the target. He looked at the cylinder the way he saw tough-guys do in movies. Six bullets, all in their places. Did bullets get old? Did they stop working? He hoped not.

Zach cranked the engine. The truck howled to life and growled as he ground the gears until he hit the right one, then pulled out and sped back toward the old house.

That damned kid. He was more trouble than he was worth.

Gary worked his shovel under the stone while Trevor and Sheriff Weston did the same with theirs. Chris and Toby used pry bars to try to shift the thing. Around them, the older men and the women stood with clasped hands and whispered voices, all of them speaking their own prayers and Hallelujahs over and over again. Angela knelt beside them, but was silent. He noticed, oh and there'd be words to come.

"It's moving!" shouted Toby. The men pushed together and the stone came free with a hissing noise. There was no odor, no ancient smoke to billow up. As they moved the stone and peered in the hole, the women's joyful cries grew louder. A couple of farm hands put nylon straps around the stone and moved a block and tackle into place so they could hoist it out of the way. When it was done, the mummified corpse of Horatio McBride lay welcoming to their stares.

"Here!" shouted Gary. "Here is what comes of betrayal! She was one of our own, and she turned her back on us! Turned her back on Shy Grove! And what happened? Her treachery almost destroyed our town!"

"Amen!" shouted Trevor.

"And how fitting is it," continued Gary. "That *I* should be the one to come back? How fitting is it that *I*, who was stolen from our *Lord*, should return to set things right?"

A chorus of "amens" and "hallelujahs" erupted from the

gathered flock.

"Tonight, we shall give back to the *Lord* the glory that has been denied him for more than thirty years! And Shy Grove will live again!"

They roared in approval, screamed out their thanks for deliverance. Only Angela seemed reserved, almost afraid. That boy had to come back. They couldn't be a family without him, their first born. Across the room, Trevor stood with his powerful hands on Cindy's shoulders. Gary smiled. First things first, he decided.

The path that served as the driveway was far enough away that no one could see the main road from the house. The full moon gave enough light that Zach could see, but did that also mean they would see him? He hoped not.

He killed the headlights for the last few yards before the driveway, then killed the engine and coasted to a stop. Maybe they could hear the truck, maybe they couldn't, but he didn't want to take the chance. When the truck was stopped, he picked up the gun and stared. It was heavy, cold in his hands. What if it kicked? What if he missed? What if he killed someone? The image of his parents flashed through his head. No matter what was in them now, they were still his mom and dad. Maybe the gun would scare them enough to let Cindy go. But that was as far as his plan got. Take Cindy, drive to San Antonio, then what? Hide for the rest of their lives?

It didn't matter. They were going to do something bad to her, he felt it in his bones. He pressed the grip to his forehead. The pounding in his chest doubled as he made his decision and climbed out into the night.

The corpse of Horatio McBride lay in the middle of a sheet pulled from Gary and Angela's own bed. They, along with the others, knelt around the preacher's husk. There were tears, praises sent to *Him* for delivering his body back to them after so long.

"Be not afraid, brothers and sisters!" shouted Gary. "For you all *know* me! Let no tears of sorrow fall tonight, because I am reborn! Look at this face and see me inside! I have returned from cold and wormy Earth to lead you once again, and to take my place among you! Yea, I have come to bring prosperity back to you, the faithful!"

Cries of joy and amens and hallelujahs filled the air.

"And you all fulfilled your duty to the *Lord*!" Gary clambered to his feet and swung his arms at every hard-hit word. "And *He* did smile upon us! But there was one..."

The congregation lifted their voices again with anger and cries of "no."

"Yes, yes," continued the sermon. "One, who did not offer up her life to *Him*! Who hid away her tithe! Who burned our church and killed our brethren. And what happened?"

"Tell us!" they cried.

"The *Lord* turned his back on us! She lied to her own flesh and blood! Sent him away to live with non-believers! And held dominion over our holy land!"

"No!" shouted the congregation.

"But tonight... tonight we set things aright again. For I am that lost tithe! And her selfishness, her arrogance will prove to be her undoing, and our salvation!"

A ragged chorus of cheers and amens exploded in the air as the congregation gave thanks to their reborn savior. Gary turned toward Angela. Though her pose was reverent, he saw fear in her eyes. It was the same fear he saw in the betrayer's eyes so many years ago.

He told the women of the congregation to do their duties, and they set to work. They anointed the corpse of Horatio McBride with oils and took great care in wrapping it up in the sheet. While they worked, Gary took his wife into their bedroom.

"Is there something you'd like to say to me?"

Angela shook her head and looked down at the floor.

"Because if you have doubt, now's the time to say so."

"No," she said. Her voice was quiet, submissive, the way it should've been, but he wasn't convinced.

Gary's fist shot out, fast as a snake, and punched her hard in the temple. She fell to the ground. Of course she did. She was weak, the weakness borne of Eve's original sin. It sickened him to see her, wallowing like a limbless pig in shit. He thought she'd learned her place, but she needed another lesson. His firm hand across her face would remind her, no doubt, but he didn't stop there. A vicious kick to her ribs took her off her knees and sent her gasping for air.

Just look at her. Pathetic. Worthless. Just like that coward son of hers. He'd get his, sure enough, but not before the whelp's mother begged him for mercy. Not until she was broken. Not before she lay bleeding and naked on his bed, and was thankful to be so. But that would have to wait. There were guests to attend.

He stood over her, the sadistic smile plastered over his face, and took hold of her hair. She cried out for only a breath, but then was quiet as tears welled in her pleading eyes. He pulled her close enough to smell her skin, to taste the fear that leaked from her pores.

"You will do as I command, as is written in the laws of Abraham, won't you?"

She struggled to nod against the clump of hair he held.

"Do I need to remind you again of what happens to you when you disobey?"

A sob escaped her throat as he pulled her hair tighter.

"You disobey me, that makes me appear weak. Weak before our congregation. Weak before the eyes of the *Lord!*"

Tears streamed down her face and slid off the sides of her quivering lips. How he wanted to taste those tears, to force his mouth upon hers and make her submit to his wishes. As it was written. But there would be time enough for that later.

"Do not cross me, woman," he hissed into her ear. "When this is all over with, I'm going to remind you who the man is around here. You understand?"

Her breath came in sniveling jerks as she nodded. It made him feel powerful, the way a man should, the way he used to before that bitch stole his life away. For a moment, he though about unzipping his fly, gracing her by allowing her to pleasure him before going back out. Let her tears and blood and spittle mix on his cock while she sobbed because she knew he was right. But there was no time now.

Gary held her hair tight as he let the threat hang for a moment, then threw her to the floor.

"Clean yourself up," he said. "We can't have the congregation see you like this, now can we?" With that, he turned and stalked out of the room, back to his adoring flock.

Angela sat on the floor and sobbed, deep and purging. It was wrong. Not only the way he treated her, but it was wrong for him. In all the years they'd been married, he'd never treated her like property, like a mule for whipping. It was wrong for *her*. She'd never let anyone treat her like that before. Her own father was a despicable man, and his hard fists and acid tongue taught her that no one was deserving of such treatment. And yet she stood there and let him. She should have fought back, should have broken his nose, broken his balls, but she didn't. What ever she was, this new person wasn't *her*.

Something snapped inside Angela, a dam of hateful images and emotion that pounded at the back of her consciousness. The screaming voice that told her to get out, the pain of Gary's abuse, the rage at being defiled. She grabbed a pillow off the bed and let it all flow out in a muffled guttural howl of anguish.

She lay on the floor, her spastic breaths pouring bile and bitterness out of her body. That son of a bitch. No one treated her the way he did. *No. One.*

She pushed herself to her feet, ignoring the ache in her ribs, and walked with slow, confident steps to the bathroom. In the mirror, she looked like a mockery of her gender. Her hair stood out where Gary'd gripped it. Her eyes stood out with mascara that ran down her cheeks. Her puffy lips looked deformed as they stood out with lipstick. She looked like a clown, a beaten doll for him to abuse and tear apart.

She turned the water on full cold and splashed her face. Was this how Ester felt? Did he do to Ester the things he did to her? She remembered her dreams and felt her gorge rise. It was Ester she saw held to that altar. And the accepting look on her face, she welcomed it, saw it as her duty. Bile climbed up her throat and she lurched for the toilet and heaved until her stomach was empty and cramped.

When she felt able, Angela stood and went back to the mirror. Someone had to stop this madness from happening all over again. She wiped her mouth with a damp washcloth, rinsed some mouthwash around, and ran a brush through her hair. He hit her in the temple, not the eye. There'd be no swelling, no split lips. The bastard knew what he was doing. A few touch-ups with her makeup and she would look "presentable." She snorted at the word. He would pay, and pay dearly. Before another innocent drop of blood was shed, he was going to pay.

She took one more look in the mirror and her mind floated to Zach. Her first and only child. Wherever he was, she prayed to any other God than what these people prayed to that he was safe.

23

Zach crept across the rocky terrain the way he'd seen guys do in movies and video games, hunched over, gun held high in one hand, half running, ducking behind anything that might hide him. That was the way it was supposed to be done, wasn't it? Only the movie tough-guys weren't fourteen years old, and video game heroes were always commandoes or spies. They had fancy guns that weren't made before they were born. They knew what it was like to shoot a gun, what it felt like to kill someone.

And they weren't piss scared like he was.

In his head, he replayed his favorite first-person shooter video games, the ones where zombies and giant spider-creatures leaped out from behind every bush or doorway, and he mowed them down with ease. Except for when he didn't. Except for when they caught him, and his computerized arms flailed as digital blood spattered on the monitor, then giant red letters flashed "GAME OVER" at his failure. It wasn't as easy as the games made it out to be.

What took four minutes in his parent's car was taking too long on foot. He didn't know how long he'd been moving, but every second ticked by, an eternity in itself. He had visions of those awful hands reaching up out of the water for Cindy, of his father holding her head under while his mother smiled and watched and wondered if he had the courage to shoot them both to save her.

The gun in his hand felt like it weighed a thousand pounds.

His arm ached, and switching hands did no good. He tried tucking it in his belt, the way he saw gangsters do, but the fear of it falling out, or worse, him shooting himself, killed that idea fast. He was out of breath and tired, and he knew he had a long way left to go. What kind of hero would he be if he stopped for a break? The kind that was too late to save the girl, that's what.

A few more feet and he stumbled on something in the dark, a rock or a root, he couldn't tell which. The gun skittered out of his hand as his knees and elbows hit the gravely ground. He flailed, searching frantically in the darkness for the gun, and prayed he didn't stick his hand into a nest of scorpions. After a few moments of panicked feeling around, he laid his hand on the cool steel of the barrel, then Zach shifted to his butt and sat for a moment.

His knees and elbows stung. In the darkness, he couldn't make out much, but he knew they were skinned, the knees of his pants torn. He wished his mom was there to kiss the scrapes and help him to his feet. Not the thing that looked like her in the old house, his *Mom*, the strong, opinionated woman who would never let anyone hurt her baby. Tears stung his eyes at the thought. Could he shoot her? His own mother?

Zach pushed himself to his feet and wiped his eyes with the back of his arm. Heroes didn't cry, or whine to their mommies when they skinned their knees. Like Jesse Ventura said in that movie with the alien hunter, he didn't have time to bleed. Not now, with Cindy in danger. Too bad that all he had was an antique pistol instead of Ventura's mini Gatling gun.

He forced his aching legs to move and his burning lungs to keep drawing breath.

"I'm coming, Cindy," he gasped. "I'm coming."

The women were almost done wrapping the body to his satisfaction. Good. A fine job they'd done, too. The strips of linen were tight. He looked almost like an Egyptian mummy. He snorted at the thought. The Egyptians and their idolatry and heathen ways. So much belief, yet they got it wrong in the eyes of the *One True God*. In fact, *every* religion in the modern world lost their ways long ago. Only Gary knew the *Lord*'s true wishes, *He* of the Old Testament.

Angela came out of their bedroom, clean and groomed. She smiled sweetly as she came to his side. Good. She knew her place.

As he watched the final strips being tied, he lost his focus for a moment. A flash of that other man, that weakling, hit his mind with all the force of a buzzing gnat. So full of indignity, so angry, so full of fear, he screamed in his head, begged for him to stop, to leave his shrew of a wife alone, to let him leave. But no, he'd escaped once before. And what came next would silence that little whelp's voice for good.

"It's done," said Trevor with a proud smile.

"Good," said Gary. "Let's get on with it then."

He crossed the room to where Cindy sat and crouched in front of her.

"You were supposed to bring him back, weren't you?"

The girl nodded as frightened tears ran down her cheeks.

"And where is he now?"

"I don't know."

Gary blew out a forceful breath and stalked back to the mummified corpse.

"It's time!" he said.

The men in the congregation picked up the body with gentle, reverent hands, and carried him through the house to the back door. Once out in the yard, Gary made his way to the barn. When he reached the door, he faltered for only a moment. Ground consecrated in that blasphemous false religion made up the floor. He spat over the threshold, but didn't cross it.

"Trevor!" The large man appeared by his side with an eager grin. "We need wood for torches."

"We got flashlights."

"This has to be done in the old way," he explained. "Fire. Now hurry up. The *Lord* awaits!"

Trevor nodded and ran into the barn. A few minutes later, he returned with wood torn from antique chairs, an old axe handle, and other strips of lumber small enough to be held in one hand. Then he wrapped the ends with cloth from a pile of rags in one of the stalls.

"There's kerosene in the loft," shouted Gary. Trevor nodded and sprinted up the ladder. In a few minutes, he came down with a can and doused the rags with its contents. The men all took one and lit the ends with their lighters.

"And now, my brethren, let us go to our holy place!"

A chorus of amens echoed through the night.

The group raised their torches up high and walked toward the back of the property. Zach crouched by the front of the house, hidden by a shadow cast by the corner. His lungs still burned from the distance. His heart pounded too, but he couldn't tell if it was from his trek from the road or out of fear. A little of both, he supposed.

He peeked around the corner and scanned the group. His father was in the lead. No, not his father. Not anymore. The thing that led the group was Horatio McBride. It had to be. But he wore his father's face, his body like a suit of skin. He glanced down at the gun in his hand and wondered if he could do it, if his father was still inside, if he'd ever come out again.

Two steps behind the preacher, Zach's mother followed. From where he crouched, she looked the same as when he left. Still under the spell of the house and the preacher. Still beaten and subservient. Still a mousey thing with no free will. If he killed the preacher, his mother would be free. He hoped so, anyway. He had his doubts about shooting his father, but his mother he *knew* he could never kill.

Among the torches and bobbing heads he spied Cindy's father, almost a head taller than the rest. The proud smile he wore was evident, even from across the yard. He held Cindy's shoulders and pushed her along in front of him.

There were so many, too many to use the gun on them all. He looked down at the gun again. So easy, to pull the trigger, but then what? Would he be arrested? Put in jail for murder? The more he thought, the heavier it seemed in his hand. So much power for one person to wield. In his heart, he knew he could never use it. He'd never admit it, but he cried in movies when someone killed an animal, and he'd never hurt anything bigger than a spider in his life. The thought of taking a human life was alien, unthinkable.

But then, maybe he wouldn't need to *really* shoot anyone. Maybe he could just scare them, make them *think* he intended to gun them down if he didn't do what he said. If he held it up and talked like he knew what he was doing, didn't let them see how terrified he was, he might be able to get out and away without anyone getting hurt. At least, he hoped so.

The echo of their voices as they sang that same diseased hymn faded as the torches became little more than bright dots against the velvet darkness. If he was going to go, he needed to do it now. Time to man up, prove that he could be a hero. Save the girl, drive off into the night.

He swallowed hard against the lump in his throat and hurried after them.

24

In the early days, the land was wild. They were brought to the pond by divine providence. He told them stories of how the pond sprang up from nothing when a good, righteous man collapsed from heat and exhaustion from working his land all day, the way the *Lord* intended. When the man fell to his knees and begged *Him* for something to drink, a great clap of thunder echoed in the sky, the ground split, and cool, clear water bubbled forth. The man, according to legend, drank his fill, then gave thanks to *Him*. That was the beginning of Shy Grove, a single thankful and righteous man.

The story made him smile every time he thought of it. Even more so now, because the town was begun by a righteous man, and now would be reborn by a righteous man. Surely the *Lord* would forgive him one small mote of pride. After all, it was by *His* grace that the lost child found his way home.

The weakling inside him struggled again, twisted inside the purgatory of his own mind. But he didn't deserve this body. He was never meant to have it. His purpose was to die so long ago, to give his soul to Glory for the good of the community. The way Horatio saw it, his life was stolen, and he was just taking back what was rightfully his.

Though the church was gone, destroyed by that sinful jezebel, the land still held a familiar scent. Even at night, he knew the path to the sacred pond as if he'd walked it just yesterday. The grass was brown now, instead of the green that it once was, and many of the lush trees were twisted shadows of their former selves, but he knew the rocks to his left, the dips in the ground to his right. It was a long hike to the pond, but that would please the *Lord*.

"Long and hard is the road out of Hell!" he shouted to his gasping and wheezing flock. "If it was easy, it wouldn't be worth doing! It wouldn't mean anything!"

The weakling's body was soft, not used to walking long distances. Too many books to cloud faith, too much philosophy and radical ideas to distract from the true way. He polluted young minds with his Wordsworth and Dante, and dared call himself a teacher. He was an abomination. His very existence was a blasphemous slur against the will of *God*. He bet the man was a Democrat, too. Probably had homosexual friends and shared space with unworthy races to boot. He knew he was a weaklng where his wife was concerned. But Horatio already took care of that problem. When they became willful, women needed a firm hand, as was written in the Holy Scripture.

After tonight, things were going to change. The weakling would die, as he should've already, and Horatio would be free again to do the *Lord*'s work.

He glanced behind at the tired old faces of the faithful. The church would have to be rebuilt. He doubted there was one capable of bearing children anymore. Except for that one, his brother's daughter. She was ripe. He could smell her. Already marked with the curse of Eve, she would make someone a fine woman, so long as he kept his hand firm. She would be the first in rebuilding the church, of re-establishing their ritual. It was her duty, after all, to the town, and it was up to her father to make her understand and accept that fact. The land couldn't thrive without the *Lord*'s blessing, and what kind of person would defy *Him*? Surely not her. And if she did, what did it matter? At her age, she was more or less her father's property, and would do as he said.

He glanced behind and saw his congregation further away. They were old, tired. Their faith weakened over the years without him to guide them. Though his body cried out for rest, his faith kept him strong and urged him forward. The voice of *God* soothed his aching muscles, called him toward the sacred pond.

"Shall we waver?" he called out. "When we arrive at Glory, will the *Lord* look upon us and find us lacking? Not me, he won't, that's for damned sure! Because *He* is my strength! *He* guides me in darkness for *He* is my holy light!"

The exhausted faces looked upon him with misery and shame. They knew he was right, and if their faith was weak, then his would just have to be strong enough for all of them.

Listen to him rave. Angela walked behind him, bitterness and hatred growing within her like another child. Whoever that was walking up ahead, it wasn't her Gary. Her husband was gentle, loving, kind. He thought faith was the last refuge of the illogical and uneducated mind. Gary would never raise a hand against her in anger, never violate her, never harm another living soul.

But the man who walked in front of her wasn't her husband anymore. The more he talked, the more she realized how deep his lunacy ran. It was one thing to be a crazy cult leader, but he really believed all his bullshit. Part of her felt sorry for him, wondered what could've produced such a warped point of view. The other part wondered how it would feel to drive him out of her husband, or, if she couldn't, to bash in his skull.

She hoped Zach would stay away, wouldn't try to do something heroic and stupid. Heroes weren't the big guys who saved the day, got the girl, and rode off into the sunset. No, heroes were the ones who did something stupid that usually got someone killed. Usually themselves.

Just keep driving, Zach. Don't try to help and don't look back.

But she knew better. As she walked, she felt him nearby, the way she always knew when he was near, or when he was hurt, or when he really needed her.

Mothers know.

She glanced toward Cindy and shivered as her dreams flashed through her mind. Could he be so cruel? Could they all? She was just a child. Could they take that innocence away from her? It was cruel and repugnant. It had to stop here, tonight.

But the time wasn't right. Not yet. She had to wait until they were all distracted, until she was able to get up close to the thing in her husband's skin. If she tried anything now, they'd be on her in the space of a breath, and she could only imagine what "punishment" such an act would bring. She shuddered at the thought of Gary's tender graces. No, not Gary, but the sadistic monster that wore his face. *Her* Gary could be insensitive, but he was never cruel. The thought of the creature using her husband's body to hurt her, to violate her, set her rage to a raging boil.

Zach stayed back as far as he dared. It was a straight shot, more or less, to the pond, but in the darkness it would be easy to get turned around. If he did, he could wander the land for hours without realizing he'd gone the wrong way. By the time he found his way back, it would be too late.

He waited by the barn until he was sure they wouldn't see him creeping behind them, then stayed low as he moved. He walked with his sneakers moving toe to heel, in slow, deliberate steps. When they stopped, he'd take his position, then leap out and surprise them.

But his legs tingled, then burned, then ached with the effort of walking crouched down. It wasn't like a video game. In real life, a body got tired. Plus he couldn't remember the last time he'd walked so far in one stretch. The gun felt heavy and his arm ached with the weight of it. Too much time in front of a computer, not enough time swimming or hiking, or even walking downtown with his friends.

But what friends did he have anyway? Most of the people he knew were nothing more than pixels on a screen. His best friends in San Antonio, both of them, he knew in real life, but when he went to their houses, the first thing they did was jack in and play some online game with headsets and keyboards to dictate their every move. Most of his waking moments were spent sitting in a chair, staring at characters he wished he could be doing things he wished he could do.

But he did have one friend, and right now she needed him to be the hero, to be the character to leap in, guns blazing, to rescue her from evil. To rescue her from that monster that wore his father's face. So he kept moving, his pace painfully slow across the moonlit night.

He dashed behind trees, hid behind scrub brush a bit at the beginning, whenever he thought they might look back, but after a while his muscles complained, his lungs burned with every sudden sprint, and every burst of speed became slower and slower until he became just another one of the pilgrimage, trudging along in the darkness behind the larger group.

If one of them turned around, he hoped the darkness would hide him. But inside he knew the moonlight was too bright for the darkness to conceal anything larger than a raccoon.

Toward the back of the group, one of the men that carried the preacher's mummy stumbled and fell. As the others scrambled to keep the body from hitting the ground, he saw his mother, and almost swore she saw him. He ducked behind a mesquite bush and lay as still as his heaving chest and pounding heart would allow. She saw him, he was sure of it. He sat with his eyes closed tight, as if he could keep them away with his terrified will alone.

"Fine!" his father's voice boomed. "We shall rest! But not too long. The *Lord* does not wait for us! He demands our devotion!"

"But we're old!" Another tired voice, a man's, sounded in the darkness. "Surely *He* would grant us a rest!"

"What have you done," demanded Gary, "to deserve such rest? While I was away, did any of you punish the betrayer? Did any of you keep the congregation alive? Did any of you do more than tuck your miserable tails and hide and pray to *Him* to make everything better? The *Lord* isn't a genie! The *Lord* only helps those who help themselves!"

Silence stretched out as Zach waited for an answer from anyone. Someone to keep the preacher talking, give him a few moments to rest.

"I say unto you, Brothers and Sisters, the *Lord* has spoken to me, and he is *displeased* with what he sees in Shy Grove! You speak of faith! You speak of humility! But none of you followed with the ways, gave your tithe to the *Lord*, and for your arrogance, the land around you died! He sent me back to lead you back onto the path of righteousness! He sent me back to shepherd this flock back with the crook of *His* staff! You older folk, you taught the children our ways, but did you see to it that they practiced them? No! No better than the rest of the Sunday-school Christians are you, with the one-day-a-week service and sin for the other six days a week! Well no more! For God did say '*I am a vengeful God*,' and vengeance shall be *his*!"

Weak "amens" drifted through the darkness as Zach stayed

still, his knees pulled against his chest and head down. He expected to feel his father's hands on his shoulders, but instead heard the older people groan as they got up together and continued their journey. Only when their voices and footsteps faded a bit did Zach open his eyes and chance a look.

They were moving on, all of them, their voices raised in warbling song as they walked. He was sure his mother saw him, but if she did, she said nothing. Maybe she was there after all. Maybe she wouldn't hurt him, and he wouldn't have to hurt her. The thought gave him hope enough to push himself to standing as he hurried after them into the darkness.

It couldn't be too far now. His stomach churned and his ears burned hot with the knowledge of what he had to do. He prayed he had strength enough to do it, though he hoped that it wasn't the preacher's *God* that listened.

25

Damned weak stock, that's what they all were. Weak of body and weak of spirit! But that would change soon enough. The *Lord* charged him with tending *His* flock, and it was a task he took to heart. With the first offering, they'd see. They'd feel young and vigorous again, and the land would bear new life and food, and *His* might would be proved!

He glanced behind. The boy was coming, but it didn't matter. He was just as weak as the rest of them. The boy had hopes of stopping them, but who was he to go against the will of the *Lord*? He would see, just as the rest of them saw, and they would rejoice in the beauty of it.

He longed for the old days, for the little white chapel where now stood a barn, for the air filled with voices lifted in joyous praise. In those days, the Sowing, as they called it, was a holy ritual. There was to be no pleasure taken, save in the knowledge of a job well done in the eyes of the *Lord* as in the eyes of the community. And yet whenever he thought upon the Sowing, his loins stirred with the demon lust and animalistic desire. The feelings weren't holy, weren't according to the *Lord*'s plan. Still, the image of him breaking a virgin girl for the first time made his pulse quicken. Many nights he sat in prayer, whipped his back raw to purge the sinful thoughts from his heart, but they grew stronger each time. In fact, he realized that he looked forward to his self-flagellation. The stinging cuts made by his whip made him almost as hard as the girls who opened their bodies for him.

The willing ones were good, but the ones he liked best stank of fear, cried a little. And when he took one of them, he whipped himself harder until he spilled his seed again.

His own wife said she understood. When he arrived in Shy Grove, a bachelor, she tempted him, professed her holy love and vowed before *Him* and the town that wherever he lead, she would follow. And for a while, he believed Ester, she who was favored above all others.

She knew the rituals, knew the one true path. But all that changed after the Sowing. She bowed to his will, endured his every whim and performed her God-given duties, as any woman should. But he should've known, should've seen. The larger her belly grew, the more she began to disobey, to get strange ideas. Still, he never expected it would be she who turned Judas on him.

Even when she locked the doors and burned the church, he still found himself disbelieving. It couldn't have been her, but, of course, it was. When she ran past one of the windows with a burning torch in her hand, her belly full to bursting with their offering, his heart broke. She was to be the one, and she betrayed him in the end. She left him to burn, left him to feel Satan's flames as they licked up and down his body. Such pain he'd never felt, and there was ecstasy in it.

The others, fifteen of them in all, mistook his cries of joy for howls of pain, and they threw themselves atop him to crush out the fires and protect him from the burning timbers. They died that way, on top of him, so the last sight he remembered before his eyes boiled and burst and struck him blind were their agonized faces, the last scent in his nostrils was the greasy odor of their burning flesh.

The last breath he uttered was not, however his forgiveness. Even *He* forgave, but she was not penitent. Her betrayal was not just to her husband or to the church, but to the community, to the families that relied on the *Lord*'s good graces to survive. She'd betrayed the *Lord* himself.

He awoke again, after the blaze, to wander the charred ruins of his beloved church, to watch as farmers came and sifted through the remains, but unable to touch or feel. The *Lord* saw fit to leave him, a guardian of the holy land. He didn't know why, but he didn't question it. His was not to second-guess the Almighty!

His was to follow *His* divine plan. So he waited while the betrayer ran away.

When she returned, it was without the offering, hidden away like Moses in the basket. But like Moses, he knew it would return one day.

He watched as she produced documents, legal to the laws of man, that said the holy land was hers, watched in impotent silence as she found his body where she'd secreted it after the blaze, and watched as she buried it beneath a stone with blasphemous symbols on it. As she laid the stone in place, he was drawn back to the charred and decaying corpse, and he could do nothing but listen as she and her ungodly mercenaries built her house on top of his grave. There he lay and waited, listened to her babble on. Sometimes he spoke to her, whispered sweetly of times spent, but she rebuked him at every turn.

The grove of trees came into view in the distance. Not long now until he could undo all that the heathen bitch had wrought.

"Do you see, Brothers and Sisters?" He pointed into the distance. "Our salvation is at hand! Quicken your pace!"

Excitement flooded his heart with joy. He looked to Angela, who said nothing, but smiled. As a good wife should.

So smug, his smile. So arrogant. But there was something in his eyes that told her more. Angela tried not to shiver when he looked at her. His plastic oozing smile was unsettling, but the fire that burned in his eyes spoke volumes. Whatever he was, her husband or the preacher, he was more than a zealot. She went cold when she realized that he was insane. There was no God that spoke to him, no all-powerful guiding spirit. There was only his madness and his need to cause harm, no matter his reason.

Angela kept in step, though her feet bled and her legs ached. She needed to be near him at the right time, needed to be close enough to stop him. But not yet. That's what the little voice inside her head told her.

Not yet.

When the time came, she had to try to make him see that what he did was wrong, that there was something else, something diseased, at work in Shy Grove. The town stank of it. The people wallowed in it. And if he wouldn't listen, there was a choice to make. Either way, it had to end.

She smiled back at him as visions of their wedding day, the day Zach was born, them making love flashed through her memory. She hoped he wouldn't see the tears that welled in her eyes, or if he did, thought they were tears of joy, or even allergies.

Zach was closer now. She caught a glimpse of him trailing them. He looked terrified, exhausted, so much the child that, to her, he would always be. But one arm hung low, and she thought she caught a glint against the moonlight. A gun? Where the hell did he find one of those? She hoped he wouldn't have to use it, and wondered if he even could. She wished there was some way to signal him, to let him know that she was on his side, but couldn't risk being seen by Gary, or whoever he was. Until the moment came, she just had to trust that he loved her, that he wouldn't kill her. And if he did, she would, with her dying breath, forgive him. He was, after all, the only son she would ever have. If she had to die that he would live, then so be it.

The grove was closer now. It wouldn't be long. Gary raved again. What he said, she tuned out. She couldn't feel for him, couldn't afford to think of him as her husband anymore. His voice plucked at her heartstrings because, in it, she still heard his off-key singing, his whispered confessions of love. His face no longer held the beautiful gentleness it once had, twisted into that face of hatred and zealotry. When he touched her now, all she felt was her skin crawl. But his voice... it still sounded like Gary.

Tears rolled down her cheeks as she walked. She pointed her face away so Gary wouldn't see, but her tears burned as they raced down, and it was difficult to breathe without her chest hitching. None of it mattered, though. All that mattered was that Zach stay safe.

She saw him, Zach was sure of it that time. Her eyes locked with his and though it was dark and he couldn't be sure, he thought he saw a trace of a smile on her face. Did it mean she was okay? Or was it a trick? Zach hoped it was the former and continued to follow just out of torch light.

In the distance, and getting closer with every step, he saw the trees around the pond. When they were in the throes of their sick ceremony, they'd be distracted enough for him to make his move. Though he didn't feel much like a hero at the moment. He felt more like a little kid as the gravity of the situation began to dawn on him.

Still, he wasn't going to let them kill Cindy.

The group ahead began to sing, the same eerie song his father kept singing. Their voices filtered up, breathy and exhausted as they walked. They echoed through the darkness in a way that gave him goosebumps, like mournful ghosts wailing away, or coyotes howling their loneliness to the moon. As they continued to sing, their voices grew stronger, as if the song itself gave their wrinkled old arms and withered bodies power. It was impressive to behold. Terrifying, but impressive.

The trees were just ahead. He ducked behind a large rock to catch his breath. It was a pretty far distance back to the truck. He knew he'd never be able to run it. Cindy might be able to, but not him by a long shot. So it would have to be a long walk back, with the gun pointed at the congregation for as long as he could keep it that way. Walking backward in the dark was not a thrilling idea, but he couldn't think of another way to do it. Maybe they'd get lucky, maybe they wouldn't.

His first priority, however, was to get Cindy. The rest, he'd have to make up as he went along. James Bond always made improvising seem so easy, so natural. Only now, when it was his own improvisational skills that were to be put to the test, the thought terrified him.

26

Moon- and torchlight reflected off the holy pond, the spring of life, in a dazzling display of color. The preacher looked down into the water. The face reflected back didn't seem to fit his mood. Where he felt a smile cross his lips, the face in the pond screamed in unholy rage, raised its fists up and pounded them against the still surface. The weakling. Even now, he screamed in the preacher's ear to stop, to let him go. He cried out blasphemy upon blasphemy, called the word of the *Lord* insanity and begged for the offerings to stop.

But of course he wanted them to stop and tried to cast doubt. His was the voice of the Fallen, the Lord of Lies, the voice of evil. He was to be sacrificed, wasn't he? Of course he would want to keep the cycle broken forever.

The preacher picked up a stone and dropped it into the center of the screaming image and smiled as the ripples tore it apart. Then he turned to his flock.

"Brothers and Sisters! Our time is at hand!"

A chorus of Amen and Hallelujah rose from the congregation, bolstered by the power given to them by their hymn. They sounded strong, their belief renewed. Such was the power of faith.

"Bring the body!"

The men that carried the charred remains of the preacher stepped forward and marched to the edge of the water.

"As this, our holy place, bringeth and giveth life, let so it receive the dead, and deliver this body back unto the dust from which the *Lord* made it!"

They brought the corpse forward and laid it at the edge of the water, then untied its bindings. When the sheet laid open, the women brought rocks and kissed them as they set them on top of the withered body. The last of them brought a rock as big around as a baby's head. She kissed it and placed it on the corpse's abdomen, then backed away. The men set to work and tied the sheets back up, tight so what lay wrapped within was plain to see.

"As the *Lord* brought forth life in this pond, so then do we rededicate this fragile form to the water."

He nodded toward the men, and they picked up the body, now heavier, and waded into the pond with it between them. They lowered the body into the water and let it sink down.

"Amen!" said the preacher. The congregation responded in kind.

He looked from face to face and saw tears in all their eyes. Though the body of the man they knew, and about whom they'd heard stories of his greatness for all of their lives, now slept at the bottom of the pond, their tears were not of sadness, but of joy. They knew, felt it in their bones, that he was returned to them, like Christ returned to his apostles. The old body was gone, but the new one remained, and it would last him far longer than if he'd stayed in the other.

He squeezed his wife's hand and smiled at her. She smiled back, but there was something behind her eyes, something that didn't read true to him. Was she, even now, uncertain? Or was there more treachery to be had? He learned his lesson from the last one. He was too soft on her and she turned on him. Not this one. When the ceremony was over, there was discipline to dole out, and she would get a double helping.

"And now," he shouted. "Bring forth the offering!"

The girl was led to the front of the crowd. To her credit, she did not cry, but he smelled her fear. Her hands shook, though she tried to hold them down to her sides, and her chin quivered. A small part of him could not blame her for being afraid. After all, she did not know the glory that waited after. But he would show her.

"Let her come before *Him* as she was born!"

Rough hands reached out and tore at her clothes. Her shirt

came first, then her own father loosed her belt and pulled at her jeans until they were off. She never let out a shout or begged while she was stripped, just stood proud and defiant. To some, she was still considered a child, but the preacher saw the fullness of her firm breasts, the curve of her hip, the thick thatch that covered her holy gift. This was no child, but a woman, firstborn and ripe for the taking. But grown woman or not, she would cry, the preacher would make sure of it. What good was contrition if there was not real penance to go with it?

"Bring her to me!"

Her own father took her by the arms and pushed her hard from behind until she stood in front of the preacher, who stared down at her nakedness. For a moment he felt ashamed, but soon shook the feeling off. It was no sin, after all, to appreciate the beauty of the *Lord*'s creations. And this girl had beauty in ample supply.

"Who gives this girl?" he asked.

"I do," said her father.

"And do you give her freely, and of your own will?"

"For the glory of God," said her father. "And for the good of the community, I do."

"Praise be!" shouted the preacher with hands aloft and face turned toward the heavens. "Is she unknown by man?"

"She is," said her father.

"Is there any who disputes her worthiness, who doubts the word and will of the *Lord*?"

"Yeah," came a voice from the back of the crowd. It was angry, dripped with hatred, and was one he recognized. "Me."

The barrel glinted in the moonlight, even as Zach's hand shook. He didn't intend to make his entrance all dramatic-like, but he had to admit, it sounded kind of cool.

He pointed the gun at the preacher in a way that he hoped was threatening. The congregation stepped back and let him pass.

"Let her go."

The thing that used to be his father grinned.

"I mean it. Let her go or I'll..."

"You'll what? Shoot me?" The creature laughed from deep in its throat. "You think you're man enough to shoot your own father?"

"You're not my father!" Tears rolled down his face as he screamed at the beast. His father would never hurt anyone, never humiliate anyone. "Let her come to me or I swear I'll blow your fucking head off!"

The creature raised its eyebrows in surprise, frowned, then gave a careless shrug.

"Come and get her."

Zach thought for a moment. If he went up there, the whole congregation would be around him. He might be able to shoot one or two before the rest beat him down. But Cindy didn't move. She might be hurt, or traumatized, or even hypnotized for all he knew. He couldn't just leave her, though.

The crowd parted enough for Zach to slowly walk through. He swung the gun left and right to make sure they all got the message to leave him alone. For the last few feet, he took extra careful steps, his eyes never leaving the preacher.

"Cindy," he said as he placed a hand on her trembling shoulder. "C'mon. We have to go."

She slowly got to her feet and turned toward Zach with tears in her eyes, fell against him in a long embrace.

"I thought you weren't coming," she whispered into his ear. Then she turned and struck downward with both hands, knocking the gun to the ground. Zach was so stunned that he didn't see her fist coming across until it struck his jaw and knocked him sideways. He lay there for a moment, staring up at the naked girl who offered him a wicked smile in return. "But I'm glad you did," she said. "Wouldn't be proper without you here."

"But... but they're going to kill you!"

She laughed at him and squatted beside his head.

"Don't be stupid," she said. "I'm a girl. I got other purposes. It's only the first-born boys they give back to the *Lord*. Remember when I said I wasn't ready to go all the way yet? I was saving myself for tonight."

Zach's mind reeled against the thoughts in his head. He loved her, truly and deeply. She said she loved him too, but it was a lie. He sank back to the ground, unwilling to go on. His body ached, but not as much as his heart and soul. His father was gone, he knew that now. The girl he thought loved him, didn't. And his mother...

A shot rang through the darkness, and Cindy's head pitched forward. Blood spattered on Zach's face as her lifeless body collapsed next to him. He scrambled backward, unable to tear his eyes from her naked corpse, until he bumped the legs of one of the congregation. When he looked up, he saw the smoking barrel of the pistol pointed at the girl, and his mother's hands around the grip.

27

The gun felt good in her hands, heavy and reassuring, as if it belonged there. When it fell at her feet, she wasn't sure if it was a sign from God or just simple stupid luck, but the girl did her a favor. Zach couldn't shoot anybody, no matter how strong a front he tried to put on. He wasn't the type, not a violent bone in his sweet body. But Angela was a different story. Especially when someone threatened her only child.

She turned the gun on Gary and took a few tentative steps toward Zach.

"What in Hell do you think you're doing, woman?" shouted the preacher.

"Getting my son away from you," she said. "And I'm going to blow the whistle on this whole crazy cult you've got going here."

The congregation cried out in anger as Gary moved toward her, but she set her stance and narrowed her eyes, the barrel trained at the bridge of his nose. He stopped short, just as she hoped he would.

"I *will* kill him," she said. Though her voice was a low growl, she had no doubt they all heard her. Their outrage quieted to a dull rumble as she backed toward her son.

Zach lay on the ground, his eyes wide, as he tried to frantically wipe Cindy's warm blood off his face and hands. It couldn't be helped. She knew what they were going to do, even before Zach did. She shot the girl to prove a point, that she had no qualms about killing anyone who threatened her child. And while she had no idea how many bullets were left in the gun – six? Didn't all these old guns have six shots? Was it fully loaded? – she was certain that four more of the congregation would fall before they took him, and the last bullet she would save for Gary.

The girl's corpse lay cooling over one of Zach's legs, but he made no attempt to move it. He loved her, or at least held the mad fascination that all boys did when they found their first girlfriend. And Angela shot her, killed her dead in front of him. She hoped one day he would forgive her, but it had to be done. The little bitch was in on it from the beginning and delivered him to them.

"Zach, honey, come on." She reached down with one hand while keeping her eyes and the gun on the preacher. When her fingers came into contact with his sweat-soaked t-shirt, she gave him a gentle pull. Zach pulled away.

"She... you... she..."

"Come on, honey." Gary shifted from foot to foot, the look in his eyes growing more hateful and crazed by the second. She couldn't keep them away for long.

"You... you fucking shot her!" His voice seemed to tear out of his throat through a blockade of tears and anger. "How could you..?"

"They're going to kill us," she said through clenched teeth. "We have to go now." The gentle tug turned violent as she grabbed a handful of shirt and yanked him backward. Zach scrambled to his feet and followed her as she backed out of the torchlight.

"Just keep going," she said quietly. "Keep walking."

"Then what?" he whispered. "You can't kill them all. They'll come after us."

"I'm working on that part," she said. "Just keep moving. I'll keep my eyes on them, you lead."

Betraying bitch! Every woman had the capacity for treachery in her heart. Since Eden and Eve, that was the way of it. Why he thought this one, the weakling's wife, would be any different he couldn't guess.

Inside, he felt the weakling roar with joy, heard him laugh when she pointed the gun at him. He didn't laugh because the thought of a woman with a gun amused him, but because he felt the preacher's fear. A true man of faith would not only show no fear, but would not *have* fear in the first place. The weakling saw through him, felt his heart rate increase, and it sickened the preacher that this man, this *academic*, felt his fear.

He watched them move out of the firelight, she backward and pointing the gun, the offering forward, leading the way. With every step they took, his rage grew until, when they were only wisps in the darkness, he could contain it no longer. He let out a bellow that burned his throat and tore the edges of his mouth. The congregation cowered in fear of him.

"Bring him back!" he screamed.

His flock traded bewildered looks, then turned and hurried after them, the youngest in front while the older of them hobbled to keep up. As they ran, he moved to the girl's corpse and knelt beside her ruined head.

Her hair was sticky, caked in already congealing blood. Flecks of bone and gray matter littered the dry ground. Where she fell, the blood sank into the earth. Her beautiful skin felt cool, no life left within it. It was a shame. He rolled the corpse over. The bullet's exit took off a large portion of her beautiful face. A real shame. He ran his hand down the length of her body, squeezed her chilly breasts and stroked her tight legs. He had such plans for her. The Sowing was only the first part. In time, she might have given herself to him as man and woman should, and their children would've been beautiful. Of course, the bitch would've had to go first, but it was a moot argument now. Cindy was dead. Her cold corpse hardly stirred his emotions or desires.

He pushed himself to his feet as anger swelled inside him. There was no plentiful supply of youth in Shy Grove, and even fewer that were female. Cindy was the only girl among them that came from a good God-fearing family. He might be able to take another from one of the outlying farms that were worked by heathens, but with the state of the world now, it would surprise him if any that were left held their virtue intact.

He took a few short steps, then broke into a run, righteous fury boiling in his blood. How dare they? How *dare* they go against the will of the *Lord*? He would catch them and bring the sacrifice back. And as for the woman, he had other plans for her. For her betrayal, her derailment of the Holy plan, no mere cuffing or punishment would suffice. She needed to suffer. She needed to beg for his, and *His* forgiveness. Her suffering needed to be so great that she would beg to die before he, and the rest of the flock's men, were done with her. And when she showed up for judgment like a used up whore, she would be cast down into the pit of eternal damnation, forever to burn as she burned him.

28

"Shit!" Angela tried to move her backward-stepping feet faster, but tripped and stumbled. They were coming, heavy footsteps and angry growls like starved animals. She spun as she ran and grabbed Zach by the wrist.

"Run!"

Zach turned his lost expression toward her. His eyes looked like those of a child who first learned that pretty glass could cut. The betrayal there sliced her deep, but there was no time to sort it out now. She gave a sharp yank and pulled him along until he seemed to get the idea and picked up his pace.

They'd never make the house. It was too far. Her legs already were stiff from the walk out to the pond, and now they burned with every panicked step. Her lungs felt as if they would burst, and Zach was slowing down. They needed to hide, find some place to make a stand when the others caught up to them. The house was the safest place she could imagine close by, but even so, it may as well have been in San Antonio. Or even the moon.

The older among the congregation weren't as pressing an issue as the few younger men. Cindy's father, her brother, Toby, and Sheriff Weston were fast enough to catch them with ease, and young enough to overpower them both. Their four against just Zach and herself would be no challenge at all. But there was the gun, and at least five more bullets. Or so she hoped.

Behind her, angry hurried footsteps and heavy breaths combined with animalistic howls and grunts. She turned in time to see Cindy's father launch. His shoulder hit her at the waist and knocked her air out before she had time to raise the pistol. She hit the ground hard and writhed on the ground as her body fought to draw breath. He rolled off and stood staring down, his face a contorted mass of rage.

"You bitch!" he screamed, and struck her with a vicious kick to the ribs with the toe of his work boot. Pain shot through her body, strong enough to force her diaphragm to contract harder and cramp. If they weren't broken when her husband kicked her, they were now. The night seemed to thicken as darkness pushed in the sides of her vision.

"Mom!" Zach snapped out of his haze when Cindy's dad tackled his mother. When he stood and kicked her, she didn't make a sound, but writhed under his boot. Fear swelled inside him and turned to panic and desperation as he ran toward the big man, full of intent to kill, but with no real way of doing harm. Out of the corner of his eye, he saw the others coming, Cindy's brother and Toby. The sheriff wasn't too far behind them either.

He changed course and ran straight for the smallest target, Cindy's brother Chris, and screamed as he flailed at him. A lucky awkward punch landed square on the boy's nose and knocked him flat. He was so surprised that he didn't see Toby until he was already on him. The young farmer hit hard, arms muscled by labors Zach never had to endure. One punch to the jaw and Zach went down on rubber legs. Dirt and rocks tore into his face as he hit the ground, then Toby was on him, raining down punches and kicks. He sobbed as he curled into a ball and tried to protect himself, but Toby's hands were like hammers. Every blow felt as if it shattered something, as if he intended to cripple him before delivering him to be sacrificed.

"Stop it!" a deep voice panted. The Sheriff Weston slowed to an exhausted jog. The rain of hammer heads ceased, but Zach couldn't stop crying. He couldn't move, it hurt too bad. And what did it matter anyway?

"Preacher wants him back," gasped the sheriff. "Alive. Can't offer up something already dead. And he says he's got plans for that one too."

He pushed Trevor aside and reached down for Angela's quivering form. Zach watched as he grabbed her by the shoulder and rolled her over. Her arm swung up as if it were on a spring, the gun pointed at the sheriff's surprised face, then a thunderclap and a flash from the muzzle. The old man's moustache ignited as his nose exploded and showered Zach's mother with gore. The bullet exited the back of his head in spectacular fashion and left the sheriff's twitching body upright for a moment before it fell to the ground.

"Get away from him," she croaked as she struggled to sit upright.

Trevor roared and ran toward her, but the gun erupted again. The bullet put a small hole in the inside of the man's thigh and left one the size of a fist on the way out. He fell to the ground shrieking in agony. For a moment, the only sounds were the echo of the gunshot and the man's screams. No one moved. Zach didn't even breathe.

"Help him up," said his mother to Toby as she pushed herself to standing. She gasped for air and her words came out as gasped wheezes around broken ribs.

Toby's bloodied hands shook as he grabbed Zach by the arms and hefted him to his feet, then he raised his hands to his shoulders and backed away.

"Zach, honey. Come over here."

Every movement hurt, but Zach obeyed. When he got within arms reach, she took his hand and guided him behind her.

"You ain't gonna get away," snarled Toby. "No matter where you run, *God*'s gonna find you!"

"Give me one good reason why I shouldn't shoot you."

His mother's voice was cold, vicious, unlike she'd ever spoken before. It was almost as if a part of her enjoyed the warm crimson spray that coated her face. Zach shivered as he placed a gentle hand on his mother's shoulder.

"Come on," he said softly. "They're coming."

"I've got three bullets left," she said to Toby with a cruel smile. "Do you want one?"

Even in the moonlight, it was too dark to see the farmboy's face, but Zach felt certain the color drained out of it. His hands shook and his feet twitched. Toby was terrified, and he was right to be so.

"Get the sheriff's gun," said Angela. Zach leaned over the bloody corpse and pulled the .38 from the steaming corpse's holster. "Now we've got more shots. I see you again, I swear to whatever God you pray to, I'll kill you."

Cindy's father's screams softened to whimpers. His pants leg glistened, soaked with blood. Mom's shot must've hit something important. The man was as good as dead, bled out from the wound. Behind him, Chris groaned and rolled off his back to his hands and knees then pushed himself to standing. In the moonlight, his broken nose lay over to one side and blood ran down his chin. He wobbled for a moment, then looked up and saw Toby with his hands raised, then he saw Zach's mother. He raised his hands too.

"Go on," she growled. "Go tell those other sick fucks to leave us alone."

When neither of them moved, she lifted the gun slightly and squeezed off another shot. They both jumped and ran back toward the pond.

"Come on," she panted. "We have to get back to the house."

At least one of her ribs were broken, of that she was certain. A few more might be as well, or just cracked. Either way, she was hurt bad. Every painful breath she took made sure she remembered. Zach looked awful, bruised and bloodied, but otherwise intact. He shuffled along beside her with his shoulder under her arm to help her up. Such a good boy.

The bullet that took the sheriff peeled his lip back in a perpetual Elvis sneer and the muzzle-flash lit his moustache on fire before it sent the bullet into his nostril. The look of surprise on his face was almost worth the blood and snot that burst forth when the bullet smashed his sinus cavity. That other bastard, the one who willingly gave up his daughter to be gang-raped, deserved to bleed out, long and slow. He deserved to feel his life slip away. She shuddered at the thought.

Murder and blood weren't supposed to be in her thoughts. They never were before. She glanced at her son, but saw nothing to betray what he felt on his stony face.

"I'm sorry," she wheezed. "I know she..."

"Don't," he said. "Not now. Okay? Later. Let's just get back to the house."

She nodded and forced herself to keep going.

The Preacher led the pack. He caught up with the rest of his flock in no time, then pushed his way to the front. When he saw two figures running toward him, he slowed and held his hand up for the others to do the same. The girl's boyfriend, Toby and her little brother waved and hurried to the preacher.

"She killed 'em," panted Toby. "Sheriff's dead, Mr. Rogers probably bled to death by now. Me and Chris just barely got out."

Rage blossomed within his breast, but he tried to put up a calm facade.

"They got away? And you two, they let go?"

The boys nodded.

"They just want to be let go," said Chris. "Said they'd kill anyone else who came after them."

"I see," he said quietly. The woman, he didn't care about. Sure, he had designs that involved breaking her will, but she was nothing to the plan. The boy, however, *was* the plan. His blood spilt could restart the whole town, and these two morons just let them go. Before they could think, he swung a vicious backhand at Chris, striking him across his already-broken nose and sending him to the ground. Toby was too surprised to react when the preacher grabbed him by the throat and drove him to the dirt beside Chris.

He rode the boy's body down and brought his face within inches of Toby's. The boy's breath stank of fear and incompetence.

"You are unworthy of *His* love," he hissed at the boy's face. "If we fail, let it be known that it is, at least in part, your fault, and I will make you suffer until your debt to the *Lord* is repaid."

The preacher pushed off the boy and stood over him, then turned to the congregation.

"They're headed back to the house," he said. "This land is ours as given to us by *God* himself. I suggest we go and reclaim it!"

A few tired shouts of approval filtered up from the group. Pathetic. None of them were worthy. They all lacked faith, humility. They were soft and wanted everything handed to them. But that would change. By *His* will, it would change. At his word, the congregation stood and hurried after their offering to God.

29

As the barn came into view, Zach's heart filled with joy. Past it, another mile or so, and the Stepside waited. They couldn't take Mom's car, he'd seen to that, and only now did he realize that it wasn't the brightest move in the world. Of course, none of his plans lately were, it seemed. Every muscle in his body hurt, along with his jaw where Cindy hit him, and the rest of his face where Toby rained down farmboy haymakers. But he was alive, no thanks to his planning skills. If he relied on them, he'd be dead now. But Mom came through. Mom saved the day again, just when he thought he'd lost her for good. Of course, she seemed different now than even before, and he wasn't certain he liked this personality any better.

Before Shy Grove, Mom baked, told him stories, kissed him goodnight. As he grew older, he didn't think he needed such babying from her, but now he'd give anything to have her kiss his forehead again. When she turned into an opinionless shrinking violet of a woman, he thought that was bad. But the woman who walked beside him, with her wild eyes and white-knuckle grip on the pistol, scared him. He watched her shoot three people, one of which was the girl he thought he loved. Of course, the other two were beating her at the time, so they deserved what they got, but Mom's panicked face didn't soften when the echoes of the bullets she fired died. He hoped there was something of his mother left inside somewhere.

"Almost there," he said.

Angela spun and pointed the gun behind them at the darkness. Her ragged breath came in gulps and her wide feral eyes twitched at every imagined sound. He had to get her into the house and calmed down.

"Mom? MOM!" Her head snapped toward him, followed by the pistol. "It's okay. It's me. Come on. We have to get to the house. We're almost there."

She lowered the gun and nodded, then picked up her pace to match his. At best, it was a slow jog, but he hoped they'd get there before the others caught up.

When they reached the back end of the barn, his mother stopped and turned. At first he heard nothing but his own heart slamming within his ribcage, but then hurried footsteps and angry grunts reached his ears. A shot of cold raced through his body as he jerked his legs faster. The house bobbled in his vision, but he kept his eyes on the back door and his hand on his mother's wrist. When they reached the door, he heaved and threw her in ahead of him before he slammed and locked the door.

Zach sprawled, panting with his back against the door. They were coming fast, and a couple of locks wouldn't keep them out for long. He looked up to his mother.

The gun sat on the kitchen table, his mother in a chair with her head down and her hands tangling in her hair. Her body jerked, wracked with sobs that came from deep inside.

"Mom?"

Her head snapped up, her wide frenzied eyes locking on him for a moment, then she looked down at her hands and started rubbing them.

"Blood," she murmured. "Too much blood. Needs to come off. It won't come off."

Zach crawled to her side and took her hands in his.

"It's okay," he said. "You had to. Thank you."

Angela's eyes slowly turned to meet his, and in them he saw a spark of his mother. Tears flooded her eyes as she threw her arms around his neck and sobbed against his shoulder.

"I'm so sorry," she wailed. "I didn't want to..."

"Shhh... it's okay. They're coming. I need you with me. Are you okay?"

She sniffed and nodded.

"I love you," she said. She stroked his hair the way she did when he was in grade-school. This time, he didn't mind.

"Best mom a kid could ask for," he said. "Help me."

He clambered to his feet and hurried into the main room. The hole in the floor gaped like a festering wound. Around them, purses and jackets, bibles and bags lay strewn where the congregation left them. For the life of him, it looked as if the floor ate all the people and spit their belongings back out.

"Get the door!"

Angela nodded and ran to the front door. She turned the deadbolt, then pushed the heavy hall tree against the little window beside it.

"We need to block up the other windows," said Angela.

"How? We've got no furniture left in here, and they'll be here any second!"

"What do we do?"

His brain raced against the question and against the passing seconds. Even if they had something to cover the windows, there was no time. They both had guns, though hers had only two shots left. If they chose to make a stand, they could only shoot eight of them before the rest came. And he just bet Horatio, because he had no doubts about who walked around in his father's skin, wouldn't be the first through the door. More likely, he'd be the last, would come in after all the bullets were spent. The truck was too far away, and they were too tired, to run for it. The way he saw it, they had one option.

"Hide," he said.

The group approached the house with labored breaths and heavy steps. The preacher urged them forward, all the while cursing their age and sloth, reminding them that the *Lord* demanded his offering, and of what awaited success or failure. He chuckled when the first of his flock tried the door and found it locked. As if a locked door could stop the will of *God*.

"Break it down," he shouted. "Break out the windows and climb through if you have to. It's not like it's going to be standing for long anyway!"

The house was a blight, a monument to Ester's treachery. The sooner he took the boy, the sooner he could have the house demolished to make way for a new church.

Hands banged on the windows and door, but they were old, weak, worthless.

"Get tools from the barn!" he said. "And bring that can of kerosene. When it's all over, I want to see this place burn."

The old people hurried to do as he instructed and returned a few moments later with shovels, a pickaxe, and broken furniture between them. None of it mattered, so long as the boy was bled and the *Lord* was appeased. As for the woman, maybe he should let her burn inside the house, let her see what it felt like to smell her own flesh cook off the bone and watch her hands melt like wax in front of her eyes before they burst from heat.

Glass shattered and a blow to the back door sent splinters flying. He waited while the others hurried inside. When no gunshots sounded, he warily approached the house. They had guns. He knew they had at least one, and the sheriff's was missing from his belt. That meant they both had one, unless the boy was too much of a child. Then his bitch mother had them both. Either way, there was danger ahead. Best to let the others go first, let the bitch waste all her bullets, then at least he could continue the good work and bring Shy Grove back to grace in the eyes of *God*. But the shots never came. As he passed through the back door, he was met by Furgeson, one of the older parishioners, a farmer from way back with more dead cattle than alive and both a field and wife that were barren.

"They ain't here," he said. "Maybe they made for the road."

The preacher looked around the main room. The door was barred from the inside, the back door locked, and he doubted they'd take the time to secure the place.

"No," he said. "They're here. They're just hiding is all. Search the house. Find them." Then, as an afterthought, "And be careful. They've got guns."

Angela lay on her belly under Zach's bed, next to her son. It was a stupid plan, but it made sense when he threw it out there. She wasn't in much of a state of mind to argue. To tell the truth, up until a few moments ago, she wasn't in much of a state of mind at all. She shot the girl, shot the sheriff, and did she shoot someone else? It seemed to her that she did, but that part didn't seem real. After the bullet went up the sheriff's nose and bathed her in a fine spattering of his blood, she didn't really think of anything else. She fell apart, plain and simple, went on auto-pilot and let her mama-bear instinct take over. But Zach kept it all together. She smiled in the darkness. Such a strong boy he turned out to be. It made her proud, though she felt shame at herself for cracking.

Zach's plan was simple: Hide. He could've picked a less obvious place than his room, under his bed, but it was a plan, and she didn't really think about it until after he'd jammed the old tire iron into the doorframe and slid under the bed next to her. Now that she thought about it, they were trapped, and at least fifteen zealots, and their leader, were coming for them. Zach, they were going to kill. But for her, the punishment would be more severe.

She wondered what would happen to her when she died, if she would fight to the last or just let go and let oblivion take her.

Glass shattered downstairs, followed by the sound of the door being hacked apart. They were in the house. She clamped her hands over her mouth to keep her hysterical sobs quiet.

"Shhh." Zach tried to keep it together, but she could tell by the quiver in his voice that he was reaching the end of his rope too. He couldn't take too much more, and she couldn't say she blamed him.

Angry voices from downstairs, more breaking glass and pounding. Then she heard the preacher's voice.

"Search the house!"

Her heart froze in her chest and she felt Zach tense next to her. Any second, the door would burst open and they'd be dragged from their hiding places like kittens. But she wouldn't go down without a fight at least.

The guns lay between them on the floor. Angela took hers and propped her arms on her elbows with the gun pointed toward the door. Zach mirrored her position with his gun. Let them come, and she and her son would together send them to meet their precious *God*.

She snorted in spite of herself. If there truly were an all powerful God, and theirs was the way to gain his pleasure, she wanted nothing to do with him.

Heavy footsteps pounded the stairs. Zach's breath quickened. Her own heart raced and pounded in her throat and temples. It was enough so, for the moment, she forgot about the stabbing pain in her ribs, the ache in her muscles and joints. She focused her eyes on the door and did not blink as first one set of feet, then another and another hit the stairs. When they reached the landing, she held her breath.

Next to her, Zach trembled. He couldn't take a life by the pond. She wondered if he could now, and what it would do to him. There was no doubt in her mind that, once the whole ordeal was over and assuming they both survived, they'd both need counseling. She hoped he would recover.

Outside, the sounds of the congregation's search continued. The door to her studio slammed open, and she heard them throw her art supplies to the floor, heard the chime of her steel tools as they struck wood. Glass and pottery shattered. With every sound, her anger grew.

The knob on the door turned and someone leaned against the other side. The tire-iron held the door in place, but as it did its job, it also gave them away.

"They're here!" came a voice from the other side of the door, followed by heavy thumps as someone tried to shoulder it open.

Thunder echoed through the room as Zach squeezed the trigger of the revolver. The bullet pierced the door a foot off the ground, and from the other side someone howled in agony, followed by the sound of a large body hitting the floor.

"My leg!" screamed the man. Zach let out a nervous giggle.

More footsteps pounded up the stairs, then the sound of something heavy being dragged away. Then another set of feet on the stairs. This one didn't rush, though, nor was it as heavy as the others. This one's approach was slow, almost casual, as it came to the door of the room.

"You in there, honey?" Gary's sugary sweet voice dripped with venom. "How 'bout you, tiger?"

"Leave us alone!" shouted Angela.

"Nope," said the preacher. "Can't do that. Why don't you come on out now. We'll talk about all this."

Another shot rang out as Zach fired one higher into the door.

"Fuck you!" she screamed.

"That's not nice," chided the preacher. "You gonna talk that way to your son's father? In front of him?"

"You are *not* his father," she growled. "His father is Gary Carter. You're some crazy asshole in his body."

"You shot Effram Green. Hurt him pretty bad too. Not a very Christian thing to do. You come on out now. Say you're sorry."

Another shot from Zach answered him. Angela put her hand over his.

"Stop it," she hissed. "He's *trying* to make you shoot. You're using up all your bullets."

"That's, what? Three shots?" called the preacher. "Down to five shots between you. Think you can kill us all with only five shots? Just let me in and give yourself over to the *Lord*. So much easier that way."

He was right, damn it all to hell. Zach's impetuous shots cut their chances of getting out alive.

"What do we do?" His whisper cracked and she knew he was crying.

"How did you get out last night?"

"Through the window," he sniffed. "I climbed out on the roof and jumped down."

She slid out from under the bed, atop which still sat the air conditioner where Zach left it. The window had fallen shut and cracked the glass, but it slid open easily and without much noise.

"Go," she said. "Hide out there. I'll get you when I can, or jump down and get to the truck."

"But what about..?"

"I love you," she said as she brushed the side of his face. "Now move it."

Zach squirmed through the window and helped her put the air conditioner back in place. When she was sure he was out of sight, she picked up the gun and calmly walked back to the door. It took a few tugs to remove the tire iron out of the door frame, but it pulled free and she let the door swing open. Gary's twisted smile greeted her on the other side.

"Where's Zach?" The sweat that coated his face stank of crude oil and he looked pale.

"Not in here," she said. "He ran for the truck while you were messing with me."

His hand struck her hard across the face.

"Thou shalt not bear false witness!" he bellowed. "Don't lie to me, bitch!"

Angela raised the gun to his face.

"I'll kill you before I let you hurt him," she snarled.

The preacher never flinched, the smile never wavered. His eyes stayed locked on hers, even with the pistol pointed between them. Inside, he felt the weakling scream for her to pull the trigger, but he knew she wouldn't. She might be able to kill, but he still wore her husband's face. And while he faltered at the pond, there was no fear in his heart. He was protected by the will of the *Lord*. He was a righteous man.

He turned and shot his arm out to meet hers. The gun went

off, but the bullet missed him and dug into the wall behind. Then he cocked back his arm and punched her right in the teeth. Angela fell backward and spit blood onto the floor.

"Where is he?" He was tired of the game, tired of the pursuit. Tired of the nagging fly in his brain that cheered when someone or something made the plan stumble. His patience and temper snapped a while ago.

"Where... is... he?" he shouted, and punctuated every word with a vicious kick to the ribs. Angela curled into a ball and coughed blood onto the floor.

"Gone," she croaked. "Gone."

"Fine," said the preacher. He leaned down and grabbed her by the hair. If she wanted to be difficult, he could accommodate. It was time she learned her lesson, and it would be the most painful teaching he could imagine. He dragged her out of the room by her hair and to the stairs. Every step he took was accompanied by the dull Thump of her body hitting the step after him.

"Brothers and Sisters!" The congregation looked toward him. "This traitor helped the offering escape." He pointed to three of the group. "You, you and you, he's headed for the main road. Catch him." They nodded and wrestled the hall tree away from the door, then hurried out into the night.

"And what shall we do with this one?" A dozen eager faces looked toward him with hate and bloodlust in their eyes. It made his heart sing. "I say she burns! As the one before burned our place of worship, burned our families, this one shall be consumed in fire!"

A chorus of Amen's rose up from the congregation. One of them dragged a chair from the kitchen and set it at the mouth of the hole in the floor. Another came with a roll of twine from Angela's workroom.

The preacher dragged her struggling form to the chair, where two of the congregation seized her arms and sat her down, then lashed her hands and feet together. When they were done, they wrapped her body to the chair tight enough for the twine to bite into her skin.

Angela thrashed and screamed, but it did her no good. She looked like a wild creature, possessed of feral rage. Had she the ability, the preacher had no doubt that she would tear him to

Scott A. Johnson

pieces with little more than her nails and teeth. He smiled at her.

"It didn't have to be this way," he said. "But the *Lord* does not look kindly on non-believers. As the fire cooks you from the outside in, I want you know that we'll find the offering, and he'll fulfill *God*'s plan. Take comfort in that at least."

She thrashed and screamed, words turned to guttural howls of pain and frustration. The chair tipped over and she hit the floor hard, but it made no difference. Fire didn't care if a person was upright or prone. It ate and cleaned away indiscriminately. She struggled harder, then she lay still. For a moment, the preacher thought she'd lost consciousness or even thrashed herself to death, but a low moan rose up from her body and he smiled. She cried. Maybe she saw the error of her ways, but it was too late for forgiveness. Penance had to be paid.

At his direction, the congregation moved out by the back door and waited. He took the kerosene can and splashed lines around the main room. It might have been kinder to douse her too, set her off first, but true penance came from reflection, thought. As the flames inched closer to her body, as she felt the heat sear the hair from her flesh and boil her skin in its own fat like bacon, she'd have time to think, time to beg forgiveness. She might be saved from damnation yet.

"Think hard on what you've done," he called out as he stepped through the back door. "Perhaps *God* will forgive your sins." He struck a match and touched it to the trail of kerosene. "Probably not, though."

Flame leapt along the liquid trail around the room and began to devour everything in its path. Greasy smoke billowed up as the source burned, but the fire was hungry and chewed on curtains and sticks of furniture where they lay piled. Tipped over in the center of the room, Angela thrashed against her bonds and screamed. It made him smile as he closed the door and went to join his flock.

"When they return with the offering, we can get back to business," he said, then turned to watch the house burn. How fitting it was that it should be consumed, and that he himself set the match. Things were full circle now, and life could get back to the way it was.

Movement on the roof caught his eye. He looked up in time

247

to see one sneakered foot disappear through the window. The bitch lied! Inside, the weakling roared, and for once the preacher agreed. The boy could not die in the fire. He had to be saved. But their opinions differed as to why. The weakling wanted his son to get away to be safe and live a full life that never should've been. But that was not *God*'s will. The boy had to be offered up to the *Lord*, that they all could start again. He gave an angry cry of frustration as he pulled an old jacket from the barn over his head and hurried into the blaze.

Zach waited on the roof, just like his mother said, hugged close to the wall and scared. He didn't dare jump down like he did before. He was already tired, too hurt to take the fall. In his mind, he saw himself jumping and breaking a leg or something. Then there'd be no chance of him getting away.

From where he sat, with his ear pressed to the wall, he heard the preacher take his mother, heard the gunshot and the smack of skin on skin. His mother's cries as that bastard dragged her down the stairs was too much for him, and he cried softly into the hot night wind.

When the congregation began to file out of the house, he felt sure they would drag her along to try to tempt him to save her. When she was not among them, his stomach sank. Then the preacher came out. Zach couldn't hear what he said, but saw that he was taunting someone inside. Mom. When he lit and threw the match, panic raced through Zach's body. Mom was alive, she had to be. Even if she weren't, he had to get off the roof, and jumping down in the midst of the preacher's followers was less appealing than running through a burning house.

Zach pushed the air conditioner through the window and climbed through after it. Smoke billowed through the open door, blackened every surface it kissed. He dropped to his knees and crawled under the smoke, though the stench choked him. By the door, he found a dirty t-shirt, which he pressed over his face. It was better, but he still coughed and his eyes stung with the smoke. Through the crackle and hiss of the blaze, a woman's voice screamed.

"Mom!"

Smoke filled his room from the ceiling down. Even the open window didn't let out enough that he could see more than a few inches in front of his eyes. He flattened out further onto his belly and crawled toward the door. When he reached the hallway, he listened again. The screams were replaced with choking and sobs.

Fire licked over the sides of the stairwell, ate the carpeted floor. Smoke curtained the room in black fog, dotted by hot orange and yellow streaks. He couldn't see her, but her chokes and sobs guided him. She was downstairs, somewhere in the main room.

"Mom!" he wheezed. "Where are you?"

She didn't answer. Maybe she couldn't. Maybe she was overcome, unconscious from the smoke. Or maybe she was dead. No, he couldn't think that way. Mom wasn't dead. She was down there waiting for him.

Zach winced as fire scorched his hairless arms. Too hot. It hurt, scared him and made him want to run. But he couldn't leave his mother. He wouldn't.

Fire consumed the base of the stairs, it's teeth snapping further up. He had to get down there, somehow, but it looked like suicide.

"Mom!" He heard her again, more a noise than actual words, but he hoped she heard him too.

As he neared the base of the stairs, heat flooded his legs. He looked down and realized his pants legs were on fire. A scream escaped him as he pounded the burning cloth with his heat-blistered palms.

"Zach!" His mother's voice was weak. "No! You have to go! Get out of here!"

He didn't answer, but swung over the rail. He hit the floor on the other side hard, but the pain was less than being burned alive, he imagined. Then he flattened out on the floor, under the smoke, again. His mother lay on her side, tied to a chair. That sadistic bastard left her to burn tied to a chair. He crawled to her as fast as he could.

"You have to get out," she said. "You'll die."

"Not without you. We're getting out of here together."

He fumbled the knot with blistered raw fingers. It wasn't elaborate, but his fingers were swollen and every movement made them feel as if they would burst. When he got the knot untied, he began unwrapping his mother. Her face looked red in the firelight, and he knew she'd already been burnt. He hoped her lungs weren't heat-damaged, otherwise she might die anyway, then he'd be alone. She'd lost a little hair and everywhere the twine touched left red angry welts in her skin. She slumped to the ground, exhausted and drained.

"We need to go," said Zach into his mother's ear. "I can't carry you. You've got to help me."

She gave a weak nod and rolled to face him. Her lips were swollen and there was dried blood on her chin, but to Zach she was a wonderful sight, one he thought he might not see again.

Her face twisted into fear. Zach turned to see the preacher standing behind him. Against the flames, he looked more like his true self, a devil of a man, cruel and twisted.

The preacher looked furious as he dove toward Zach. The boy moved, but wasn't fast enough to avoid him completely. One of the preacher's arms hit him near his neck and knocked him flat. Zach scrambled backward as the preacher crouched by his mother and stroked her hair.

"I can pull her out of here," he said. Though his voice was low, Zach heard him fine over the fire. "All you have to do is come with me. Be the offering to the one true *God*. And I promise, your mother will live."

Zach reached into his pocket for the pistol. Only three shots left, and his fingers hurt to touch the grip. They were so swollen he doubted they would fit through the trigger guard. But he raised the gun as if he knew what he were going.

"Get away from her."

"Don't you get it? This is bigger than you, or her, or even me! This isn't about killing babies or anything else. This is about the town! This is about the community! This is about pleasing the *Lord* almighty!"

"It's about murder!" screamed Zach.

"How many people have you two killed tonight? How many did Ester kill when she burned my church down? I don't think you've got a whole lot of room to talk!"

"Shut up!" Zach squeezed the trigger. The gun kicked and the bullet flew wide, missed its target by at least a good foot. Two bullets left.

"I'm not going to argue with you," said the preacher. "Every second she stays in here she comes closer to dying. Your life shouldn't even be. Just do the right thing."

His swollen finger split as he pulled the trigger again. This time he was ready for the kick, but didn't know how to aim. The bullet grazed the preacher's ear. He jerked his head to the side in pain.

The preacher retreated. Gary felt him slide past, felt the searing pain in his ear and grabbed hold of it, used it as an anchor to keep himself in control. The heat from the blaze was unbearable, but he had to endure to get his wife and son to safety.

Zach looked terrified, beaten and angry. The gun he leveled at him wouldn't miss again, and Gary knew it.

"Wait!" He threw up his hands and covered his face. "Take your mom and get out of here!"

Confusion clouded his son's face.

"Dad?"

"No time! Help me!"

He moved to Angela. Her bruised face and burned skin brought tears to his eyes, and the fact that the preacher used his body to inflict such damage made him sick. He took his wife under one arm. Zach crawled to his side and took the other. "I'm sorry," said Gary. "I couldn't stop him. You need to get both of you out of here. She needs a hospital."

Zach nodded and coughed. They *both* needed medical attention. The boy's hands looked like raw hamburger and there were blisters forming on his skin. If they lived through it, his hands would have plenty of scars to show for it.

They worked their way toward the front of the house. Fire engulfed the door, but the heavy hall tree hadn't caught yet. Gary hurried over to it and gave it a shove. It slammed through the fire-weakened wood.

"Come on," he said as he resumed his place at his wife's arm.

He helped Zach climb up onto the hall tree, then helped him drag his mother through the door into the night. Once they were in the yard, he turned back toward the house.

"Where you going?!" Zach's voice cracked with either emotion or smoke damage.

"I can't come," said Gary. "Someone's got to put a stop to all of this."

It was true, the cycle of death and pain had gone on too long. While the preacher was in control, Gary saw his thoughts, saw his past, and was horrified by the number of dead that lay in the little pond, but even more frightening was the zeal with which everyone in the town followed him. Horatio McBride started off as a huckster, a con-man of the highest order, who dealt in the greatest commodity known to man: faith. But somewhere along the way, he started to believe his own bullshit, became drunk with the power it afforded him. In time, he thought of himself as God's representative, then as the son of God himself. Every young woman he took, every life he ended weighed heavily on Gary, especially because he knew his mother was one of them, and that he should've died long ago.

"I can't come," he said. "The preacher's a part of me. He won't let go."

Even as he spoke, the preacher clawed at his psyche, dug in and fought his way back up for control. But Gary wasn't about to let him hurt his family again.

"Hurry. Get to the truck and get the hell out of here."

Then he turned and walked back into the burning house.

The preacher's need was a physical pain, more than the heat from the flames or the burns that covered his flesh. He wanted back up, wanted to take the boy while he was exhausted, and let the mother choke on her own blood. But Gary wouldn't let him. He focused on the burns, on his wounded ear, on anything else that distracted him from the preacher's influence.

He hurried toward the back door and looked out over the dozen faces of the preacher's flock. They were older, desperate, willing to cling to anything that promised relief. They weren't evil so much as they just didn't know any better. But they were also set in their ways, sure that what they knew was right and mistrustful of anything that didn't fit in with their dogma.

"Come, brothers and sisters!" he called out. "Faith will protect us! Come and help me drag the offering out!"

They shuffled forward, not a doubt on their faces that what he said was true. He felt guilty for tricking them, but it had to stop. He couldn't think of any other way. When he was gone, when the preacher was again dead, they might spread their diseased religion, and he couldn't accept the possibility. Nor could he abide the notion that someone else might come, some other child of Horatio McBride, and take up the practice again. It was better this way, better to finish what his mother started.

As they filed past him, the preacher raged and screamed, but Gary put on his best smile and ushered them in, helped them to avoid the flames and directed them to the main room, where the inferno was hottest and where there would be little chance of escape. The hall tree caught and burned in the open doorway. All he had to do was wait for them all to die.

When they were all inside, he pulled the kitchen door shut and turned the deadbolt. It was a stupid gesture, to lock the door on a burning house, but it was more out of reflex than anything. He joined the flock in the living room. They looked scared, but he knew how to ease their fright.

"The offering is gone," he said. "Dead in the flames. We have succeeded! The *Lord* is pleased with us, and will bless the town with his loving bounty. So we must now prove our faith in *Him*! *He* has spoken unto me, told me that the flames would hurt none of us, for such is *His* power, such his *His* love for the faithful!"

The congregation shifted and looked from one another. Their fear might be greater than their faith, but he knew how to soothe them, knew the words, picked from the preacher's own vocabulary, to say.

"Do not fear!" he shouted as timbers cracked and glass shattered. "For when we meet our *Lord*, we shall be rewarded as people of faith! We will be given seats at his right hand, and our suffering will be over."

A few weak and choked "Amens" answered him as several of the older people collapsed from the heat. They deserved it, Gary reminded himself, even if it didn't ring true.

"Come on now," he coughed through the smoke. "I think we'd all feel better if we sang a song."

Those that could joined him and lent their voices in praise of their cruel God.

Let our pleasures be thy pleasures, let us share in all your pain, let us sing unto your praises, beneath the blooded rain...

32

The eerie sounds of the mournful hymn reached Zach's ears as he cradled his mother's head in the front yard. She opened her eyes and smiled at him.

"How?" she croaked.

"Dad." Superdad came through, got them out and went back to make sure the job was done. His raw skin stung where tears streaked down his face.

The sounds of the congregation stopped slowly as voices dropped out, succumbed to the heat he supposed, until only one voice remained, one that he knew. His father's. They sat and watched as the supports on the upper floor gave way, and the top story collapsed inward, sending sparks into the night sky. It wouldn't be long before there was nothing left to mark the presence of the house except for a black scorch on the ground.

"We need to go," said Zach. "Can you walk?"

"I'll try," she said.

Zach helped her to her feet as best he could, but in truth he wasn't in much better shape than she. Whenever he drew clean air in, his lungs fought to expel smoke and soot. She coughed and gagged beside him before she seemed to get her legs under her. Then they walked slowly down the driveway toward his truck.

As they walked, they heard voices and hurried footsteps, but they were too tired to hide, too exhausted to run. Zach's gun held one more bullet. He wondered if he would have to kill one of them, and what the others would do when he did.

From down the driveway, he saw three figures, members of the congregation the preacher sent to get him. They stopped when they saw the boy and his mother, and the gun that Zach held pointed at them.

"They're dead," coughed Zach. "All of them."

The three looked at each other, then at him. For a moment they seemed to consider, as if they knew how many bullets he had left. He felt a tug at his shirt and his mother stepped in front of him.

"Preacher's dead," she said. "Burned to death. You want to do something, go tend to them."

The three didn't say a word, but looked at each other before walking past and giving them a wide berth.

It took them the better part of an hour to walk the mile-long driveway, but the longer they walked, the better Zach felt. Sure, he still hurt. His hands would be unusable for a while, which meant his video game days were on hold for a while, but it didn't matter. What mattered was they were alive. That his father sacrificed himself to save them hurt deeply, but even more that all he could remember the two of them doing was arguing. He knew his father loved him, always loved him, but he pushed him away because...why? No good reason he could see, especially now that he was gone and there was no chance to correct it.

His mother put her hand on his shoulder and squeezed.

"Your father loved you."

"I know."

"You have to know that he wasn't the one that tried to..."

"Kill me? Yeah. I know."

Up ahead, the thicket that separated the road from the driveway came into view. Zach increased his pace and Angela did her best to match it. As they came around the thicket, the old Stepside sat waiting. A gift from his father, something that would carry them home.

"Yeah," said Zach. "Dad loved me."

He looked back toward the house. The orange glow of the fire flickered against the trees, then grew softer. It was done. By morning, there would be nothing left but more stories and a barn, if the barn didn't catch too. He climbed into the truck and realized he couldn't fit his hands into his pockets to get the keys.

Angela had to get them for him, which was awkward and weird.

"I can't grip the steering wheel," he said.

"I don't know how to drive this thing," she replied. "I've had an automatic since I was sixteen."

She had to turn the key for him, and he steered with his wrists while he told her when to shift gears. They pulled the truck around until they headed down the road toward Luling and the hospital therein.

The nurse on duty took one look at them and called the police, then hurried them to the back. Apart from a few contusions, first and second-degree burns, and smoke inhalation, Zach seemed fine. He waited impatiently for the doctor to return with his mother's diagnosis.

"Dehydrated, three broken ribs, first and second degree burns... what the hell have you two been doing tonight?"

Zach laid back and waited for the police to arrive.

EPILOGUE

A month went by slowly in San Antonio for Zach, especially without the benefit of video games or his computer. His fingers still wouldn't respond the way he was used to, and the bandages made his hands look like Mickey Mouse gloves, but at least he was alive. His friends visited, but he wasn't interested in talking to them. Not yet. After a few visits, they got the hint and stopped coming by.

The police listened to his and his mother's stories, then drove out to Shy Grove to investigate. A few follow-up visits later, and the police left them alone. It wasn't until a week later that a story ran in the San Antonio Express News about bones dredged from the pond and the strange cult. Their names were left out of the article, but it still made Zach feel weird, as if he were being watched. A religious ceremony gone bad, that was what it was. Angela and Zach were to be considered blameless, case closed.

When the lawyer from Luling showed up on their doorstep, Zach's first urge was to slam the door in his face. But, the man explained, there were papers to be signed and legal issues that needed attention. He sat and fidgeted when Angela came to the kitchen. He wasn't prepared for the bandages she still had to wear, or for the oxygen tank she rolled behind her. The smoke did a number on her lungs, scorched nearly forty percent of their usability away. Her hair was growing back, but the scars would remain forever, Zach feared.

The money Gary inherited belonged to Angela, said the

lawyer as he made a conscious effort not to stare at her face. The land too, though the barn caught too and only half of it still stood. He offered to drive them out to survey the damage, but Zach cut in and told him that would not be necessary. Shy Grove was the last place on Earth he ever wanted to revisit.

"Not much of a town there anymore," said the lawyer. "All the businesses just didn't open one day. Even that auto parts store is just left to rust."

"Good," said Zach. "Let the whole town rot. I don't care."

The lawyer finished up with his papers and handed them their copies, then left them to grieve.

Angela's sculpting tools and clay sat unused in her studio. It wasn't that she couldn't sculpt anymore. Unlike Zach's, her hands were fine. But she only left her bed to wander the halls and cry. The thought of sculpting again only brought more choked tears, and Zach eventually learned to not mention it. She'd get back to it some day, he told himself, even if he didn't quite believe it. They both had therapy, physical and emotional, to go through. Maybe, when the bandages came off for good, she might come out for more than just meals.

In the living room, on the wall, a bare spot stared where a picture once hung. Zach took it down because his mother cried whenever she saw it. Sometimes he didn't know if it was from fear or loss, but whenever she saw Gary's smiling face, it brought too many emotions with it. It was bad enough that he resembled him, that glimpses of his father looked back at him in the mirror. But the picture was too much. He couldn't stand to look at it himself for a while, but weeks went by and he grew to miss his father's face. After a time, he even stopped imagining that the eyes followed him.

ABOUT THE AUTHOR

© Lily Coy Johnson

Scott A. Johnson is the author of nine novels, three true ghost story guides, a chapbook and a short story collection. He currently lives somewhere near Austin, Texas, with his wife, daughter, four cats and a pug.

For more information, look to his website at
http://www.creepylittlebastard.com

OTHER BOOKS BY SCOTT A. JOHNSON

An American Haunting

Deadlands

Cane River: A Ghost story

The Journal of Edwin Grey

City of Demons

Deadlands: The definative edition

The Mayor's Guide: The Stately Ghosts of Augusta

The Ghost of San Antonio

Haunted Austin, Texas

Droplets: A Short Story Collection

The Stanley Cooper Chronicles:
>   *Book One* - **Vermin**
>   *Book Two* - **Pages**
>   *Book Three* - **Ectostorm**